The John Reddisson Saga

–

My Early Life

Freddy Johnson

Grosvenor House
Publishing Limited

This book is published by
Grosvenor House Publishing Ltd
28-30 High Street, Guildford, Surrey, GU1 3EL.
www.grosvenorhousepublishing.co.uk

A CIP record for this book
is available from the British Library

ISBN 978-1-78148-657-3

To My Father and Mother
And to My Sister Lori
Who all stayed calm and carried on

CHAPTER 1

My father Samuel Reddisson was born in July 1889, the son of a quarryman employed in Hessle near Hull in Yorkshire. His mother had been in service at 'the big house' nearby. She was illiterate and had signed my father's birth certificate with a cross – 'the mark of the mother'. My father went to school locally but left at fourteen to become an engineering apprentice in the Hull dockyards.

When the First World War arrived in August 1914, he joined the Royal Naval Division (RND). He saw action at the defence of Antwerp. After a lengthy period of training, his unit moved to Egypt preparatory to the Turkish Gallipoli campaign of 1915. The RND were retained under Admiralty control even though they were fighting on land as infantrymen in Gallipoli alongside army units. They still used naval language and ranks and bells to signal time.

Two divisions landed at Gallipoli in April 1915 – the RND and the regular Army 29th Division. My father's unit was sent to Anzac Cove to reinforce the Australian and New Zealand troops. It was at Anzac Cove that he suffered a most serious eye injury as a result of shrapnel debris. The purpose of the amphibious landing had been to capture the Turkish forts on the heights above that controlled the passage of the Dardanelles Straits.

The Turkish troops were lying in wait on the heights and many of the invading Allied troops were killed or injured. 'We were minced at Gallipoli', my father would later tell my mother. It was solely to my mother that he ever spoke about Gallipoli and then only during their courting days. His harrowing experiences had affected him so deeply that the subject was never discussed with his children.

My father was evacuated back to the UK as one of the many casualties where, unusually, he was sent to a civilian hospital. He suffered long periods of having both his eyes bandaged, leading to admittance to St. Dunstan's Hospital – an independent charity for the rehabilitation of blind and partially-sighted servicemen. Whilst undergoing treatment there, he was taught basket weaving. There was a period of time when it was feared that he had not only suffered irreversible damage to the optic nerve in one eye but that the optic nerve in his other eye would fail, too. After months of specialist treatment and enduring long periods of bandaging to both eyes, he was discharged as a war casualty and granted a war invalid's pension for life. Despite his impaired eyesight, he managed to find employment in London in due course in his trade as a qualified engineer. He married his first wife in 1916 and they had a son. Sadly, his wife died in the Spanish 'Flu pandemic of 1919, having already been weakened by tubercolosis.

Samuel Reddisson found lodgings for himself and his young son in the Southwark area of London. The owners of the boarding house had a daughter, Ella, who was my mother's best friend. Ella's parents had come to London in the 1890s as German immigrants. Her father had taken the precaution to change the family name from Herschell to Henshaw in the early years of the twentieth century in an effort to fade into the London background. As a result, they were not targeted during the First World War. Many German immigrants were not so lucky. Some were verbally and even physically abused, German-owned shops were damaged and some men were interned. Fortunately, Ella's family were known as London Jews and not as London Germans. The national anti-German feeling came to involve the Royal Family itself. In 1917, King George V was advised to change the family name from Saxe-Coburg- Gotha to Windsor as a patriotic gesture. Prince Louis of Battenberg, who had married a granddaughter of Queen Victoria and had served in the Royal Navy, also changed his name. It became Mountbatten, a new British name that would become world-famous in due course, his grandson being Prince Philip, Duke of Edinburgh.

My mother Flora was born in November 1906, the daughter of John Cartwright and his wife, who lived in Southwark. Her father had employment as a turncock, whose main job was to regulate street water supplies. My mother left school at fourteen and found work as a messenger-girl, carrying company mail and accounts information from one part of London to another. She would relate how she received one penny bus or tram fare but, pocketing the money, she would walk the distance involved instead of taking public transport and handing over the precious penny as fare. With my father living in the same house as Ella, it was inevitable that the widowed Samuel and the young Flora should meet. There was a seventeen-year difference in age and so it was natural for Flora to address him as Mr. Reddisson rather than the informal 'Samuel'.

Family entertainment in the 1920s often took the form of a singsong one or two evenings a week around the piano in the parlour. In addition to everyone joining in a rousing chorus, there would be solo performances of well-known songs together with recitations of monologues and poems. Samuel was in great demand for he not only played the piano and had a fine tenor voice but he could also deliver many popular recitations. Flora and Ella would attend the family musical evenings, especially enjoying Samuel's performances. A favourite of theirs was a nineteenth century sailor's lament called 'The Maiden's Prayer'. Samuel's rendition never failed to bring tears to the eyes of the ladies, both young and not so young, although a few port and lemons helped to create the right mood.

The Maiden's Prayer

'As I came home from work one night, to find my house without a light,
I went upstairs to go to bed and then a thought came to my head.
I went into my daughter's room and found her hanging from a beam.
I took my knife and cut her down and on her breast this note I found:
O father dear I died in shame to bear a child without a name.
Please dig my grave and dig it deep and place white lilies at my feet.
At my head, please place a dove to show that we had died for love.'
Another tear-jerker was 'The Skylark', which Samuel sang thinking of his motherless young son:

'Skylark, skylark, winging your way so high, Skylark,
skylark, when you are up in the sky,
If among the angels, mother you should see,
Ask her if she will come back to poor daddy and me.'

Samuel had enjoyed visiting the London music-halls during
and after the First World War. He had seen the famous
Marie Lloyd (1870-1922) perform on a number of
occasions. She was acknowledged as one of the best music
hall artistes of the day. Londoners loved the innuendo and
double entendre in many of her most popular songs. She
would perform them with endless winks and gestures. The
straight-laced Licensing and Watch Committees of the day
objected to the suggestive wording of one of her most
famous songs – 'Oh, she sits among the cabbages and peas'.
Without any fuss, she changed the wording to 'Oh, she sits
among the cabbages and leeks', - which brought the house
down and and encouraged half a dozen encores.

My father recalled how one evening in the early
1920s he had watched a Charlie Chaplin lookalike/
walkalike contest in his tramp role as part of the
programme at a London music hall. Unknown to the
unsuspecting audience at the time, Charlie Chaplin
himself had arrived heavily disguised at the music hall
and, on a whim, had entered the contest. He had been
staying at a nearby hotel on a rare visit from the United
States. The thought of participating in the contest had
intrigued him. Unrecognised, he was given limited time
to use the music hall make-up and costume facilities.
He failed to make a major impression on the audience
and the contest judges. He came third.

Relatives of my father's first wife had emigrated to
Australia in the early 1920s. They contacted my father

and asked if his young son might join them. My father agreed as he felt that conditions in the boarding house were not ideal for a growing boy. He boarded a ship in 1924 and sailed off to a new life in Australia. My father never saw him again.

Despite their difference in ages, Samuel Reddisson and Flora Cartwright began courting. Flora was one of over a million 'surplus' young women in Britain in the early 1920s, known as the 'mateless multitude,' such had been the slaughter of young men in the War. Most young women at the time found it very hard to meet any suitable boyfriends, especially ones of their own age or thereabouts. Samuel and Flora married on Boxing Day in 1925 and set up home in my mother's parents' house in Southwark.

My parents would relate how there were many unusual and colourful characters in Southwark in the 1920s. My father would enjoy telling us about the exploits of a character called 'Odd Sox', whose professional title was 'Official Rat-catcher to the Borough of Southwark'. Locals suspected, and some even claimed it was true, that Odd Sox also bred rats in order to increase his income from the borough once he had released them. He also had a 'fancy rat' that was the champion rat fighter of Southwark. There was a particular tavern near 'The Elephant and Castle' which ran illegal ratting competitions where terriers fought live rats in a large rat-pit. The betting hinged on which terrier could kill, say, twenty rats in the quickest time. The terrier owners were known to wager large sums of money on the outcome of such competitions.

Odd Sox would fearlessly catch rats by hand when they were cornered, as well as training his 'rat' terrier to catch them. He would often have a couple of ferrets in his pockets – they were also expert ratters. He never wore gloves and would just laugh off the many bites he suffered. He maintained he had only ever had one rat-induced infection fever in his entire professional lifetime. He refused to use poison, claiming that a poisoned rat would often creep into the recesses of premises to die and the resulting stench could be unbearable.

Odd Sox only worked at night. After one successful night's work with his strong hessian sack containing six live rats destined for 'The Elephant and Castle' rat tavern, he was walking along Great Dover Street when a constable approached him. It was a young constable only recently attached to the local police station and he had never met Odd Sox before. He clearly thought this man walking the streets at night with his terrier and with a large, bulging sack was up to no good. Odd Sox as a professional rat catcher knew that six rats in a dark sack would remain absolutely still, even if prodded. The constable asked him to open the sack. Odd Sox refused and so the constable arrested him and took him along to the local police station where, he was told, the sergeant would make him open his sack. When they arrived at the station, the sergeant happened to be at the rear, talking to one of the overnight prisoners in a cell. Again, the constable insisted that the sack was opened. 'All right', replied Odd Sox, 'but it'll be you to blame for any problem.' With Odd Sox firmly holding his terrier on a leash, six rats ran out of the sack just as as the sergeant returned to the duty room. 'What the hell's going on here?' he asked, as the rats sped past him. It all ended up with Odd Sox and his terrier recapturing the rats – and a handsome fee was forthcoming for the additional work. 'That'll come out of your next week's pay,' growled the sergeant looking at the red-faced constable.

My mother would also relate a tale of life in Southwark in the 1920s but I suspected it of being apocryphal. It was on the subject of tapeworms. One species parasitises humans after being consumed in unprepared meat or in food prepared in conditions of poor hygiene – not uncommon in the 1920s. The worm's head attaches itself to the wall of the human intestines and absorbs nutrients from the food being digested by the host. They can grow to several feet in length. Tapeworms in the system usually cause no symptoms apart from some upper abdominal discomfort and loss of appetite.

My mother claimed to have witnessed a 1920s old wives' recommended procedure for getting rid of a tapeworm without having to pay a doctor's fee. The patient was starved for several days. Then a long meaty sausage was held half in, half out, of the mouth. The starving tapeworm appeared in the mouth and followed the sausage length. At that point, the expert old wife seized its head with pincers and with one deft pull carefully dragged the tapeworm up the patient's oesophagus making sure not to let it break into sections.

The collapse of the US Stock Market on 29 October 1929 precipitated a world-wide collapse of international share values and financial chaos. My parents had been married less that five years. Living in Southwark within the sound of Bow Bells, they'd had two children – Ruth, born in 1927, and George, in 1928. Amy was to follow in 1930 and I appeared in 1933, less than six weeks after Adolf Hitler became the German leader or Fuhrer. They named me John.

It so happened that only four days after I was born, (and not many people know this), another London cockney boy made his appearance less than a mile away in St Olave's Hospital, Rotherhithe, Southwark. His parents were Maurice Joseph Micklewhite, a fish-market porter, and Ellen Micklewhite, a cook and charwoman. The son was also named Maurice. He and I duly ended up together as 'new boys' at Wilson's Grammar School, Camberwell, London in September 1946. Maurice Micklewhite had transferred to Wilson's after one year at a grammar school in Hackney and I had arrived after one year at Llanelly Grammar School for Boys in South Wales. He later became one of Hollywood's most successful and easily recognised film stars and a top box-office draw – Sir Michael Caine – brilliantly portraying a varied selection of roles over many years.

The 1929 crash signalled the beginning of a ten-year long Great Depression affecting the USA and Europe. My father, along with millions of others in Britain, was thrown out of work. He was reduced to pushing a barrow in the local fruit and vegetable market in Southwark to earn a few shillings to try to make ends meet. When work in the Borough Market dried up, the family went onto the unemployment benefit system with money being paid out to claimants according to need. To the day she died, my mother would recall the strict means test we underwent to qualify. A government official visited the family. The radio and gramophone were seized as being non-essential items and surplus to basic requirements. It was all so unfair and humiliating.

It wasn't until 1935 that my father was able to obtain work again as an engineer. It was in that year that the family moved from a rented house in Falmouth Road,

Southwark to a council flat in Brockley, south London. They were subsequently allocated a 'dream house' in nearby Bellingham which had a feature my parents had never enjoyed previously – their own garden. Their mutual joy in their new accommodation was short -lived - war against Germany was declared a few months later.

I was six years old when war broke out on 3 September 1939. I was well aware that unusual things were happening in Bellingham. Public air-raid shelters were being constructed in the area and barrage balloons appeared in the sky. They were anchored to the ground and were intended to bring down low-flying enemy bombers. The word 'evacuation' was in constant use and I soon found out what it meant. All the pupils of Ruth's school, Mary Datchelor Girls' School, Camberwell, were to be 'evacuated' to Llanelly in South Wales. My brother, George, and I were to be 'evacuated' to a village called Otford in north Kent, and Amy to Wadhurst in Sussex. We had all now been issued with gas masks, which we had to carry with us everywhere in case the Germans resorted to a gas attack. The gas masks were in cardboard boxes with string attached to form a thin strap over the shoulder.

Otford was not to be a pleasant experience for me. I lived alone with a semi-sadistic spinster with ultra house-proud principles and habits. George, on the other hand, ended up living nearby with a warm-hearted, kind and thoughtful host family. My hostess hated having a 'scruffy London kid' foistered onto her by the authorities in her spotlessly clean house and she got her revenge on them and on me in several special ways: regular banishment to my freezing cold bedroom because of too much sniffing; serving up to me – I always ate alone – appalling, meagre food consisting mainly of bread and dripping (a congealed animal fat scraped off oven baking trays), potatoes and turnips – as my brother later recalled hearing from me. When I looked back in later years, I was positive that the woman was scoffing all my rightful ration-book coupon monthly allowance of meat, bacon, sausage, fish, eggs, etc., for some attractive kitchen smells used to drift up to my freezing bedroom some evenings.

As I was forever falling into ditches and ponds on my rambles and prone to kicking stones along the street, she took away my shoes and made me wear wellingtons all the time – but not in the house, of course. Finally, considering scruffy little London urchins looked even scruffier with their hands in their pockets, she sewed up all my pockets even though a harsh winter had arrived.

Eventually, my brother, George, who had patiently been teaching me the names of birds, butterflies and plants on our rambles, relayed by letter to my parents the facts of my misery. My mother arrived to take me back to south London and the joys of the Luftwaffe, but not before giving the spinster a good piece of her mind.

As my Otford home had been only a dozen miles from the RAF fighter station at Biggin Hill, I had watched a number of aerial dogfights between the RAF and the Luftwaffe. The dogfights over south London were more numerous and seemed to be much more dramatic. They were often quite high up as Spitfires and Hurricanes fought with Messerschmitts 109/110, with us boys later combing the nearby streets in search of souvenir metal. At night, there were the searchlights and parachute flares with the sky frequently lit up by ack-ack flashes, almost like sheet lightning.

At the start of an air-raid after the warning siren had sounded, my father, mother and I would make for the Anderson shelter in the garden. My father had scoured far and wide for mattresses and they arrived at the house perched on an old pram which he pushed along the pavement. He knew all about their life-saving anti-blast value when they were propped up against house windows or fixed to the door, walls and roof of the Anderson shelter. Some evenings before a raid, we would sit – I can't say relax – in the living-room behind the blackout curtains and the mattress at the window. If we hadn't drawn the curtains properly, an ARP warden was bound to appear and shout, 'Put that light out!' There would perhaps be a smoky fire in the grate while my father listened to the wind-up gramophone playing records by such 'stars' as Albert Sandler and the Palm Court Orchestra or Count John McCormack, an Irish tenor. When the sirens inevitably began their air-raid warning signature tune, he would turn off the gramophone, put on the wireless in defiance for a few minutes and then we all trooped off to the garden shelter. The whole thing became a routine procedure, sometimes a nightly one. It never once occurred to me that our house could be a target: I was safe with my parents and therefore any bombs would fall safely in the distance, never in our street. To give them the credit they deserve, my parents never showed any fear, just a defiant resignation – the 'Blitz Spirit', if you like. There was a slight bickering occasionally as to what to take into the shelter but my mother's knitting was an essential item. Sometimes in the near darkness of the shelter,

I would hear the 'crump, crump' of bombs falling in the distance, or not so distant, and the sound of local ack-ack activity. When the 'all-clear' sounded, we would emerge bleary-eyed, make our way back to the house and get on with our lives, but not before my mother had put the kettle on for that morale-boosting cup of tea, and my father had put on the wireless again. Our old-fashioned wireless set required a two volt glass-cased accumulator for the valve filaments. It was my job to take the accumulator to the local garage for recharging as required. I would leave it there and bring home a newly charged one. I do recall how heavy they were for a young boy.

The early months of the War had seen an increase in food shortages as a direct result of German U-boat activity in the seas around Britain. The government encouraged people to grow their own food, and the 'Dig for Victory' campaign began. My father had filled our garden – as much as our Anderson shelter allowed – with vegetables, mainly potatoes, but also a few root vegetables. My mother would make a pie containing vegetables and oatmeal with a potato pie-crust. My father and I would comment that it tasted just like chicken pie – but without the chicken. Fresh fruit, especially previously imported items such as bananas, oranges and lemons vanished from the shops. All staple foods such as bacon, cheese, tea, jam, eggs and so on were strictly rationed and the ration-book allowances were very meagre, such as two ounces of butter per person per week and one ounce of cheese. No wonder that we children were always hungry.

My parents had made it clear that my stay in south London was only a temporary measure. It was duly arranged for my sister, Amy, to join me for evacuation to the Plymouth area, well away from the London bombing. We were put on a train at Paddington Station with some other children – all equipped with a small suitcase, cardboard-boxed gas mask and a name label – under the close supervision of some Women's Voluntary Service (WVS) ladies. They accompanied us to Plymouth and then in a coach to a reception centre in the church hall in nearby St Germans. The scene inside the church hall must have resembled a cattle market. Potential foster parents were wandering around selecting children as evacuees in their homes. Inevitably, girls went first, as it was considered that they would give far less trouble than boys. As other children left with their new host families, I began to feel somewhat abandoned. A scruffy London boy of eight was certainly not at the top of anyone's shopping list. Amy had meanwhile disappeared but she now returned with her new foster parents. Feisty as ever, she told the WVS ladies that she was going nowhere without her brother. Her foster parents lived in Polbathic, a village about a mile from St Germans. Another Polbathic couple about to leave the church hall without an evacuee, heard the commotion. They came over, scrutinised me and the wife said, 'All right, we'll have him, if we must. What's his name?' 'John Reddisson'.

In fact, my new foster parents, who ran the village shop in Polbathic, proved to be extremely understanding and kind to me. It was a welcome change from the harridan in Otford. The only thing I didn't enjoy in their house was my weekly bath, administered by their twenty year-old daughter with the help of a large kitchen scrubbing brush. Its bristles were harsh and unyielding but the daughter maintained it was the only way of cleaning me up.

Our primary school was in St Germans. Ten year-old Amy would collect me from the village shop and take me to school. While the daughter was in the hall getting me ready, Amy would stuff her coat pockets full of raisins and sultanas from the two open barrels which stood just inside the shop entrance. Those pilfered items helped to sustain us through the day as we always seemed hungry. Whatever the weather, Amy and I used to walk the mile across fields to St Germans. Amy would later recall that I often didn't bother to go the whole distance, especially if the weather was fine. There was a deserted barn and some haystacks in the fields and I would spend the day chasing rabbits or just wandering around. Amy would tell the teacher that I was ill and then collect me on the way home after lessons. No-one seemed to bother too much about my frequent absences from school. The teacher must have thought that it was just one of those evacuee children having attendance problems.

One afternoon, I met up with Amy on her way home to Polbathic from school in St Germans. I showed her a fruiting apple orchard I had discovered. I left my shoes at the base of a tree and climbed up to scrump some ripe eating apples in the upper branches. I passed them down to Amy who stuffed them into her blouse. At that moment, the farmer appeared. Amy was stuck at the bottom of the tree weighed down by the apples and holding my shoes. She told the farmer we hadn't eaten all day and we were starving hungry. To his credit, he let us off and said we could keep the apples we had – but if we ever returned to his orchard, he would let the local policeman know and we would be in trouble.

Having been brought up in suburban London, I loved the freedom of the fields. There is no doubt that children inhabit a world of their own, far removed from the thoughts, worries and decision-taking of adults. They put their own interpretation on what is going on in the real world, embellishing it with their own unsophisticated imaginings. Amy, my fellow field-wanderer, loomed large as my real minder in the evacuee world. The strong bond between us certainly developed during those far-off days in Cornwall and then strengthened during the later challenging times to come.

Amy's host family received a letter from my mother informing them that our house in south London had been destroyed by the Luftwaffe. We would later learn that my parents had been in the Anderson shelter at the time. When they eventually emerged from the shelter after dawn, having been dug out by rescue workers following the 'all clear' siren, the Air Raid Precautions (ARP) warden was flabbergasted that they were not only alive but uninjured. He had already jotted them down as casualties. In fact, my resourceful father's action in lining the shelter with mattresses, specifically against blast effects, had saved the day. A number of neighbours had not been so fortunate and had been killed.

It is interesting to note that, at the time, my parents received no post-trauma counselling. After being bombed-out and still suffering from shock, they were then expected to walk to the local church hall, which they duly did, each carrying a routinely packed emergency suitcase taken with them into the shelter. Those suitcases, in addition to the clothes they were wearing, now became their sole worldly possessions.

At the church hall, the only counselling on offer for losing their home and almost their lives was 'a nice cup of tea with biscuits' and, as my mother later recounted, a poster on the wall advising everyone to 'Stay Calm and Carry On'.

My mother had a previously planned emergency evacuation to South Wales to join Ruth and her host family in Llanelly, the town to which Ruth's London school had moved on the outbreak of war. My father braved it out in London, stayed with his job and moved into temporary lodgings for a few months – until his factory was destroyed by bombing. He then joined my mother and Ruth in Llanelly.

A few weeks later, it was arranged for my father to travel to Polbathic to collect Amy and me and take us to join the family in Llanelly.

CHAPTER 2

The train carrying my father, Amy and me left Plymouth station and we were now bound for South Wales. We had only been travelling five minutes when it came to a sudden halt. We could hear an air-raid siren in the distance. 'They are probably after the railway line,' said a man in the corner of the carriage. 'They are probably after the docks,' retorted my father. 'We don't want to distress the children, do we?' he added, fixing the man with a glare. As far as I was concerned anyway, Amy and I couldn't possibly come to any harm with our protective father sat next to us – an impossible development.

We caught a bus from Llanelly railway station to Thomas Street where my parents were renting a flat. It was in a cold, damp Victorian dwelling with small, musty rooms. My elder sister Ruth would now have to share her small bedroom with Amy while I slept in my parents' bedroom. My brother George was away at boarding school in Sussex with Wilson's Grammar School which had been evacuated from Camberwell, London at the start of the war. Within a month, we had moved to another rented property in Fellinfoel Road near the 'Thomas Arms'. It had previously been a shop but the Jones brothers who owned it had carried out some work to convert it into living accommodation. It still had the large shop window facing the road. As you entered, you went through a hall into the living-room from which stairs led up to three bedrooms. There was a scullery and kitchen at the back and the lavatory was across the rear yard. There was no bathroom, so a tin bath was put in front of the fire in the sitting room on 'bath night'. The Jones brothers were cobblers and their shop was adjoining our 'house'.

Amy aged ten and I, eight, attended the nearby Old Road Primary School. There were formal lessons in the morning of English, Welsh and arithmetic. The afternoons were devoted to singing in English and Welsh, learning poetry and art lessons. Amy duly passed her Eleven Plus examination and joined Ruth at Mary Datchelor Girls' School, evacuated from Camberwell, London to Llanelly.

I enjoyed learning Welsh at my school and it was a challenge that I accepted with pleasure. Some of my friends were frequently speaking in Welsh to one another and I wanted to join in. In class, I learned useful phrases, numbers, days of the week, months and seasons of the year and common social phrases. Little did I realise at the time that I was being conditioned to treat language learning as something enjoyable, valuable and worthwhile. It all bore fruit in later years in my formal studies of a number of foreign languages. Unlike in North Wales, there was never any strong tradition of speaking Welsh. Some parents in Llanelly, for example, insisted that their children spoke only English at home. That would help to ensure that they would make progress in life in the larger world. There was one teacher at Old Road Primary School, however, who always made us use the Welsh word for 'toilet' as and when necessary. It was one of the first Welsh words

I learned and quickly, too. The same teacher tried to teach us a little French through Welsh, when many of his pupils thought only in English. It quickly led to total confusion and the idea was soon abandoned.

Unfortunately, my carefree days at the primary school soon came to an abrupt end as a result of several periods of hospitalisation. My mother took me to Dr. Llewellyn our local GP, to discuss my frequent sniffing. It resulted in my being booked into Llanelly General Hospital for a sinus operation. One minute I was lying on the operating theatre table, the next minute a nurse appeared from nowhere and clamped a chloroform pad over my nose and mouth. Ther first thing the nurse did when I came round after the operation was to give me a metal bowl in which to be sick – such was the known effect of residual chloroform in the system. Apparently, after a bit of scraping, they found nothing wrong with my sinuses. My mother had been urged to press for the operation by my elder sister, Ruth. She was not the most relaxed or patient of sisters and she had repeatedly complained to my mother that my frequent sniffing prevented her enjoying reading her books. Ruth's iron will and uncompromising attitude were already much in evidence and my mother usually chose the easy way out in order to keep the peace. Her unsisterly action solved nothing for I carried on sniffing – deliberately sometimes so as to get my own back for the unpleasant operation I had endured unnecessarily. I was only nine at the time and lots of nine year-old boys sniff, or they did in 1942.

It was an early indication of the fact that one crossed or irritated Ruth at one's peril and of the undesirable hold she had over my mother, even as a young teenager. My brother George also had some sort of fascination effect over my mother. As the 1940s unfolded, our family seemed to split into two camps – mother, Ruth and George in the one and father, Amy and I in the other. In my mother's eyes, Ruth and George could do no wrong whereas it was often the case that my father, Amy and I could do no right. Family life was forever accompanied by tension and angst. The favouritism extended into food allocation. My father was often out or late home from work and he usually ate alone in the evening. For the rest of us, fish and chips were a regular wartime meal – well, fish and chips for Ruth and George, but chips and chips for Amy and me. On some occasions, Ruth would graciously pass me the batter from her fish as she didn't like it. I know I was grateful as chips on their own could be boring.

Very occasionally our bland war-time food was livened up with something totally different. My father had become acquainted at a local pub with a part-time poacher. As a result of being treated to the odd pint or two, he would produce a food item for our family, perhaps a pigeon, a rabbit or even a pheasant, as he did one Christmas. In addition, I would go down to the local Llanelly Docks and fish for eels on a hand line. My mother thought nothing of skinning eels and rabbits or plucking birds for the pot.

A friend at Amy's workplace had given her a pet rabbit on her birthday. My father made a hutch for the animal and it lived in the back yard near the outside lavatory. Amy and I would visit the local waste areas to find suitable food for the rabbit, which she named Alfie. Supplies of hutch straw were obtained free from the nearby greengrocer's. Amy ensured that the hutch door was always kept firmly shut. She was adamant that she had seen the odd rat or two in the back yard and didn't want Alfie to be attacked by them. My mother claimed that there weren't any rats there – only the large local Welsh mice. Although Alfie was Amy's pride and joy, Ruth often complained to my mother about the smell from the hutch in the back yard, being obliged to walk past Alfie on her way to and from the outside lavatory. Amy countered by saying that she thought Alfie's hay smelled fine.

One evening we all sat down to a fine rabbit meal, presumably as supplied by my father's poacher contact. As usual, Ruth and George had the best cuts. Afterwards, Amy went out into the yard to feed Alfie. The hutch door was open and the rabbit had gone. 'Where's Alfie?' Amy exclaimed. 'You've just eaten him', said Ruth with a smirk. 'It was Alfie or nothing for dinner. Mum didn't have any money for anything else.' It was rabbit stew on the menu the next day but Amy went to bed hungry and in tears.

I accepted the family living system as I was young and didn't know any better system existed. Amy, being two years older, was prone to analyse it all and she harboured resentment at the two grade treatment. Nevertheless, it became an established pattern of family relationships for many years to come. My father had given up the struggle of fighting against the combined will-power of my mother and Ruth and he tended to keep in the background of family life. It probably all went back to the distressing circumstances of my parents' early married living conditions with its continual lack of money, cramped rented accommodation and having four children in six years. As far as my mother was concerned the first two babies were welcomed and much loved. Amy had overheard my mother and father arguing over the fact that the next two were unwanted pregnancies. They, that is Amy and I, compounded the existing deprivation and hardship – a fact mainly presented as my father's fault.

Irritations and disagreements which in most families would have soon been forgotten, in Ruth somehow aroused an implacable desire for revenge. If some excessive reaction was initiated, as in the case of my sinus operation, there was never a subsequent glimmer of remorse for the consequences. She undoubtedly had a controlling and manipulative side to her nature and never forgot a slight. Ruth was academically brilliant and went on to win an Open Scholarship in classics (ancient Greek and Latin) to Cambridge University but her personality left much to be desired. Having crossed Ruth more than once in Llanelly, my father became a marked man. It was to lead to future family upheaval and misery. It is a valid truism that when families are happy, they are all happy in much the same way; when families are unhappy and dysfunctional such as mine was, they are so in their own uniquely different and varied ways.

The scraping of my sinuses during the operation may well have interfered with my immune system. A few months later, I took to my bed with a high fever. Dr. Llewellyn was summoned. He took one look at my throat which had developed a thick greyish curtain across the back and then uttered the one word 'Diphtheria' – a highly contagious disease with death not uncommon. The ambulance duly arrived and took me through the Welsh countryside to Ammanford Isolation Hospital. Meanwhile, Dr. Llewellyn had placed a total fumigation order on the house. I was placed in a bed in an isolation ward with six other children. The boy in the next bed was also called John and we became friends – for a few days. The screens were then erected around his bed one night and his distressed parents arrived in the building. They were not allowed into the ward. John died soon afterwards and I had already lost my new friend.

Diphtheria was not an uncommon disease in the 1940s but was later virtually eradicated in Britain by means of widespread vaccination. A generation of doctors has now practised who have never seen a single case.

Isolation hospitals lived up to their name. No visitors were allowed into the wards. As the weeks passed and my health and strength improved, I was allowed to stand at a closed window in the ward and wave to my mother and father in the garden below. After some three months' incarceration, I was discharged and sent home. After a couple of weeks convalescing, I was able to resume my schooling – but not for long. Within three months, I took to my bed again with another fever.

The rash first appeared on my face and neck but soon spread to my chest and back. My mother diagnosed scarlet fever, another deadly contagious disease. Before the availability of antibiotics, as in 1943, scarlet fever was a major cause of death amongst children under twelve. Dr. Llewellyn returned to our house and confirming my mother's diagnosis, he exclaimed, 'Oh! Poor lad! It's back to Ammanford, I'm afraid and house fumigation once again.'

Arriving back at the isolation hospital, I was destined to spend another three months isolated from my family and from the outside world. The second time around, the days passed even more slowly but the staff made every effort to encourage me to read – after all, there was nothing else to do. On returning home I had a few weeks' convalescence before returning to Old Road Primary School. I had now lost the best part of an academic year as a result of the sinus operation, diphtheria and scarlet fever. Further, in the near future my Eleven Plus examination was due.

The papers had to be sent from London as I was taking a London County Council (LCC) version of the examination as we knew we would be returning to London in due course. Mr Dai Rees, my form-teacher, told me that he was sure the composition question choice would include 'My School'. He gave me a long sample composition with that title which I was to learn by heart. He also coached me in arithmetic. He made me sit several practice tests and eventually seemed satisfied. As I was the only pupil taking the LCC examination in the small Welsh primary school, it was arranged for me to attend to sit the papers on a Saturday morning under the supervision of Mr. Rees. Question one was the composition question with a choice of subjects including 'My School'. Most of the arithmetic questions were very similar to those I had been practising with Mr Rees. He had prepared me well and I duly passed the examination. I think I must have repaid him for all his extra coaching by eventual selection for Cambridge University many years later and proceeding to a BA and then an MA.

Having passed my Eleven Plus examination meant that in September 1944 I could join my brother George as a boarder at Wilson's Grammar School at their wartime location near Horsham in Sussex, well away from the dangers of London. One advantage in having an older brother at the same boarding school, in his fifth year in fact, was that I was never subjected to bullying. At the first sign of a problem, George would readily sort out the perpetrator and rapidly nip it all in the bud.

With one or two notable exceptions, the teaching staff treated their boarding-school evacuees with an 'in loco parentis' care and due attention. Whether the boys treated all the staff with the respect they deserved is another matter. Music classes inevitably presented mischievous boys with the chance to play the fool and misbehave. Our Form 1A music teacher, Mr. Simpson, would patiently overlook a number of misdemeanours and it proved difficult to upset or annoy him. One particular morning, however, was different. Half-way through our lesson, he suddenly burst into tears and rushed out of the music room. The Headmaster soon appeared and, to a hushed class, he announced Mr Simpson had that very morning received news of the tragic death of his wife and two young daughters. They had all been killed by a German 'doodlebug 'or buzz-bomb in London.

While I was at the school, Victory in Europe (VE) Day arrived on 8th May 1945. The senior boys constructed a huge pile of wood and combustible rubbish and, along with the teaching staff, we sat around a magnificent bonfire. We sang songs to celebrate the end of a war which had lasted over five years. The Headmaster delivered a patriotic speech. The World War may have been over but our family was still at war, and we had well over a year of chaos and deprivation ahead.

On my return to Llanelly with George for the school summer holidays in August, I little dreamed of what lay ahead of us as a family. All six of us were now living together in the 'house' in Fellinfoel Road by the 'Thomas Arms'. Several times I entered the living-room in which my mother, Ruth and George were deep in conversation, only for a sudden silence to descend. They would all look in my direction with a clear joint message – 'You are interrupting us'. I was soon to discover the subject of their private discussions. I returned home one afternoon from my usual ramble in the local countryside to find my mother, Ruth and George surrounded by suitcases, shopping baskets and bags. 'We are leaving', said Ruth. 'What do you mean, we are leaving?' I asked. 'Where are we going?' 'We are all going to live with Mrs. Clarkson and her family in Pembrey. We are just waiting for Amy to come home from work and we'll be off.' 'But what about Dad?' I continued. 'He won't be home for a couple of hours.' 'Dad isn't coming with us. Mum is leaving him.' The bombshell didn't really register. I couldn't exactly take in what was happening. At that moment, Amy, who had been sent out to work at fourteen as a window-dresser in a large store in Llanelly, arrived home. The same news was sprung on her. 'Either you come with us,' snapped Ruth, 'or you can stay here on your own with your father. Which is it to be?' Amy had no real choice but to accompany us to Mrs. Clarkson's. 'There's a suitcase on your bed,' said my mother. 'Fill it as best you can. It's time we were off.' She then turned to me. 'I've already packed your things in a basket and a bag. You'll have to carry them yourself, John.' Amy appeared with a suitcase and a couple of large bags. 'I've had to leave so much,' she protested. 'I'll have to collect it all another time.' 'No,' said my mother firmly. 'None of us will be coming back here. We are leaving for good and that's final.'

Our pathetic family group of five now emerged from the 'house'. It was a good fifteen minutes' walk to the bus-stop to catch the bus to Pembrey, about ten miles away. Laden down as we were with an assortment of battered suitcases, baskets and bags, we must have looked like a sorry band of gypsies or vagabonds to passers-by. George and Ruth were in the lead, followed by my mother and Amy, with me bringing up the rear and trying desperately to keep up with them all as best I could. I had two carrier bags in one hand and a heavy basket in the other, and they became heavier by the minute. 'Hurry up, John', said Ruth. 'We'll miss the bus if you dawdle.'

There were several inquisitive stares from passengers in the bus, especially as my mother didn't have enough money to pay for all our fares. It took additional contributions from both Ruth and George to settle the correct amount. As I sat there on the bus, I still didn't fully understand what was going on. Mrs. Clarkson, also an evacuee from London, had visited us a number of times in Llanelly, and she and my mother had become firm friends. As far as I knew, she had no husband but there were no fewer than five children, all living with her in rooms in a war-requisitioned stately house called 'Pembrey House'. Other evacuated London families occupied additional rooms in what had once been the country residence of the Earls of Ashburnham. Our family of five was now on its way to stay with Mrs. Clarkson and her five children. It made no sense at all to me.

It was another long trek of fifteen minutes from the bus-stop to 'Pembrey House'. The large front door was open and there were some toddlers playing in the entrance hall. Nearby, a woman was sat knitting. 'Can I help you?' 'We are looking for Mrs. Clarkson.' 'She's got rooms at the bottom of the corridor.' We trooped along and came to an open door. Mrs. Clarkson was having tea with her children in a large kitchen. Seeing all of us in the corridor with our assortment of luggage, she exclaimed, 'Oh! You've come! I knew you would but I didn't know when. Come in and have a cup of tea and a biscuit.'

There were only four spare camp-beds available from the store, so for a few nights until a fifth could be obtained, I slept in the bath. Coming from the Llanelly house with no bath, it was ironic that I was now sleeping in one. Life for the next three weeks was anything but orderly or normal. Mrs. Clarkson's children, consisting of four girls and a boy.were aged from three to twelve. The local council had allocated her three bedrooms, a kitchen, a living-room and a bathroom in Pembrey House. An odd drawer, here and there, was allocated to us for all our family's worldly possessions. Mealtimes were arranged in shifts, first the Clarkson family and then the Reddissons moved into the kitchen.

Pressure eased after three weeks. Ruth returned to Cambridge to begin her second academic year at college. She planned to stay with a college friend during future vacations until further notice. George returned to Wilson's Grammar School which had now relocated to its pre-war buildings in Camberwell. London. A host family had been arranged for him where he would spend both term time and school holidays. For whatever reason, I couldn't accompany George back to London to resume my studies at Wilson's. Instead, I had been allocated a place at Llanelly Grammar School for Boys and started there in early September. A school bus did the return journey via Burry Port and Pwll. Amy left to lodge with a friend of Mrs. Clarkson's in Llanelly, but not before overhearing some snippets of conversation between my mother and Mrs. Clarkson, and which she passed on to me. It appeared that my mother had not been too keen on the idea of leaving my father but Ruth's insistence that it was the right thing to do, had won the day. Ruth had subsequently escaped from the living conditions at Pembrey House after only three weeks and had returned to the comforts of Cambridge. My mother and I were destined to spend a whole year there.

The one and only saving grace regarding my time at 'Pembrey House' was the splendid surrounding countryside. 'Pembrey House' itself was surrounded by parkland, woods and heaths. One could ramble for miles and never meet a soul. My love of birds, butterflies and wild plants certainly dates from the time I spent there. My country walks brought me the peace and happiness that were denied to me in my family life and they laid the firm foundations of an enduring love affair with Natural History. With the money earned from collecting basket-loads of blackberries and selling them to the local village greengrocer at sixpence a basket, I was soon able to buy two important books in a Llanelly second-hand bookshop. The first was 'The Observer's Book of Birds' soon followed by 'The Observer's Book of Butterflies'. I also acquired a hardback exercise book which I entitled 'The Diaries of a Birdwatcher'. I was now fully equipped to retreat from the grim reality of life inside 'Pembrey House' and embrace the welcome reality of life in the countryside outside Pembrey House. Somehow, 'The Diaries of a Birdwatcher', begun in September 1945, has survived the many subsequent moves and upheavals in my life. It is now lying there in front of me on my study desk as I pen these words over sixty-seven years later. The original book had become full by 1949, but there were many subsequent 'Diaries' as the years passed.

Llanelly Grammar School for Boys must have done a good job in furthering my education and in teaching me the basics of English grammar and spelling. The following extracts are taken from my 'Diaries' exercise book: (aged 13):

6 July 1946

'I was rambling over some gorse- clad hills dotted with clumps of dried bracken, when I flushed a greyish bird, which silently sped away. I immediately recognised the bird as a Nightjar and commenced to search for its 'nest'. Eventually, after a very long search I located the two eggs lying on some dried bracken. They were long and elongated, white mottled with brown and mauve and were quite inconspicuous. However, when I quietly approached the 'nest' a few days later, I was really amazed at the inconspicuousness of the adult bird brooding, and I am sure that if I hadn't known beforehand the exact spot where the eggs were, I would have mistaken the bird for a piece of lichen covered log (18 July). On 21 July, only egg shells remained in the 'nest'.

LOCALITY – Near Pembrey House grounds, Pembrey.'

13 July 1946............. 'I was shown a Buzzard's nest by Mr E J Cooke [note – the local RSPB 'watcher'].

Two eggs had hatched by 30 May. However, on 13 July, only one nearly fully fledged youngster remained in the nest. The adult Buzzard, which had rounded wings, had a mewing call, and uttered this note upon our arrival in his territory. The nest was situated at the top of a large pine – about 75 feet up – and from the ground appeared as a large platform of sticks. The ferns around the base of the tree were sprayed with white lime which showed young hawks had been or were in the nest. I also picked up several large feathers from the ground beneath the nest'.

'Mr Cooke climbed the tree and photographed the young bird. Suddenly, it scrambled to the edge of the nest and launched itself out into space. However, this was rather imprudent, for as yet it was unable to fly and only half-fluttered into a clump of brambles from which we managed to rescue it. It had a brown back but white upperparts below the breast. After we had examined and photographed the young Buzzard we placed it just below the nest and left the wood. LOCALITY- A wood near Fiveroads, near Llanelly.'.............. I still have a photograph of me holding the young Buzzard, taken by Mr Cooke.

Throughout the first half of 1946, my mother had been corresponding with housing authorities in London with a view to our returning there. She received a letter in July with the address of an establishment where we could stay pending the grant of council accommodation. I was personally sorry to leave my nature haunts around 'Pembrey House' but pleased to be escaping the cramped living conditions there. Little did I know it was a case of out of the frying pan and into the fire.

CHAPTER 3

The place where we could stay in London turned out to be a Rest Centre in Waterloo Road, situated near some bridges close to Waterloo railway station. It would have been hard to find, or even imagine, a more depressing and wretched establishment in the whole of post-war London. It almost had echoes of Dickensian times. It was for homeless, pre-war London families waiting to be rehoused in council accommodation in the London area after the War. Several large rooms had been sectioned off by curtains and behind each set of curtains a cubicle measuring a few square yards was allocated to a family. Privacy was zero; washing and bathing facilities were at a minimum. To emphasise the lack of space, beds had been replaced by three-tier bunks.

The first night, Ruth, on a vacation break from Cambridge, had the top bunk, my mother the middle and Amy the bottom bunk. I was allocated an armchair in the cubicle but spent most of the night stretched out on the floor. Ruth managed to turn over and fall out of her bunk that first night, narrowly missing me but not hurting herself overmuch. Amy was then allocated the top bunk. The curtained-off cubicle next to ours was occupied by a woman and grown-up daughter with what sounded like a drunken Irish husband.

The management of the Rest Centre declared on the third day that I couldn't remain any longer as there were no four-person cubicles available and my presence with the rest of my family was 'not convenient'. Fortunately, George had only recently left his host family to live at a classmate's house closer to the school in Camberwell. Within a couple of days, I had relocated to Mrs. Brown's house in Catford, south London, where I was to spend the next six months. The number 58 tram passed the door and later travelled on to Camberwell and Wilson's Grammar School, so the journey to school was not difficult.

In late September, Ruth returned from the Rest Centre to Cambridge, where she was reading classics (ancient Greek and Latin), to complete her final year. In college, she mixed with the cream of the cream of young ladies. As an Open Scholar, in addition to her own bedroom-study and an en-suite facility, she had three good meals a day in hall. She also enjoyed the services of a gyp, or college servant – the very antithesis of the life she had left behind at the Waterloo Road Rest Centre for homeless families.

Amy celebrated her sixteenth birthday at the Rest Centre in the October. George arrived with a classmate, Derek, aged seventeen, to help celebrate the occasion. As a special treat, Derek gallantly invited Amy to accompany him to the cinema. They walked along Waterloo Road together and came to two cinemas on opposite sides of the road. One was showing a Judy Garland film, which brought a smile of anticipation to Amy's face. Derek, however, couldn't afford the entry price for two. So they ended up in the cheaper cinema opposite, to watch some dreary documentary film.

As the lights went up at the end of the showing, a heavy package arrived on Amy's lap. Derek explained it was a birthday present which he had brought with him all the way from their garden in Dulwich. He added that it would go very well with custard. It turned out to be an enormous green cooking apple. It was to be the only present Amy received for her sixteenth birthday – none of the family had any money to buy her one.

The Rest Centre saga continued for another five months including, according to Amy, a very forgettable Christmas, although the management did string up some decorations consisting of coloured strips of paper glued together.

In March 1947, my mother received information that a three- bedroom council flat had been found for the family in Downham, south London on a large housing estate. She was put in touch with Miss Park, a wonderful lady who worked for the Red Cross in nearby Catford. She provided a grant of money to enable my mother to furnish the flat to a modest degree. My mother, George, Amy and I moved in and Ruth joined us for the Easter holiday. We all had a 'home' again at long last.

My father had tracked George and me down to Wilson's Grammar School. Within a few weeks, forgiveness was in the air and he joined us in the flat. The family was reunited but its sad tradition of frequent dramas continued. Ruth became the star performer in her own ancient Greek-style tragedy played out over the first six months of 1947. At the time, I was blissfully unaware of what was going on but, a few years later, Amy informed me of the sequence of events which she herself had gathered piece by piece over a long period of time from my mother.

In the first term of her final year at Cambridge, Ruth had started going to 'Dorothy's Cafe' in the centre of town where afternoon 'tea dances' were regularly held. It was a venue frequented by American airforce personnel and Royal Air Force servicemen from air stations dotted around the Cambridge area. Ruth soon fell for the charms of an RAF flight-sergeant by the name of Frank, who was ten years older than her. Their relationship blossomed and by the time the Christmas vacation was over, she had become infatuated with the man and with the idea of their future happiness together. By March she suspected she was pregnant. It was the very month my father returned to live with the family in south London. The pregnancy was confirmed in April. Her studies now began to suffer as she largely ignored them, despite the fact that her final degree examinations were looming on the horizon in early summer.

During the Easter holiday back at the flat in south London, Ruth confided in my mother regarding her pregnancy. It was agreed that my father wasn't to be told, or anyone else for that matter. Ruth insisted that Frank wanted to marry her and they had even planned an autumn wedding, a few months before the baby was due. Frank actually visited us in the flat one Sunday afternoon towards the end of the Easter break. He professed his love for Ruth and even confirmed the likelihood of an autumn wedding. My mother was not fully convinced whereas my father was totally sceptical and commented that everything was moving too quickly. I was away from the flat at the time and so I didn't meet Frank.

While cleaning Ruth's bedroom one morning soon after Frank's visit, my mother happened to find an envelope on Ruth's bedside table bearing Frank's RAF address. It was sealed and must have contained a letter to Frank that Ruth was going to post later in the day. Something prompted my mother to copy out the address.

Ruth returned to Cambridge for her final term convinced that no-one would notice her 'condition' as term would finish in June. Meanwhile, following a hunch, my mother wrote to the commanding officer of Frank's unit as his potential mother-in-law, asking for a character reference. A reply arrived within the week: there was no need for a character reference. Frank was a married man, had been married for over six years and had three small children. He lived in a married quarter on camp with his wife. He had confessed to his commanding officer that Ruth was a 'romantic interlude' and that he had no intention whatsoever of leaving his wife. He had then been posted to a unit in Scotland at two days' notice. His wife and children would join him there in due course.

My mother had no option but to show the letter to my father. He hit the roof. A letter was written to Ruth stating that my parents needed to visit her in Cambridge to discuss a very important matter. They would arrive on the Sunday a week later. They showed Ruth the letter. She was totally stunned and devastated. Her first reaction was to say that she would kill Frank. My mother reminded her that he was no longer in the Cambridge area but somewhere in Scotland. My parents left Ruth in total turmoil but they had to return to London.

Ruth took her final degree examinations but instead of achieving her supervisor's predicted First, she only managed a Third Class degree. Just before the end of term in June, Ruth wrote a letter to my mother to say that she would be moving to London to find a job and 'to sort out the other matter'. She gave no forwarding address. Apparently, on arrival in London, Ruth made certain enquiries. Having borrowed the necessary money from George, she proceeded 'to sort out the other matter' at about nineteen weeks' gestation. She remained living and working in London for another three years before returning to south London to live with my parents and me.

Two natural events caused chaos and disruption during my school years at Wilson's Grammar School. The first was the horrendous winter of 1946/47. It was considered the worst winter for a hundred years. December, January and February were bitterly cold months. Insufficient supplies of coal and electricity caused many factories across the country to close. Over four million people were to claim unemployment benefit. Blackouts became commonplace and life by candlelight was an established norm – until the supply of candles ran out. With no heating, we shivered indoors; ice formed regularly on the inside of the single-glazed windows and we went to bed early in an effort to keep warm. We had no television set but for those few who had, the limited television services that were available were suspended completely and radio broadcasts were dramatically reduced. Trams in London stopped running as their electricity feed was cut off. There were supplies of coal at the pits and depots but they had frozen solid and couldn't be moved. Snowdrifts prevented movement of coal by road and most of the railway rolling-stock was trapped by snow. In some areas, food supplies began to run out. Potatoes became rationed as the frost had destroyed a large percentage of the crop. Some root vegetables had to be drilled out of the ground by farmers.

The national misery was compounded by the melting snow in March. The River Trent burst its banks in Nottingham, as did a number of rivers in Yorkshire. Sheep farmers lost up to a quarter of their flocks and tens of thousands of chickens had perished as a result of the weather. Getting to and from school was a nightmare but one managed to attend lessons one way and another.

A few years later, the pea-souper fog, or smog, of early December 1952 arrived. It was a dense, yellow-green fog and so thick that the buses, with headlights blazing, only just crawled along with visibility a few yards. On my way to school by bus, the closer we got to Camberwell and the centre of London, the thicker the fog became. As the temperature dropped, people began lighting more and more coal fires. Much of the available coal was heavy with dust and of poor quality.

It produced a great deal of smoke which then combined with the smoke from factory chimneys and vehicle exhaust fumes. There was little if any wind and the resultant mixture was a dense, toxic cloud. Within a day or two of the smog arriving, the health authorities were stating that air pollution had already soared well above levels considered hazardous. Once inhaled, the tiny particles hanging in the smog made people more vulnerable to respiratory infections as well as constituting a strong potential for increased mortality from lung cancer and heart disease. There had been a sharp increase in people seeking treatment in the capital for respiratory complaints. It particularly affected the lungs of small children and of people already suffering from bronchial complaints, such as my father. The dreadful conditions persisted for almost a week without respite. One particular rumour doing the rounds was that undertakers were running out of coffins. The Great Smog for those of us who experienced it was truly horrific. It was estimated that it killed many thousands of people in just four days.

There were other smogs later in the Fifties but none as bad as that of 1952. Debates in Parliament led to the Clean Air Act of 1956 which stipulated the use of smokeless fuels in homes. It led to a rapid improvement in the quality of London's air.

Once a week at eleven o'clock, my Upper Sixth French set (all nine of us) would assemble in the school's Great Hall to listen to a 'French for Schools' wireless programme. On 6th February 1952, we and our French teacher were surprised to discover only sombre music and bell-tolling on our usual programme. We then heard an announcement, 'The King is dead. God Save the Queen.' King George VI had died overnight and the news was only just being released. Our French programme had been cancelled.

A few months later, Wilson's Grammar School entered three candidates, of which I was one, for the award of the prestigious London County Council (LCC) French Travelling Scholarship. Most of the London grammar schools entered candidates but the awards were limited to seven. I was called to County Hall alongside the River Thames and was interviewed in French for a good half-hour by two university lecturers. A month later, I was informed that I had been selected for a scholarship along with a classmate, Derek. The award was a very generous one in financial terms. It covered travel expenses, university fees, full board and lodging for a month's course in Boulogne, followed by a further two months living with a French family 'anywhere in France'. There was also a pocket money allowance. The school received a comprehensive list of French host families which had registered for the scheme. Derek chose a family in Tours in northern France. I was more adventurous and selected a family living in a village near Grasse, in the Maritime Alps of southern France, a town perched in the foothills and overlooking the French Riviera towards Cannes. I had already enjoyed a two-week study holiday in Paris with a school party a couple of years previously, but a three-month study holiday was something quite different.

Leaving school a week early in mid- July, Derek and I travelled to Boulogne where we shared the same host family, but never speaking in English in front of them, such as at mealtimes. We learned a great deal of French during our one month's University of Lille sponsored course at a Boulogne college. The next part of the study holiday then began. Derek and I travelled together to Paris. He continued his journey on to Tours while I made for the Gare de Lyon to catch my train to southern France. I faced an overnight journey of more than twelve hours before we reached Cannes on the French Riviera. An hour's bus journey saw me arrive in Grasse and after a further bus journey I arrived in the small village of St. Vallier deThiey. It was late afternoon as the bus driver dropped me off at 'Le Pilon' as requested. I found myself standing at a pair of metal gates, with a long drive beyond leading to a very large house or chateau in the distance.

I trudged up the drive with my heavy suitcase. I eventually reached the open front door as a spaniel came out and started barking. A young woman appeared and I introduced myself. 'Ah, you are John,' she exclaimed in French. 'My father is expecting you.' She led me into a spacious room where my hosts were sitting – Monsieur Antoine Dor and his wife, together with four more children. Speaking in French, Monsieur Dor welcomed me to France and to St. Vallier deThiey in particular. To my astonishment, I learned that the chateau was only a summer residence, as the family lived in Grasse for the rest of the year. Further, not only did the Dors have nine children but eight of them were at present on holiday with them in the chateau. The ninth was the eldest daughter, married to an architect and living in Cannes. Monsieur Dor confirmed that he and his family would only speak to me in French. The final piece of information was that Monsieur Dor's brother, a surgeon, and his wife were also on holiday with them in the chateau, together with their five children. He went on to say, 'Dinner will be at seven and as usual there will be nearly twenty of us sitting down to the meal.' I was shown to my room, which I found very comfortable, with a view of wooded hillsides and a mountain in the distance.

I freshened up and appeared downstairs at seven o' clock. The family were already taking their places in the large dining-room and all eyes turned to focus on me. 'This is John,' said Monsieur Dor, 'our welcome English guest.' One other person was not only present at the table, she presided over it. The lady was Madame Dor's mother and was referred to as 'Grand-mere' by one and all. I discovered that the Dors' nine children ranged from twenty-five years of age to twin boys of seven. The Mediterranean-style food served up that first evening, and also on subsequent evenings, was absolutely delicious - garlic and all. It was, to say the least, such a marked contrast to the standard fare served up by my mother in south London. That first evening was also the very first time in my life that I had drunk wine. When I commented on that point to Monsieur Dor, he replied that wine at the table at every main 'repas' or meal was part of the French 'patrimoine' or cultural heritage. 'It complements whatever is on our plate', he added 'and it encourages an atmosphere of conviviality at the table.' He then proposed a toast - 'To our English guest, who is already enjoying our French ways. A votre sante (to your health), John.' 'Tchin' (cheers) was also said by some of the grown-up children. Glasses were raised before we took our first sip.

Throughout my two months' stay, the Dor family treated me like an honoured guest. The eldest sons, Michel, twenty-two and Vincent, nineteen, drove me far and wide. We visited towns along the coast including Frejus, Cannes, Antibes and Nice. One inland trip took us through the foothills of the Maritime Alps to the Gorges du Loup near Vence and the mountain village of Gourdan, passing by some spectacular waterfalls. Returning to St. Vallier de Thiey via Grasse, often called the 'Perfume Town', we visited the Fragonard perfume factory, surrounded by whole fields full of fragrant blossom.

A memorable afternoon was spent in Monte Carlo in the tiny state of Monaco. I twice went on picnics with members of the family to the Lerins Islands off Cannes – a magical experience. As it was 1952, and long before overseas travel became the norm for most British people, there would have been very few British tourists around who had to exist on just an average income. I was also delighted and bewitched by the Mediterranean birds, butterflies and flowers which were all so abundant around 'Le Pilon' itself.

Early October arrived only too soon and the Dor Family, accompanied by me, left 'Le Pilon' and moved back to their Grasse residence, an enormous detached house at the edge of the town, overlooking the perfume fields towards the coast. Monsieur Dor's father had been the mayor of Grasse. His overriding passion had been literature and he had amassed an amazing number of antiquarian books. They filled the spacious library and Monsieur Dor showed me his father's collection with much pride.

My last day was tinged with sadness at leaving the Dor family amid the beauty of the Maritime Alps. The memorable summer spent with them had been a sun-drenched, cultural and linguistic experience that seemed to have taken place in a magical, parallel world far removed from the real world I was now returning to in a cloud-filled south London. Moreover, I had witnessed a happy family at first hand.

As my schoolboy years at Wilson's Grammar School passed, my academic ability in a broad range of subjects improved to a considerable degree. I won form prizes in languages, history, geography and English. In the sixth form, I represented the school senior teams at football, cricket and chess, and was awarded the 'School Challenge Cup' as the best athlete of the year. I had also been appointed Company Quartermaster Sergeant (CQMS), the school number two in the Combined

4 4

Cadet Force. Perhaps the icing on the performance cake was in scoring 146 for the School Cricket Eleven against St. Dunstan's public school in the annual challenge match at The Oval Cricket Ground in June 1952. I was appointed House Captain and School Vice-Captain. I passed my A Level examinations in French, Latin, history and geography and was awarded an LCC Major County Scholarship for study at university leading to a degree.

I was particularly pleased with my academic results. We hear so often that when children are moved around different schools it will have an adverse effect on their academic progress. As a result of my family's frequent moves, together with my evacuation upheavals during the war years, I had attended no fewer than seven different schools in the nine years from 1937 to 1946. Further, during that period, I had spent the best part of a year in hospital and had moved to a dozen different 'permanent' addresses in various parts of England and Wales.

I had continued my birdwatching hobby from my Pembrey House days. I often visited parks in nearby Beckenham and Bromley as well as other areas which weren't so green or productive of wildlife. Ones which immediately spring to mind were the depressing and derelict bombsites around St. Paul's Cathedral in London in the years just after the War. As members of the junior branch of the RSPB, the Junior Bird Recorders Club (JBRC), a school birdwatching friend and I would travel up on the red London bus to the St. Paul's area. The bombsites were full of willowherb, starlings, house sparrows and feral pigeons – plus a new London bird, the black redstart. Equipped with a single pair of borrowed 'ex-naval surplus' binoculars which weighed a ton and which we shared, we would tour the bombsites, looking and looking. We did our best to avoid the local bobby on his bicycle. Sad to relate, we never did see the target black redstart but we did see lots of willowherb, starlings, house sparrows and feral pigeons.

I was a very keen birdwatcher, as we called ourselves, not that we dared admit at school that we were into such a 'soppy' hobby. I certainly wouldn't have dared talk 'birds' (feathered variety, that is) to a certain birth-month fellow pupil, the London streetwise Maurice Micklewhite, later aka Sir Michael Caine.

I joined the RSPB at the earliest opportunity at the age of fourteen in 1947. I have been a member ever since. In 1947 they only had some 5,000 members. The HQ was in Victoria Street, London and I visited it a few times after school, arriving there well before the office closed at 6.00. The visit I particularly recall was with my school birdwatching friend after we had claimed to have seen and heard a corncrake on migration at a south London sewage-farm. We had agreed by letter to present ourselves in Victoria Street to explain and give fulll details of our sighting. Two RSPB officers gave us a real grilling and finished by telling us we had been mistaken. To soften the blow, they gave us some printed material on the avocet, then a new breeding bird in East Anglia. The RSPB later moved to 'The Lodge' in Sandy, Bedfordshire and their membership increased to well over one million.

In the late 1940s and early 1950s I was a fervent supporter of Charlton Athletic, a team in the top First Division which had won the FA Cup in the 1946/47 season, defeating Burnley 1-0. I played for Wilson's

Grammar School football teams in that period and our school games finished on a Saturday morning before midday. After a shower at the ground, I was able to return home for a quick meal and then catch the train to Charlton for the afternoon matches. My entrance fee was one shilling and sixpence (7p) and I would watch the games from the terraces. The main characters in the Charlton team of those days were Don Welsh, the captain and Sam Bartram, the goalkeeper, a fiery redhead who also played for England.

One memorable match I watched was against Blackpool, with the legendary Stanley Matthews playing on the right wing. He had a great turn of speed and that, coupled with his stunning footwork, just bewildered the unfortunate Charlton left back, time and again. Matthews never acknowledged the crowd at all. When one of his crosses from the wing resulted in a goal, the Blackpool players made no attempt to rush towards him or towards the scorer for that matter. That reaction or lack of reaction was commonplace in First Division matches. 'A goal had been scored – now let's get on with the rest of the game'.

Matthews, along with most of the other players on the pitch that day, was on the maximum footballers' weekly wage of £14, about double the average weekly wage for the working man but still hardly a fortune. If I arrived early at The Valley, Charlton's home ground, I might well be on the same train as some of the players. Taxis were too expensive for them and a number of players didn't own a car. Many of the young, unmarried First Division players still lived at home with their parents or in rented rooms in guest houses. Some married players also lived in modest rented accommodation.

Walter Winterbottom was the England football team manager from 1946-62 and the Football Association Director of Coaching. In the 1950/51 and 51/52 seasons, he ran a coaching course for the Wilson's Grammar School First Eleven team at our sportsfield in Dulwich. I found his courses most valuable and thought Winterbottom an excellent and considerate coach. He had played top level football for Manchester United before the War but prior to being appointed the England team manager, he'd had no previous professional managerial experience. Notable games during his era were a 10-0 away victory against Portugal and a 3-6 defeat at Wembley to Hungary in 1953. Walter Winterbottom was succeeded as the England team manager by Alf Ramsey and many claim he had laid the firm foundations for England's World Cup victory in 1966.

In the summer holidays when at Wilson's Grammar School, I would often watch cricket matches at the Kennington Oval, Surrey's home ground. I would spend my week's pocket money on the number 58 tram or 36 bus fare from Downham (Catford) and the two shilling (10p) entrance charge. I was a keen Surrey supporter and a great fan of Eric and Alec, the Bedser twins.

One of the most memorable county matches I saw was between Surrey and Middlesex in August 1947. Middlesex won the toss and, in glorious sunny weather, decided to bat. By the close of play on day one, Middlesex had scored 537 for the loss of only two wickets. Bill Edrich was not out at 157 and Denis Compton was similarly not out at 137. Middlesex went on to win by an innings and 11 runs, with Compton taking 6 wickets in each of Surrey's innings. It was indeed a glorious summer for Denis Compton. He made a record 18 centuries, amassing a record total of 3,518 runs for the season.

The most memorable day's play I saw at The Oval was the opening day of the fifth and final Test Match between England and Australia in August 1948. England were always captained by an amateur in those days and Norman Yardley led a team which included Len Hutton, Denis Compton, Bill Edrich and Alec Bedser. I got up very early that Saturday morning and caught the first tram to Kennington. There were already a lot of people queuing in front of me; some had queued all night in miserable weather. The main attraction was that Don Bradman, the Australian captain and brilliant batsman, was making his last appearance in international cricket before retirement.

Because of a rain-affected pitch, play didn't start until after midday. England were skittled out for only 52 with Len Hutton making more than half the total. The England players just couldn't cope with the pace and swing of Australia's Lindwall and Miller. Australia passed England's total without loss of wicket. Their first wicket fell at 117 and Don Bradman, as batsman number three, was due to arrive at the crease.

There was an air of great expectation as Bradman appeared and walked out onto the field. He received a standing ovation from the crowd and three cheers from the England players. He needed just four runs to secure a Test batting average of 100. He faced the leg spinner, Eric Hollies. Arguably the greatest batsman ever was out second ball, bowled between bat and pad for a duck, or no runs scored. The crowd, the two teams, just everyone was stunned – and so Bradman's test career run average ended at 99.94.

Australia went on to win the match by an innings and 149 runs. They had won four of the five test matches played, thus retaining the Ashes.

I began my National Service as a private in the Royal Army Service Corps (RASC) in February 1953. I had only been a national serviceman two weeks when news broke of Joseph Stalin's death on 5 March. It is interesting to note that of the three notorious dictators, Stalin, Hitler and Mussolini, whose combined actions let to the deaths of tens of millions of people, Stalin was the only one of the three to die in his bed. Benito Mussolini had been shot by Italian partisans in April 1945 and Adolf Hitler had killed himself in the Berlin Fuhrerbunker in the same month. Nikita Khrushchev eventually succeeded Stalin, and he went on to denounce Stalinism in a speech in February 1956. As raw recruits, our squad did hours of parade square drill ('square bashing') in an effort to turn us into disciplined servicemen. We carried out the usual menial tasks allotted to the lowest of the low, including the seemingly senseless ones of painting coal white and mud-stained grass green. At least, our corporal tried to explain the apparent idiocy of such duties. He claimed the reason coal was painted white was simple: if someone was stealing coal from the unit's central stock painted white, it very soon became apparent when black areas appeared. The military police could then take appropriate action such as inspecting domestic coal bunkers at the married quarters patch to see if some enterprising soldier had white coal. To a sergeant-major's eye, especially before a big inspection by a high-ranking officer, brown marks on a lawn where soldiers had taken a short cut, were anathema. Those areas had to be painted green to harmonisewith the rest of the lawn. After we had touched up one large brown patch on the lawn near the unit flagstaff in freezing weather, I asked the corporal if the following day we could paint the sky blue with a big yellow blob on it. He was not amused. As with most national servicemen I can still remember my eight digit Army number to this day.

'Soldier, did you use a mirror when you shaved this morning?' 'Yes, sergeant.' 'Well, next time I suggest you use a bloody razor!' - was one of the many witticisms employed by our drill instruction staff. They were amusing the first time round but not quite so witty after the tenth hearing. There was no such thing as a minimum wage in 1953. As a recruit, I was paid four shillings (20p) a day, resulting in the grand sum of £1 – 8s (£1.40p) per week.

I applied to be selected for officer training. Those of us who had passed the Unit Selection Board (USB) were then 'groomed' to proceed to the War Office Selection Board (WOSB). The selection unit was situated at Barton Stacey in Hampshire and applicants hoping for a commission were sent there for three days. During that time, one underwent educational, military and personality tests plus practical problem-solving tasks. Commanding a six-man group, one was given planks, ropes and barrels. The task was to get the men, weapons and ammunition across a wide stream without anything getting wet. Of course, the planks were never long enough, the ropes were too short and so on. The trick was not to panic under pressure, to remain in command of the group throughout and to accomplish the task, perhaps by imaginative use of the barrels. I managed to pass. This meant I would then spend sixteen weeks at an Officer Cadet School before being commissioned as a second lieutenant.

Returning to our USB barrack room from Barton Stacey, I noticed one lad was in tears. 'I can't believe it,' he exclaimed. 'I failed as a public schoolboy and yet you, Reddisson, passed as a London grammar schoolboy. It's all unbelievable!' Later, during officer cadet training at Mons Barracks, Aldershot, I was informed by another public schoolboy how fortunate I was as a grammar schoolboy to be selected to join the officer class. Those two comments were not untypical of social class divisions in the early 1950s.

Our regimental sergeant-major at Mons Officer Cadet School was RSM Ronald Brittain of the Coldstream Guards. He was the archetypal RSM, a most imposing figure at 6 feet 3 inches tall and built like the proverbial brick wall. He had a sharp eye for detail and particularly disliked even traces of hair on a cadet's neck. He would stand next to the unfortunate miscreant on the parade ground and bellow, 'Am I hurting you, sir?' 'No, sir.' 'Well, I should be. I'm standing on your hair.' He called us 'sir' as officer cadets, and we addressed him as 'sir' as the RSM. However, he would say, 'I call you sir' and you call me 'sir' but the difference is you mean it.' One of his stock phrases was, 'You 'orrible little man, sir.' Brittain was credited with having the loudest voice in the British Army and his words of command were certainly deafening when delivered nearby. Apparently, Mrs Ronald Brittain was softly spoken but could silence her RSM husband at fifty paces with one of her steely stares.

RSM Brittain was a great character with much charisma. He proved to be a great trainer of young men. They don't make them like him anymore.

As Second Lieutenant John Reddisson, I thoroughly enjoyed my posting to a Command Supply Depot in Nottinghamshire. I knew that when I had finished my National Service, there was a place waiting for me at London University to read geography. As my elder sister, Ruth, and my brother, George had both graduated from Cambridge, I thought I would try my luck to secure a place there. In early November 1954, I wrote to three colleges in Cambridge – Emmanuel, Downing and St. Luke's. By return of post, I received 'regret' letters from Emmanuel and Downing. A day later, I received the following letter from Dr. H.R. Jamieson, the Senior Tutor at St. Luke's College:

'9 November 1954

Dear Mr. Reddisson,

Thank you for your letter of 6th November. I am afraid it is not very likely that, at this late date, we could find a place for you in this College in 1955 to read for the Geographical Tripos. I should, however, be glad to do whatever is possible and if you would care to carry negotiations a little further, please complete and return to me the enclosed admission form, although I must warn you not to be unduly optimistic as to the upshot. When you return the form I should be glad if you would let me know whether you would be likely to be able to get leave to come and see me at 2.0pm on Saturday, 20th November or at the same time on Saturday, 27th November.

Yours sincerely, etc.'

I duly presented myself in Dr. Jamieson's study in St. Luke's College, Cambridge at 2.0pm on the second of the suggested dates. He had done his homework and had telephoned my headmaster at Wilson's Grammar School for a verbal assessment of my scholastic potential. He stated that he was more than satisfied with the headmaster's comments. Fortunately, Dr. Jamieson was interested in cricket and the headmaster had mentioned my score of 146 at The Oval in the summer of 1952. My interview also included discussions on classical music, literature, travel and English history. Geography was never mentioned.

I returned to my army unit feeling that I had acquitted myself reasonably well in Dr. Jamieson's study. One week later, I received the following letter from him:

'7 December 1954

My dear John,

It gives me great pleasure to be able to tell you there will be a place for you here in October 1955 to read for the Geographical Tripos.

If you accept this offer, you should send me (Tutor's Account) the College Administration Fee of £2.0.0 so that I can put forward your name for formal admission, and you should also arrange for your 1950 General Certificate of Education to be sent to me for registration purposes.

I shall be very glad to have you in residence in due course.

A Merry Christmas!

Yours sincerely, etc.'

I extended my statutory two years' service by an extra six months (and received promotion to lieutenant) to take me up to September 1955 – the month before I entered St Luke's College, Cambridge as an under-graduate. Meanwhile my parents, accompanied by the unmarried Ruth, had moved from the flat in south London to a house in Crawley, Sussex. The move came about as the firm my father worked for as an engineer had relocated from London to Crawley and had arranged houses for those employees who accepted the move. It was the first time my parents had experienced the joy of their own garden since leaving their bombed-out house in Bellingham, south London in the early years of the War.

CHAPTER 4

I went up to St. Luke's College, Cambridge in September 1955 as a grammar school product of Wilson's Grammar School, London, to read geography. I was following in the footsteps of my sister, Ruth, who had read classics (ancient Greek and Latin) as an Open Scholar and of my brother, George, who had read modern languages (French and German). Ruth later became something of a recluse, and only worked in menial office jobs in order to pay the rent of a succession of dingy one-bedroom flats as she passed her life reading and sleeping, sleeping and reading. She also spent periods living with my parents. George subsequently worked for the publishers Harrap's, producing a number of German and French textbooks as well as a French-English slang dictionary. My other sister, Amy, opted out of academia, attended a technical institute and became a successful dress designer in a well-known fashion house in the West End of London.

Pensioners will remember learning at school all about the numerical value in yards of chains, furlongs and miles – one chain equals 22 yards, one furlong equals 10 chains (220 yards) and 8 furlongs equal one mile (1760 yards). At my grammar school in London just after the War, we also learned in our geography lessons where continents and countries were on a map of the world and which countries produced which crops and minerals. We coloured forests and jungles green on our maps, deserts yellow and so on. Rainfall area maps were also considered important. An emphasis was thus placed on regional, physical and economic geography with a dash of meteorology.

Geography, however, as studied in year one at Cambridge came as a complete shock to me. It consisted of two main parts – historical geography and what might be termed 'physical' geography. I never fully understood the purpose of the historical geography part – to me, it seemed more like history, pure and simple. The 'physical' geography part was indeed very physical. In my first term at Cambridge, I spent several days a week with two partner students physically carrying out survey work in the area of the nearby Gog-Magog Hills. The three of us would report to the Geography department first thing in the morning, sign out a theodolite measuring instrument together with a chain set which consisted of a linked metal material neatly sectioned into 22 pieces.

In the 1950s, the chain was commonly used to indicate land distances and particularly in surveying land for legal and commercial purposes. A rectangle of land one furlong long and one chain in width had an area of exactly one acre (4840 square yards). The chain survives today as the length of a cricket pitch, the distance between the two wickets being 22 yards.

Fortunately, one of my survey partners happened to have permission to borrow his uncle's 1937 Riley Kestrel motorcar which was garaged at his uncle's house in Cambridge itself. The vehicle had been one of the sporting icons of the 1930s. Riley had pioneered the 'fastback' style with the introduction of the Kestrel in

1933. At the time it was the epitome of modernity, being fitted with a one and a half litre, four-cylinder engine plus twin carburetors. The car's main attraction to us, however, was that it could just about manage to transport three Cambridge geography students plus a heavy metal chain of 22 yards and a theodolite to the Gog-Magog Hills. There we would carry out the regular but intensely boring survey tasks allotted to us. Other less fortunate students had to somehow transport their heavy metal chain and theodolyte by bus or on dodgy bicycles. Moreover, we all had to contend with the Cambridge fen-type autumn weather of mist, fog and rain, especially the frequent rain.

After a couple of months of this ghastly geography misadventure, I'd had enough; in fact, more than enough. At Cambridge, each undergraduate was allocated an 'in loco parentis' (or, in the place of parents) moral tutor. It was a high-flown title but essentially the tutor was tasked to look after our welfare needs. My moral tutor was a certain Dr. John Hargreaves, a noted historian, who would later progress to become a history professor and the Master of St. Luke's College. A short, balding, rotund figure, and hardly a bundle of fun, he agreed to see me in his rooms at the college in early December, a couple of weeks before the end of the Michaelmas Term. His metier was history in all its aspects – research, lecturing and monitoring research graduates working towards a history PhD. Having to deal with an undergraduate with a personal problem was clearly an imposition on his valuable time, so our meeting was brief.

I explained my antipathy towards the Geography Tripos content and politely suggested that he considered my switching to another tripos. 'So, Mr Reddisson,' he exclaimed, 'you don't particularly care for the way we treat and structure geography at Cambridge. What alternative subject do you have in mind so as to redress this unfortunate imbalance in your undergraduate life here?' 'Well, Dr. Hargreaves,' I began, 'At school, I studied geography, history, French and Latin to State Scholarship and GCE 'A' Level but, of course, Cambridge only offers Latin with ancient Greek, and a modern language with another modern language. That severely curtails the choice of subject area I could read here. However, I do know that Cambridge offers the opportunity of combining a good knowledge of one modern language with learning another from scratch.' Having achieved a high mark in my written and spoken French examinations at GCE 'A' Level, I had come to the meeting with Dr. Hargreaves with that nugget of information up my sleeve. 'The alternative I have in mind,' I continued,'is to combine my existing French knowledge with Italian'. 'And how much italiano do you know?' he asked, with a distinct pursing of the lips. I reckoned that the truth was the best line to follow with a character such as this discerning, brainy moral tutor sat in front of me, reminding me of Mr. Pickwick as drawn by Phiz in the illustrated Dicken's novel. 'Virtually none,' was my brief reply. Dr. Hargreaves looked at me in a rather quizzical manner and then fastened on to his perceived answer. 'Right,' he declared, 'it's now 5th December. Lent Term will begin in about five weeks or so. You have that period of grace to advance from 'virtually none' as you put it, to a virtual GCE 'O' Level acceptable grade in Italian as I might put it. Come and see me at twelve noon on 11th January and, if you haven't changed your mind yet again, I'll arrange for you to be interviewed by Mr. Limentani, a senior lecturer in the Italian department. He will decide your future. Good morning, Mr. Reddisson.'

Needless to say, the next five weeks were frenetic. Dr. Hargreaves, the supreme intellectual, had set me the intellectual task of teaching myself Italian to a level which secondary school students hoped to achieve after five years of classroom lessons – GCE 'O' Level. He had known that my brief study period would include the festive season of Christmas and the New Year but I felt that he had probably considered that factor as part of the challenge. That feeling was an essential spur that drove me on in my efforts to master the rudiments of the Italian language in the allotted five weeks.

I spent the Christmas and the New Year at my parents' house in Crawley, Sussex. They were very understanding and I virtually took over the dining-room most of the time; otherwise I studied in my bedroom. I drew up a rigid daily study programme which I resolved to follow at all costs. I worked three hours both in the morning and in the afternoon with an additional two hours in the evening. Sundays and Christmas Day were to be study free. I equipped myself with a good Italian dictionary and two or three textbooks, including the English Universities Press (EUP) 'Teach Yourself Italian' and a Hugo's Language Institute primer.

The major drawback to my self-taught efforts was that there was no way I could listen to spoken Italian. I had to concentrate very hard on the written instructions for the pronunciation of the language but any high level achievement in following such instructions was far from guaranteed. Further, just one early

misunderstanding in following the written pronunciation guide would inevitably lead to a continuing and
compounded pronunciation fault being repeated and
maintained day after day. By having more than one textbook guide, I hoped to eradicate that problem. Reel
to reel, open reel tape-recordings of spoken Italian,
did not exist for standard public purchase in 1955. Even
if they had been available for purchase, the necessary
machine on which to play them would have been well
outside my limited purchasing power. Cassettes were
still ten years away. So, I soldiered on in not only teaching myself Italian grammar and vocabulary to the best
of my ability but also its pronunciation. Waking up at
night, I sometimes wondered if I would indeed overcome
the looming hurdle as embodied by Dr. Hargreaves'
'Mr. Limentani'. Then, in my restless state, I would think
of an English word, turn on my bedside light, look up
the Italian for it and jot it down on a nearby notepad
before turning off the light and going back to sleep.
Christmas came and went as did the New Year. I found
that my apparent progress was now giving me some
encouragement.

By 11th January, I had a certain confidence that all
would go well. Dr. Hargreaves saw me, accepted my
confident belief in my own ability and he arranged for
me to meet Mr. Limentani in his house three days later.
The Italian lecturer's warmth and charm settled my
nerves at once. We worked through translation texts for
about an hour. Mr. Limentani then smiled broadly and
greeted me as a newly enrolled student into the Italian
department. 'Bene, molto bene,' he intoned. I had done
well and had successfully switched from the dreary
geography tripos to the modern and mediaeval languages

tripos in French and Italian. That one event would lead to a lifelong love affair with Italy and its beautiful language. Although I had already lost a whole term of study, the Michaelmas Term of 1955, my keenness together with my determination to do well bore fruit. Within six months, I had received in my St. Luke's letter pigeonhole in the Porters' Lodge, an unexpected but gratifying personal note from Dr. Hargreaves himself.

16 June 1956
'Mr. Reddisson,
I think you should be very pleased with yourself. Your preliminary Part 1 examination marks show that you did not just scrape into the 2:1 class but got in at a high level. Your translation paper from the French was a first class mark, your composition in French was not far below it. Both your Italian marks were very good considering how little time you have been able to spend on the language. Naturally, your composition in Italian was the weakest of your papers – a lowish second class mark. However, this should be a great encouragement to you and you should have a chance next year of getting a First.
Best wishes, etc.'

Further, in the same year, I achieved a First Class result in the viva voce/oral examination in Italian. I was informed by Mr. Limentani that it was the first mark at that level for some years. Prior to the examination, I had spent my 1956 summer vacation period attending a university language and literature course in Rome, lodging with a delightful Italian couple in the city centre. This led to another congratulatory letter from my supervising modern languages tutor at St. Luke's:

'14 October 1956

'I am so glad to see that your prolonged stay in Italy has been rewarded with a First.' (signed) Dr. P. Buffon.'

The following summer of 1957, I had the opportunity to perfect my spoken Italian to a higher level. It came about in a most unexpected way. One morning at the beginning of the Easter Term in April, I found a note in my college pigeonhole in the Porters' Lodge. It was from Henry Mullin, an undergraduate reading French and Spanish at Peterhouse. Would I be interested in working for a travel company in Italy for the coming summer vacation? The job came with good pay and excellent working conditions. If I was interested, he'd be in 'The Anchor' pub by the Cam off Silver Street at 8 o'clock on Saturday evening to take the matter further. He added that he knew me by sight.

As I walked up to the bar at 'The Anchor' on the Saturday evening, a young man approached me, introduced himself as Henry Mullin and promptly bought me a beer. Apparently, he had worked for a Liverpool based travel company, YTG Universal Ltd, during each of his long summer vacations and was now in his final year. He had been based at a hotel in Majorca and now that General Franco was welcoming tourists to the island, business there was booming. Would I be interested in working for the same company on the Italian Ligurian Riviera based in Alassio? The dates would be from late June to mid- September, neatly bracketing the forthcoming Cambridge vacation break. Someone at St. Luke's who knew I was reading Italian, had pointed me out to Harry when I was leaving a French lecture. The job involved being a travel representative or courier working at a hotel in Italy looking after the needs of a series of holidaymakers during their fortnight stay. I stated on the spot that I was indeed interested in the job vacancy. A week later, a letter arrived for me from Mr Lewis Williams, Managing Director of YTG Universal Ltd, confirming the job, subject to my attending a two-day training course in London with an overnight stay provided, and my performing satisfactorily. In those days, one had to apply for an 'exeat' to spend a night during term time outside the walls of Cambridge. Dr. Hargreaves was sympathetic to my application, realising that the stay in Italy would further improve my Italian. 'I expect further good news from Mr Limentani in exchange for this exeat,' he declared.

All went well on the two-day course. The next stage would be to meet my first group of holiday- makers. An eagerly awaited late June day eventually arrived. It had been arranged for me to meet a group of eleven Liverpudlian tourists at the ticket barrier to the Dover boat-train at Victoria Station on an early Friday afternoon. The group arrived on time, with ages ranging from an estimated early twenties to late fifties. They had already travelled from their Liverpool homes to London by rail and then by tube, across to Victoria Station. The remainder of their jouney to the Italian sun would take another twenty-four hours, thankfully on a series of pre-booked train seats and a Channel crossing – but such were the delights of overseas travel in the 1950s.

The onward journey took us to the Dover cross-channel ferry, on to Calais, the Calais – Paris train and the nightmare metro underground system in Paris to the Gare de Lyon for our train to Italy. We had been lugging our aptly -named luggage around for most of the day and our spirits rose as we realised we were now on the final part of our journey. We left the Gare de Lyon late in the evening and within a few minutes an attendant arrived to convert our two six-seater compartments into couchettes. This involved pulling out bunk-type beds from the middle and the top of the compartment walls. The existing seats on both sides were converted into the lowest bunks or couchettes. Each compartment now consisted of six couchettes for the six passengers. We were travelling second class but in first class compartments there would be just four beds. The attendant provided a blanket, sheet and pillow for each passenger. People didn't undress – they merely removed footwear. It was all very cosy if somewhat uncomfortable. At least the twelve of us sharing our two 'bedrooms' had got to know one another up to a point. Other travellers on the train would have found themselves sharing the cramped sleeping arrangements with five complete strangers – a somewhat unusual and perhaps unpleasant experience. The couchette system was never adopted in Britain for overnight journeys such as from London to Scotland. This was probably because it involved mixed-sex sleeping arrangements with a total loss of privacy and a certain loss of dignity in a country where both were highly valued and where reserve was widely practised.

As the train rattled southwards through the night, the noise it made helped to muffle the mixture of sounds coming from my five travelling companions. The quality of air was not improved by one of our number being a compulsive smoker, although his indulgence helped to mask the rising body odours filling the compartment.

I had one of the two middle bunks and found that the bottom of the bunk above me was only a few inches from my face. Awaking in the early hours of the morning while it was still dark and negotiating my way to the corridor loo took a considerable time. Despite the subdued lighting, I still managed to tread on somebody's hand. There was a yelp and then silence from the unintended victim. The train called at Dijon and Lyon during the night and in the morning we reached Marseille. Food and drink so far had consisted of sandwiches and bottled water or fruit juice purchased at the Gare de Lyon the previous evening. During the long wait at Marseille we were able to purchase further food and drink from the vendors moving along the corridor.

Spirits rose considerably as we travelled along the Mediterranean coastline heading east to Italy. The railway ran through a series of tunnels occasionally and it was rather like travelling down an enormous flute. Eventually, we reached the Italian border. Customs and passport control took place on the train with the Italian officials inevitably flirting with the young women in our group – not that they complained. In fact, they undoubtedly enjoyed their first exposure to the Italian male's foremost social habit. Taxis, paid out of my lire float, took us to the 'Hotel Solara' in Alassio for the start of my clients' summer holiday. It was YTG's first group to 'Hotel Solara', but all passed without any hitches or teething problems.

My group, without exception, loved the Italian experience. All too soon, I was taking them back to Alassio railway station and putting them on the Paris train for the gruelling return trip to their eventual destination of Liverpool – some thirty hours or so of travelling ahead. My summer passed happily, with my welcoming and then saying 'ciao' to group after group. In September, I accompanied the final group back as far as London. My summer mission had been completed successfully. It was now time to return to Cambridge.

At the beginning of a new term and especially so at the beginning of a new academic year, I would go to sample as many French and Italian lecturers' offerings as possible. In that way I could weed out those which for me would be a waste of time. After an hour's listening to a particular lecturer, I could usually make up my mind as to whether I continued in future or not. Attendance at lectures was a decision left to each student on the Arts side; missing lectures for students reading Natural Sciences was not so easily achieved. Questions were not allowed after a lecture had finished.

Some of the lecturers in the French and Italian departments were natural communicators and their lectures were invariably well attended. One sparkling lecturer specialising in French literature of the eighteenth century would bring the house down with his collection of seemingly impromptu, off-the-cuff anecdotes. He was programmed to deliver the same lecture on a Monday as well as on a Thursday in the week. Having mislaid my Monday notes, I went along to hear the repeat on the Thusday. Amazingly, the lecturer recognised me in his audience from the Monday. When he had finished speaking, he followed me out of the lecture hall and approached me. 'I don't see the point of your attending my repeat lecture', he exclaimed, 'and I would not recommend your doing so again'. It was a warning-off, in effect. What had really miffed him, of course, was the fact that in his Thursday lecture, just as he was approaching a seemingly impromptu, off-the-cuff and amusing anecdote, he happened to catch my eye, rather spoiling the theatrical impact for him.

Some of our lecturers were dismal performers, droning on and on about some obscure author and his work. One or two of the more easily self- satisfied amongst them would look at the students smugly at the end of a lecture as if they had somehow distilled all the mysteries of the literary universe and the wonders of the academic world into their one hour at the lectern. Along with other students, I was more prone to classify their offerings as pure gobbledegook dressed up to appear as the epitome of academic profundity. Bah! Humbug!

In addition to Mr Limentani, I also came into contact with two other teaching members of the Italian department. All lectures were delivered in English, never in Italian. One senior lecturer in post since 1938 was virtually on automatic from the moment he walked into the lecture hall in his long academic gown, until the moment he exited. His lectures would last an hour and throughout their delivery he would scrupulously avoid eye contact with any of his students listening to what he had to say. He managed to achieve this unbelievable feat despite the fact that our small number of only a dozen or so students were all grouped together only a few feet away from the lectern. Not infrequently, he would stray off the main topic of his lecture and start talking about some (to us) totally unknown but (to him) favourite authors. There is nothing so boring as a blinkered academic on his hobby-horse. When his hour was up, he would shuffle his papers together noisily and then shuffle himself out of the lecture hall, again without a glance towards his erstwhile audience. He was just one of the many strange, unusual and eccentric characters walking the streets of Cambridge, and many of them were employed by the University.

The other member of the Italian department's staff that I would meet a couple of times a week on a one-to-one supervision basis was a young lecturer, probably in his mid-twenties. He had completed his PhD doctoral thesis only a few years previously. Our supervisions were devoted to the study of the poet, Dante Aligheri (1265 - 1321), especially of his major work 'La Divina Commedia'. The long poem is divided into three parts – Inferno, Purgatorio and Paradiso. It was written between 1304 and 1321 and is considered to be one of the world's great literary masterpieces. Because Dante wrote his work in the regional dialect of Tuscany, ignoring the usual custom of the day of writing in Latin, he is often referred to as the 'Father of the Italian language'. Other literary figures of the time are said to have remonstrated with him for writing on his lofty themes in the vernacular instead of in Latin. Parallels may be drawn between Dante Aligheri and our own Geoffrey Chaucer (1343-1400), author of 'The Canterbury Tales'. Chaucer was a pivotal figure in the development of the English vernacular at a time when the principal literary languages were French and Latin. He helped to stabilise the London dialect as the burgeoning English language, just as Dante had helped to stabilise the Tuscan dialect to form the basis of the Italian language. Modern English has moved on considerably since Chaucer's day whereas modern Italian is still close to Dante's written language. As a result, today's schoolchildren are baffled by Chaucer's English while their Italian counterparts have little difficulty in understanding Dante's Italian.

The young Italian lecturer who specialised in the works of Dante had one glaring fault and I shall soon explain what it was. Having spent the summer vacation of 1956 on a study scholarship in Rome at the prestigious Dante Aligheri Institute, and having lodged with an elderly but attentive Italian couple, I had acquired a certain fluency in the spoken language. The study scholarship had given me the opportunity of practising my spoken Italian for several hours every day throughout the vacation. Naturally, on my return to Cambridge for the Michaelmas Term in late September, I was eager to continue talking Italian as much as possible: 'Use it, or lose it', as they say.

It so happened that I was scheduled for a one-to-one supervision with the fourteenth century poet doctor on the very first day of term. As I entered his study, I greeted him in Italian and then indulged in small talk in the language for a few minutes. I could see that his face was becoming redder by the minute and I soon discovered the reason. He had let me ramble on, injecting an infrequent monosyllabic comment. When I asked him a direct question about how he had spent his summer break, he suddenly broke into English. 'I say, Mr. Reddisson, do you mind awfully if we continue this supervision in English? My spoken Italian is somewhat rusty, you see.' That certainly deflated my eagerness. Further, I was surprised and disappointed that a Cambridge don in the Italian department was not competent to converse fluently in Italian.

I had noticed that the Italian department announcements on the main information board referred to the

Professor as with a PhD and also with regard to the young lecturer. However, it appeared that Mr. Limentani had no PhD qualification, hence the 'Mr.'On checking a central University staff list in the University Library, I discovered an entry reading 'Uberto Limentani PhD', with the doctorate award from an Italian university. Following enquiries, I learned that Cambridge University, in their domestic staff lists and announcements, only recognised PhDs from Cambridge itself, Oxford and Trinity College, Dublin. How snooty was that? In most other British universities, or in an Italian university, Mr. Limentani would have been known as Dr. Limentani but at Cambridge he was just plain 'Mr.' Anyway, Uberto Limentani, whom I greatly admired, had the last laugh. On the retirement of the department's professor, he was appointed the next Professor of Italian at Cambridge University.

Several of my fellow students in the department had also started Italian from scratch at Cambridge, although they had the advantage of having begun their studies at the start of the academic year, whereas I had switched from geography in the January of the Lent Term. A couple of students had lived in Italy with their parents, their fathers being employed there. One such student was ER 'Ted' Dexter up at Jesus College. I would chat to him occasionally before our Italian lectures but I didn't see a great deal of him. Rugby, cricket and golf were three additional subjects he was studying and he excelled at all three. I found him easily bored by social small talk. He had a distinctly reserved manner and an aloof self-confidence. He had attended Radley College public school, as had Peter Cook, the comedian. Cook later recalled how he had been caned by 'an imperious, cricket-playing prefect called Ted Dexter.' To be struck on one's rump by one of England's finest batsmen is not the sort of fate to be enjoyed and hopefull y Dexter wasn't practising his famous coverdrive at the time.

Once Dexter left Cambridge, success followed success on the cricket field. He duly captained Sussex, and then the England cricket team in the early 1960s. He was an aggressive batsman and a delight to watch. In 1961, he was named 'Wisden Cricketer of the Year.'

During my time at Cambridge (1955-58), it was compulsory for undergraduates to wear a dark, knee-length gown on a number of occasions, including going to lectures and supervisions, dining in college and leaving the college grounds after dark. Gown-wearing distinguished us from the Cambridge town populace and emphasised the phrase which had developed over the centuries,'town and gown'- the non-academic townspeople and the university members. For me, it was merely a non-adversorial distinction and I don't recall encountering very much friction between the two groups. However, in the past, there had been much animosity. The Head Porter at St. Luke's College used to say that the enormous front door of the college hadn't been built to keep the students in but to keep the townspeople out. History relates how the very foundation of Cambridge University was the result of bitter animosity between 'town and gown' - in Oxford. Fearing for their lives after a series of acrimonious confrontations with the townspeople, some Oxford students decided to move to a new area and the town of Cambridge was chosen. A charter establishing the new university was granted in the thirteenth century. The first Cambridge college to be founded was Peterhouse in 1284 during the reign of Edward 1.

The gown was often referred to as 'academic dress'. Mine was a recycled one bought second-hand from a special section in a Cambridge tailor's. Formal dress even extended into the Porters' Lodge at St. Luke's – the Head Porter always wore a morning suit and a bowler hat.

In the evenings, one had to keep a sharp lookout for the University Constables or Bulldogs, smartly dressed in their top-hats, and sometimes accompanied by another University disciplinary individual, the Proctor. They would patrol the Cambridge streets after dark, keeping an eye open for any misbehaving undergraduates, especially those not wearing a gown or trying to gain access over walls to their college room after the Porters' Lodge had closed for the night.

I often went to the 'Arts Cinema' in Market Passage in the centre of Cambridge. It specialised in showing French and Italian films often without subtitles. Our language supervisors would recommend our going to watch these films but the truth was most of us couldn't make head or tail of what was going on. The inevitable series of Gauloises in the hero's mouth and the fact that the black and white films seemed to have been shot at night compounded the problem. Nearby, was another 'pleasure centre', a cafe called 'Dorothy's' or 'The Dorothy'. They would hold 'tea dances' with live music throughout the week. Well into my second year, I still hadn't been to 'Dorothy's', but Jeremy, a good friend of mine who was also reading Italian, declared one day that it was high time to attend to that omission. He assured me that a visit there would not be disappointing.

I had heard that the cafe's customers were very varied. In addition to male undergraduates hoping to meet foreign language students learning English at the local English language schools, there would be office girls and female undergraduates from the ladies' colleges of Girton and Newnham. Good numbers of servicemen from the local RAF bases also attended, together with a fair sprinkling of United States Airforce personnel from units dotted around Cambridge. It was a constant source of irritation that with their attractive Hollywood accents and their ready cash, the American servicemen would sweep the girls off their feet. They earned three times as much as the British servicemen and could easily afford to take girls out to dinner or at least pay for their cinema ticket. The RAF lads would complain that the Yanks were 'oversexed, overpaid and over here', drinking British pubs dry and filling up the nurseries. It was indeed true that a number of British girls were left literally 'holding the baby'.

The majority of the male undergraduates at Cambridge in the 1950s were virgins, especially those arriving straight from school. Others had done two years National Sevice and may well have seen more of the world and its ways. A much larger number of the female undergraduates had acquired little if any sexual experience. Dr Hargreaves, my moral tutor, would not have lost much sleep in worrying about the morals of his students in the sexual sense. During my three years at Cambridge, the subject of 'sex' never seemed to surface to any meaningful degree, at least in my circle of friends, despite what one may have read in certain biographies and autobiographies of the period by authors with highly imaginative memories or an eye on book sales.

Promiscuity was something quite foreign to 'nice' middle class young men and women at the time. The young men might well have welcomed it but the answer was invariably 'No'. Sleeping around was seen as more of a pastime indulged in by the so-called upper classes and by actors and actressess. If however, in Britain at large, working-class or middle-class girls did become pregnant, the matter was invariably hushed up by the parents. The girls would be sent away to places where they could give birth in secret, with the child then being taken away from them and put up for adoption. The girls would return home alone. The parents would tell friends and neighbours how nice it was to have their daughter home again after her unselfish act in looking after poor aunt Lilian in Swindon for a few months. Whether the parents' tales were ever believed was another matter.

Jeremy had related to me the story of one Girton College undergraduate (or undergraduette, as they were sometimes referred to), whose overall naivety in matters of lust and love bordered on the unbelievable. One afternoon at 'Dorothy's', she was said to have asked an American airman to remove his revolver from his trouser pocket as it was uncomfortable for her when dancing cheek to cheek, stomach to stomach. For his part, the American replied laconically that his revolver wouldn't fit into his jacket pocket, so they carried on dancing regardless, she with a rather pained expression on her face, he with a look of smug satisfaction. For that particular US serviceman, dancing was indeed a vertical expression of a horizontal desire.

After what I had heard about 'Dorothy's' before ever setting foot in the place, I found my first visit with

Jeremy quite disappointing. First and foremost, men far outnumbered women by a ratio of about three to one. You had to be very quick off the mark to get to ask a girl to dance. The Americans and the RAF servicemen kept in their own separate groups. On occasions, there were some vicious glances between them and several verbal exchanges but thankfully, nothing more. I managed to have a couple of dances with a German girl who was attending a month's English course in Cambridge. She was pleasant enough but in addition to having what seemed like two left feet, she was very formal in her attitude. When, after the second dance, I asked if I could buy her something to drink, she simply said the one word 'No' – and left the dancefloor to rejoin her companions. Polite exchanges were not her forte: perhaps her class hadn't yet reached that subject in their lessons. Surprisingly, Jeremy didn't bother to dance at all. Perhaps he couldn't, but then it hadn't stopped me getting onto the dancefloor. He said he took a lot of pleasure from just watching all the activity. We went to 'Dorothy's' a few more times together but it didn't become a focal point of my life at Cambridge.

CHAPTER 5

The arrival of spring in any city in Britain is a time dominated by the renewal of nature's presence in all its glory but in Cambridge it is especially captivating and invigorating. The picturesque area called 'the backs', running along the rear of several colleges with the attendant quietly flowing River Cam, is breathtakingly beautiful in spring with its spacious green lawns, massed ranks of daffodils and other early flowers. The awesome college architecture rises as a brooding backcloth to the whole. Little wonder that on warm spring days, undergraduates flock to the area to relax before acute preparation begins in earnest for the academic year's final examinations in June.

One such warm April morning in 1957 was to be the start of my involvement in an unexpected career move that was to provide a dominant factor in the next fifteen years of my life. I had left my college room and made my way to 'The Anchor' pub in the centre of Cambridge just off Silver Street. I was sitting outside in the sun enjoying a lunchtime beer, watching the punts go down on the river and the pints go down nearby. Suddenly, there was a tap on my shoulder. As I turned round, a middle-aged man sporting an outsize pair of sunglasses thrust a note into my hand. Nothing was said by either of us and before I could fully realise what was happening he had made his way through the assembled throng and had disappeared towards the city centre. The unsigned typewritten note said starkly: 'John Reddisson, if you have a taste for adventure of a most unusual kind be here at the same time next Saturday.' I straightaway thought the whole thing was some sort of stupid hoax perpetrated by my college friends back at St Lukes's. As a result, I thought I probably wouldn't return to 'The Anchor' the following Saturday.

Several of my college friends shared my staircase in the second court at St. Luke's. One entered the college itself from the main road and passed the Porters' Lodge before coming to the first court with its enormous lawn surrounded by impressive, linked buildings in the classical style. To access the second court, one passed through a further entrance on the far side leading to the dining-hall and the Junior Common Room bar. I had been allocated accommodation on D staircase which comprised six units in all. We shared a gyp or college servant called Harry. He was a heavy smoker, pleasant enough but a somewhat lugubrious individual aged about fifty. His job included looking after the specific needs of his 'six gentlemen' – a cup of tea first thing in the morning, bed-making, washing up any glasses, plates and coffee mugs, cleaning shoes, tidying up and so on. He also served at table in the dining-hall at lunch and dinner. I had already served my National Service and had managed to satisfactorily fulfil the requirements for the Queen's commission. Life at a Nottingham Royal Army Service Corps unit as a subaltern had been a pleasant, even 'cushy' experience. The rank of second lieutenant entitled me to a batman who looked after my needs in much the same way as

Harry would later do at Cambridge. As a result, I had become accustomed to receiving some pampering attention from a third party but for the rest of my staircase companions it was a novel experience.

The week following my Saturday lunchtime encounter at 'The Anchor' was a busy one, dominated by the fact that an increased study workload was required as my second year examinations were scheduled just a few weeks later. Further, a pair of new medic friends on my staircase who were reading Natural Sciences had arranged a very special visit for me on the Wednesday morning. Anatomy formed a large part of their studies and as I had innocently expressed an interest in their work, they had insisted that I accompanied them on a visit to their anatomy study workplace.

The study of anatomy is one of the most basic and most important subjects for medical students when they begin their medical studies. Its importance cannot be overestimated because it helps to lay the firm foundations of all future learning. It will be understood therefore that the decision of an individual to donate his/her body for anatomical examination is a vital contribution towards the advancement of medical science. The provision of cadavers for the medical profession has had a very murky past. In the early nineteenth century only the criminal dead could be given to science and as cadavers were in short supply, bodysnatching became prevalent. Bodies fresh from burial were much in demand and they supplied the deficit. Two notorious villains, Burke and Hare, changed their 'modus operandi' from robbing cemeteries of bodies to actually murdering people. The very fresh cadavers of murdered victims earned them a premium on top of the usual cemetery cadaver fee. The Anatomy Act of 1832 allowed unclaimed bodies and those donated by relatives to be used in medical establishments for the study of anatomy. As a result, bodysnatching was essentially finished as a trade. Medical students have to learn about the human body somehow and somewhere; it is considered preferable that they make mistakes on the dead rather than on the living.

On the morning of my visit with my two medical student friends, I wasn't really prepared for what lay in store as the three of us entered the Dissecting Room of the Anatomy Building. There were about twenty well -separated slabs in a large hall and on each slab there was a body. Each body was attended by six students. Two were working on the head and upper torso, plus one arm and hand; two on the remaining torso plus one arm and hand; and two on the legs. The age range of the bodies was complete – from children to young, middle-aged men and women and old people. Many of them had died during an operation as their chests or stomachs were very crudely stitched. My two medic friends took me to their subject, a man in his fifties whom they called 'Fred' and they began to work on their section – the lower torso plus one arm and hand. Various body parts had already been removed but the hands were still untouched, large knobbly fingers and a skin turned yellow by the preserving formaldehyde. I watched the students at work but I'd really had enough of practical anatomy studies after twenty minutes or so. 'Oh, you must come and look at the storeroom before you go, John,' said one of my friends. 'It'll be another experience for you.' I wondered what could be in the storeroom but I soon found out. It was a temperature controlled room with two long metal poles stretching away from the door rather as in a clothes-shop. But it wasn't clothes hanging from the rails but more bodies, held in place by metal clothes-hanger attachments. The coldstore operator announced that another 'customer' was required in the Anatomy Hall. With a long pole, he deftly whizzed a waiting body to the front and, helped by a porter, the body was transported to its appointed slab and its six students. At least, I now knew what happened when one made the decision to donate one's body for anatomical examination as a vital contribution towards the advancement of medical science. 'Fred' had made that decision at some time when alive and, looking around the busy hall, I felt honoured to have known him.

It so happened that at dinner in the St. Luke's dining-hall the same evening, Harry was on duty and serving my table. The main course was a plate of unappetising - looking beef with more fat than meat. The fat was reminiscent of some I had seen earlier in the day in the Dissecting Room. When Harry came to serve me, I couldn't help noticing his nicotine-stained yellow, large knobbly fingers. Needless to say, I didn't touch the food at all.

On and off during that week up to the Saturday, I had been reflecting on what to do. Should I go back to 'The Anchor' just to see what, if anything, would happen or should I not turn up? If anything, my inquisitive nature got the better of me and I returned to the pub towards midday. I sat in the same seat in the pub garden where I had been when the note had been passed to me. Time passed and nothing happened except that someone fell off a punt into the river, accompanied by much applause and cheering from the assembled throng. I had finished my beer and was thinking about returning to college when I spotted him making his way towards me. Yes, it was definitely the same middle-aged man with the same outsize sunglasses.

He approached me and muttered, 'Shall we walk?' Hardly without stopping, he set off for the bridge over the river towards the backs. I drew level with him as he turned right and walked along the river path towards King's College. 'Do you mind slowing down,' I grunted, 'and then you can tell me what all this is about.' Within a couple of minutes, we found an empty, isolated bench-seat and sat down. He removed his sunglasses, looked me straight in the eye and started talking. His opening gambit was, 'I suppose you really must be wondering what all this is about. Well, let me explain.'

The gist of his explanation was that he was a member of 'the British state security organisation' which recruited suitable Cambridge University men – and Oxford ones, for that matter – to carry out certain low-key assignments. I immediately asked, 'But, why me?' 'Let's say we've done our homework, John,' he countered. 'You are older than the average student here, having already done your National Service rather than waiting to do it after your studies. You were commissioned into the Royal Army Service Corps and served in Nottingham. You are studying French and Italian at St. Luke's College. You were talent -spotted by one of our contacts in the University who pointed you out to me a couple of weeks ago. I followed you from St. Luke's last Saturday and now here we are a week later. We've checked on your pastimes and hobbies with the college authorities. Your interest in birdwatching as a member of the University Birdwatching Club and in chess as a member of the St. Luke's Chess Club complete your profile – certainly most satisfactory as far as we are concerned. Think over what I've said. If you want to follow it up further,' and he hesitated, 'well, it's up to you. A note in your pigeon-hole in the Porters' Lodge next week will give you a guideline as to how to proceed if you are interested.' Ever an inquisitive one, I confirmed then and there that I would like to go the the next stage. 'Excellent,' he exclaimed. 'In that case, you should soon have a gentleman visitor from London. Check your pigeon-hole for details. One final point, we'd very much prefer if you didn't discuss this business at all. Mum's the word, as they say. By the way, my name is Paul. Good-bye!' He shook my hand and off he walked, retracing his steps back to 'The Anchor' bridge and beyond.

I had to wait until the Thursday of the following week before the promised note surfaced in my pigeon-hole in the Porters' Lodge. It was in a sealed envelope, again typewritten and unsigned, although the capital letter 'K' appeared at the foot of the text:

'John Reddisson........... RV 1500 hrs THIS Sunday in D4.

K'

D4 was my room number on D staircase in St. Luke's second court. This forthcoming meeting would be with 'the gentleman from London'. The plot was thickening. The St. Luke's College clock had just finished striking three on the appointed Sunday, when there was a knock on my door. I opened it to find a man standing there, smartly dressed in a grey suit. He was probably in his late forties and had a pronounced shock of black hair. I ushered him in. He motioned me to sit down on one of my two easy chairs as he took up a position opposite me.

His first words were most unexpected: 'No notetaking, please.' 'So,' he then exclaimed, 'according to our Cambridge man, Paul, you came through your first test with flying colours. Congratulations! I need to verify his good opinion of you during the next hour or so in order for me to be sure of your suitability to carry out an assignment here in Cambridge that we need to bring to a satisfactory conclusion.' For the next hour, I was subjected to a variety of questions constituting a weird sort of job interview. At one stage, I offered him a mug of tea (Cambridge students didn't possess cups) which he accepted. I was glad of the short break in the ongoing conversational pressure.

I was in the middlle of giving an answer to a particularly angled personal question, when he brusquely interrupted me. 'Right,' he declared, 'enough is enough. We may now move on.' He explained that he was speaking on behalf of British Intelligence adding, rather apologetically, that it had been subjected to a bad press in recent months due to some miserable failures. 'But,' he exclaimed, 'we are now committed to driving up standards. You may have read of some wilful mischaracterisation of our Service, but ignore it totally. Hopefully, success will characterise our future operations and you could well be part of that success. In our line of business, we seek to celebrate the cult of the brightest not the cult of the average. We are not interested in low achievers but rather high achievers. It must be stressed that the Service is in the front line of Britain's national security.'

'Now let's move on from the general to the specific. A lecturer in the Modern Languages department in Cambridge is suspected of recruiting to the communist cause undergraduates who are reading modern languages. We believe he himself was turned in his own student days here in Cambridge in the 1930s. It was a time when for some members of the University, many of them so-called intellectuals, communism was seen as the only way forward to a truly just and equal society. We have it on record that he joined the International Brigade fighting in Spain on behalf of the Republicans against General Franco and the Nationalists during the Spanish Civil War. During the Second World War, he remained a sleeper, disappearing as it were until he arrived in Cambridge as a lecturer in 1950. Once he had settled in after his arrival, he would have been waiting to be reactivated as an agent to the communist cause when the time was ripe. We believe that time arrived three or four years ago but we have only got wind of his recruitment activities in the last year. Heaven knows what else he has been up to. We believe that his wife is German. She is said to suffer from agoraphobia, thus never leaving the house to give us a chance to check on her.'

'It's very difficult to prove anything against the lecturer unless we have someone on the inside. That's where you come in, young man. A major reason for our choosing you to be of help is that the lecturer is a specialist in German, Russian and French language and literature. You already go to him twice weekly for French one-to-one supervisions.' There was only one lecturer who gave me one-to-one supervisions for French and I pictured his face. His house was in Devonshire Road near the railway station. 'Your task will be to ingratiate yourself with the lecturer, gain his confidence and give him the impression that you are ripe for recruitment. Once this term ends, you'll be continuing in October with much the same timetable, so you have plenty of time.'

'You are to have regular meetings with our Cambridge man, Paul. He will leave messages for you in your St. Luke's pigeon-hole. If for any reason you cannot make a suggested appointment with him, your fall-back position is to go to 'The Anchor' pub and inform Chris the barman that 'Smith of St. Luke's can't make it on such and such a day.' Paul will later suggest other arrangements. Is that clear?' I nodded but to me it was as clear as everything else he had said. My concentration span was now beginning to shorten – there was so much to take in and remember.

My visitor still hadn't finished. 'Three final points,' he continued. 'First, you must work out some modus operandi so as to convince the lecturer of your sincerity to the communist cause. Secondly, you must now take on board a code-name, a new professional name or cryptonym, if you like. I have christened you 'Pluto' and I shall be the only person to address you as such. Just use 'Smith of St. Luke's' if leaving a verbal message for Paul at 'The Anchor'. Thirdly, it goes without saying, although I will not only say it but also stress it: not a word of any of the details of this assignment to anyone. Not to a college friend, not to a family member – nothing at all. I won't insult your intelligence by asking if you understand.'

There was then a pronounced pause in our conversation. I looked enquiringly at 'the gentleman visitor from London'. From his expression, he seemed to be juggling with some important point and had a certain indecision as to how to proceed. He finally decided how he might continue. 'Young man, it is only right that I inform you regarding your origin in this intelligence matter. You are essentially a figment of my imagination, a brainwave of mine, let's say, which it was necessary to clear at the highest level in London. You see, in effect, you don't exist anywhere on paper – there's no file marked 'Pluto' and not even one with your baptismal name for that matter. You are a one-off. You are the result of a mental project I conceived when faced with the problem of how to deal with this talent-spotting lecturer. Paul, your contact in Cambridge, has been told that you are a floater for this one assignment only and, if it all reaches a satisfactory conclusion, he'll soon forget that you ever existed. My plan is to use you further in the future. As a student of Latin and French, you will remember that Descartes, the seventeenth century French philosopher said, 'Cogito, ergo sum.' 'Je pense, donc je suis.' 'I think, therefore I am.' Well, in your present Intelligence persona, it's more a case of 'I think and you exist.' Without my thoughts, you are a non-person and without my breathing you are also a non-person. As I said before, you are the embodiment of a figment of my imagination, a formula number one version, so to speak.'

A further pause ensued then, 'I wish you good luck, Pluto, and of course good judgement in your first endeavours.' As a final point, I asked him if there was any name, real or coded, by which I should know him. He replied, 'Well, for the time being, 'K' will do.' – and that was that. 'I now have to dash to catch my train back to London. If you have any further queries, Paul will do his best to answer them. Good-bye!' He thrust out his hand, gripping my hand firmly. He opened the door and was gone down the staircase.

The lecturer in question had a large detached house in Devonshire Road near the railway station. I was timetabled to go to him twice a week for one-to-one supervisions on Tuesdays and Thursdays at 2pm. We students understood, as did my visitor from London, that he had a German wife, Anna, but no children. I had seen his wife a few times during my supervision visits but I had only exchanged a perfunctory 'good afternoon' with her, nothing more. The lecturer's study was on the first floor, comfortably furnished with easy chairs, bookcases and an enormous desk. Several large pictures hung on the walls and the window overlooked Devonshire Road. He and his wife used to organise 'At Home' evenings every Friday, inviting along foreign students from a nearby language school teaching English as a foreign language (TEFL), plus his ten or so supervision students. Tea, coffee and biscuits were provided and the evenings gave the foreign students useful practice in mastering their English in a social setting. They also gave his supervision students useful practice in chatting up foreign students of the female kind. The lecturer had already mentioned the Friday 'At Home' evenings to me on more than one occasion but I had declined the invitations. That would now be rectified.

What I also discovered later was that the 'At Home' evenings provided an excellent cover for the lecturer to extract his talent-spotted students during the evening. This gave him the opportunity fo further any communist themes in his upstairs study, aided by his wife and by occasional Friday evening visitors from London.

My one-to-one supervisions now took on the extra dimension of my looking out for clues the lecturer might give as to his considering me a potential recruit to the

communist cause. As we went ahead with the usual translations from English into French and French into English,
little of note seemed to surface during the first few weeks
from my two- dimensional supervisions. Then one afternoon, he introduced a passage for translation from
French into English that had a distinct flavour of 'liberty,
equality and fraternity'. After I had exhibited a reasonable degree of proficiency in my translation into English,
we discussed the aforementioned themes in French. Here
was my chance. I declared my lack of satisfaction in what
I saw as a most unequal social system in Britain. Further,
my father had been an ardent communist in his later
years, eagerly devouring the news as printed in the 'Daily
Worker'. Warming to my subject, I continued that as far
as I was concerned, true equality could never be achieved
in Britain with its rigid class structure; one could but
admire the Soviet system with its aims mirroring the
French 'liberty, equality and fraternity'. The lecturer
moved the conversation forward carefully – and still in
French. 'But I suppose when you vote, you vote Labour,
don't you?' I replied that in the confines of his study
and for his ears only, I voted Communist. 'Well, well,
Mr. Reddisson,' he exclaimed, 'I am surprised, not only
at your honesty but also at your politics.'

A couple of weeks later, I was extracted from the
Friday evening 'At Home' and, along with another
student, Michael, I was invited up to the lecturer's study
on the first floor of the house. Present in his study were
also his wife and a husband and wife on a visit from
London. Surprisingly, alchohol was on offer – a choice
of beer, sherry or vodka. I had never drunk vodka
before. His wife explained that the Russians never
sipped vodka but always drank the contents of the glass

at one go – usually uttering the Russian phrase 'do dna' meaning 'to the bottom'. I followed that procedure along with the two guests from London. It was clear from their spoken English that they were of eastern European origin and as the evening wore on, I guessed Russian. Indeed, at one stage the man produced from his briefcase copies of a magazine in English with articles translated from leading Russian magazines. I made every effort to stress what an interesting evening it had been and promised to read the articles most closely.

My assignment regarding the Cambridge lecturer now approached a totally fallow period of some four months. First, I had to sit a number of papers relating to my French and Italian studies for my second year examinations. Once they were over, it was time to set off for Alassio in Italy for a summer season as a travel representative with YTG Universal Limited of Liverpool – an adventure I have described earlier. The job was not really very demanding but for me it was essentially an opportunity to spend the summer in a country whose way of life suited me admirably. Further, my ability and confidence in speaking fluent Italian developed rapidly. On my very first visit to Devonshire Road in the Michaelmas Term of 1957, I made a most interesting discovery. I had arrived a few minutes before the appointed time of 2pm for my supervision. I happened to get into conversation with the lecturer's neighbour clipping a privet hedge in his front garden. I casually mentioned what pleasant people the lecturer and his German wife were. 'She's not German,' he declared. 'She's Russian. During my National Service I was in the Intelligence Corps and I did the intensive Russian course in Crail, up in Scotland. I've overheard his wife speaking to visitors in the garden on more than one occasion and she was most definitely talking perfect Russian – she's a native. I've never seen her go out anywhere. Her husband says she suffers from agoraphobia.'

My conversation with the lecturer about the comparative merits of the British and the Soviet social systems must have had the desired effect. In late October, I was invited to dinner – my recruitment potential had obviously registered. Six of us sat down to the meal: the lecturer and his wife, the same Russian couple I had met previously, the other favoured student, Michael, and myself. The meal did indeed begin Russian style with bortsch, a very tasty beetroot soup. Vodka appeared again and the Russian guests from London proposed a toast: 'to Anglo-Soviet friendship', accompanied by 'do dna' as we drained our glasses.

Chatting after the meal had finished, the lecturer said he would ask me to carry out a special favour for him – a favour which Michael was already doing. He stated that for a number of reasons which he wouldn't go into, certain postal items were being sent to Michael's pigeon-hole at Emmanuel College which he later delivered to Devonshire Road. Would I agree to have some postal items sent to my pigeon-hole at St. Luke's, and then bring them along to Devonshire Road on my next supervision? Michael nodded and agreed that it was no problem for him, so I agreed to the suggestion without further hesitation. During the following couple of weeks or so, no fewer than three packages arrived in my college pigeon-hole, all stating 'for Devonshire Road'. I delivered the first two as promised, but the third package I handed to Paul, my Cambridge Security Service contact, when we next met up. Apparently, all hell broke loose in the Security Service circles when, as I later learned, the package was found to contain copies of highly confidential details pertaining to electronic equipment being designed for an MOD contract. The company involved was one of many located in the Cambridge area, attracted by the kudos of the University presence. Further, unknown to me, MI5 had taken a strong interest in the Russian couple that frequently visited the lecturer and his wife. It turned out that they both worked at the Soviet Embassy in London.

The fourth package delivered to my pigeon-hole in St. Luke's led to the unravelling of my assignment. It was arranged for me to take it to Devonshire Road on the evening of another arranged dinner date in mid-November. Michael was present again as were the two Russians from London. Michael and I had just handed over our packages when the front doorbell rang. Anna went downstairs to open the door. I could hear a policeman explaining that he was calling in connection with a burglary next door. Could he and his colleague come in for a moment to ask a few questions? Anna let them in so that they could continue talking in the hall. Before she knew what was happening, the two policemen moved rapidly up the staircase and into the dining-room. They immediately seized the two packages which Michael and I had brought and had put on the sideboard. Anna now joined us as did another policeman and a plain-clothes detective who promptly declared that all six of us were under arrest. 'You can't arrest my wife and me,' shouted the Russian. 'We are Russian diplomats and we claim diplomatic immunity.' 'We'll sort that out at the police station, sir,' replied the detective. 'Before I leave the house,' interrupted Anna, I must check the coke boiler – I don't want it to go out.' Seizing her handbag, she made to leave the dining- room. 'Just a minute, madam,' said the detective, 'you don't need your handbag to attend to the boiler.' He signalled to one of the policemen to take possession of the handbag and then said, 'It's time we were all moving to the station, if you don't mind.' Through all these events, the lecturer had remained sitting at the table as if transfixed, saying nothing at all and just staring straight ahead.

According to Paul, it later turned out that Anna's handbag contained not only incriminating photographic material but also some microdot messages – photographic reductions of sensitive documents – actually transcribed onto our French-English and English-French translation passages, making them so much easier to smuggle to the Soviets in London. Further, when a thorough search of the Devonshire Road attic was later carried out, it was found to contain spying equipment, including codebooks, false Australian passports in the lecturer's name and his wife's name, together with a large sum of money in banknotes of various currencies.

The lecturer had been uniquely placed to carry out his subversive activities. The University of Cambridge attracted to the surrounding area a number of state of the art electronic, aeronautical and light engineering companies, many of them at the cutting edge of scientific advancement. Although he was primarily concerned with 'talent-spotting' and recruiting students, the lecturer was also involved in his wife's main job: receiving classi-fied technical and scientific material from agents work-ing in local scientific and engineering establishments, processing it and passing it on to the Soviet Embassy by a courier system. The occasional visitors from London were really Soviet Embassy officers who couriered the gathered information to London. The Cambridge spy ring was part of the ongoing Soviet espionage campaign aimed at collecting intelligence on UK economic and defence sectors.

Michael and I were soon released from custody as being innocent stooges in the whole affair. The two Russians pleaded diplomatic immunity and were also released. However, on their return to London, the British Government declared them both 'persona non grata' – that is, in effect, not welcome here – and they were expelled from Britain.

Further information duly surfaced from Paul that after the War, the lecturer had taken up a post in East Germany lecturing in English studies. He was later subjected to a 'honey pot' trap in the form of Anna, a trained Soviet intelligence officer. They had married in Leipzig in 1948, two years before they arrived in Cambridge. Anna didn't suffer from agoraphobia at all; she had used that as an excuse for not leaving the house. She was paranoid about being traced and exposed. If ever the house was put under surveillance, it might lead to her being recognised as a previous agent working at the Soviet Embassy in London.

The two packages seized by the police from the dining-room were traced back to two local engineers. They had copied details of highly classified equipment relating to War Office contracts placed with two separate electronic companies in the Cambridge area. They had been working independently of each other, ignorant of the other's existence.

I met up with Paul again a few weeks later. I asked him when the details of the whole affair would be appearing in the national press. 'The case won't be appearing in the national press at all,' was his unexpected reply. 'It will be held in camera, behind closed doors. Further, we liaised with the Americans on a number of matters in the case and their information will be vital in securing convictions in court. We mustn't forget that benefits flow in both directions – that's what a good alliance is all about. Security cooperation with our closest ally would be put at risk in an open court and they might well stop feeding us their regular supply of vital facts that we so often need. After all, security information is passed from country to country on the basis of strict confidentiality and in full trust that it won't surface in the public domain. The protection of such confidentiality is sacrosanct as far as British Intelligence is concerned – hence secret courts. Such a control principle is mandatory in our eyes. The Americans can be ultra-sensitive, almost paranoid, about certain aspects of shared intelligence and the British govern ment has to tread very carefully. In additlion, it goes without saying that we must avoid the disclosure of all secret information, the identity of members of British Intelligence and their modus operandi. Any release of such details in the short term would clearly damage our national security. If it all surfaced, say, in fifty years' time and entered the public domain, circumstances will have changed. The main players will probably all be dead and British Intelligence and its procedures will have moved on. But I am talking about the here and now and confidentiality is the current keyword.'

In due course Paul contacted me and agreed to brief me on the results of the trial. It was confirmed that both engineers had betrayed their country for financial rather than political reasons. They disclosed that before the lecturer had hit on the idea of using students' pigeon-holes for the onward transmission of classified material, there had been awkward and dangerous clandestine exchanges in the Cambridge railway station left-luggage office and in telephone kiosks The students' pigeon-hole system had been much more to their liking and had presented less danger to their being traced, or so they had thought.

Following conviction, the lecturer, his wife and the two engineers were all sentenced to a substantial number of years in prison. The secret court had done its job. Meanwhile, I had received a warm letter of congratulation from 'K' with the promise of further contact early in the New Year.

CHAPTER 6

In early January before the Lent Term began in Cambridge, I travelled up to London from Crawley to attend an arranged meeting with 'K'. I was now entering my final six months at St. Luke's and the important matters of future employment and a career were looming large on the horizon. Graduate recruitment often began with the 'Milk Round', when the largest companies in the country toured Cambridge and Oxford in an effort to recruit the most promising candidates. It was a conventional route to a conventional job. The 'Milk Rounds' usually took place in the Michaelmas (autumn) Term and in the Easter (summer) Term. I had attended some of these circuses but nothing special had attracted me. I had been interviewed by the personnel managers of several blue-chip companies including Ford, Marconi and various well-known drug firms. They offered about £650 per annum as a trainee executive – a good starting salary at the time. Mr. Lewis Williams, the managing director of YTG Universal Limited for whom I had worked in Italy as a courier/travel representative during the summer of 1957, had indicated to me that courier employment would be on offer only periodically. There would be work opportunities for about four months in the summer and possibly around Easter and Christmas but there would be nothing available on a twelve month basis.

Nevertheless, I had begun to consider a career in the travel industry with one of the larger companies such as Thomas Cook. My French and Italian would be very useful in travel work but the exact type of job I could do hadn't yet crystallised in my mind.

It was against this background of vague future job employment that I made my way to 'K' by train and tube that early January morning. He had previously hinted at my 'future', so I was intrigued by how he might see a possible career for me.

I was most impressed by his spacious office in a large building in Curzon Street. No-one else was present during our meeting. He began by congratulating me on the successful outcome to 'the Cambridge talent-spotting lecturer saga' and he added that he was confident it could be the first of several assignments. He then moved on to a planned agenda. 'That now brings us to the question of your future career, young man,' he said. 'What exactly are your own thoughts on the matter?' I replied that I had attended the Cambridge 'Milk Rounds', but that nothing on offer had appealed to me. I was increasingly attracted by the idea of a career in the travel industry but had no fixed idea as to what that would really involve.

'Well, I have a totally different career in mind for you,' 'K' began, 'and once you have considered it and mulled it over, it may indeed appeal to you. It also recognises the value of foreign language proficiency and, in addition, it could well give you the opportunity to learn new languages and also to use those new languages. I'm talking in general about a career as an Army officer and specifically as an Army officer in their Education Branch. I've done some research with contacts in the War Office and I am given to understand that language training and filling posts using a wide variety of languages are considered a top priority in that Branch. Further, overseas postings to such places as Hong Kong, Singapore and Germany are very likely to occur. At twenty-five years of age, and having proved yourself a competent officer during your National Service days, you are just the sort of recruit the Army is looking for and, more to the point, what the Education Branch is looking for. What do you think?'

The uncanny aspect of the suggestion 'K' was making was that on a number of occasions when thinking about a career, I had considered the Army but I had repeatedly relegated the idea to the back of my mind. The information that the Army could lead to a 'career in languages' now gave the matter an additional emphasis and attraction. I replied that the suggestion as now presented to me had undoubted appeal. 'K' interrupted me to say that if I did become an Army officer, I would probably be a captain within a couple of years or so. The salary I would then receive would constitute an approximate fifty percent increase on any trainee graduate post salary or on that offered by an initial appointment in the travel industry. 'That's an extremely valid point,' he added, 'and one well worth considering.'

'K' now continued in a totally different vein. 'I have never been less than honest with you ever since you materialised as Pluto. As I've said before, you are the embodiment of a figment of my imagination; you don't exist anywhere on paper. Should you decide to join the Army, you could be valuable to me as a sort of hybrid agent. You would be working as an officer under the strict control of the War Office but I might task you with a specific assignment with my Service. It would be an assignment about which the War Office would have no knowledge at all. Anyway, first things first. You have six months left at Cambridge and you have previously indicated that you would like to return to Italy as a courier this coming summer. Let's say you have until mid-October to make up your mind as to what you want to do in the future. I'll fix a date for you to come and see me then. If you do choose the Army, it appears from my enquiries that a formal written application to join would take about six months to be processed. That means that if you choose the Education Branch, your three-month induction course will not begin until May next year, at the earliest. It would be held at their training centre at Wycombe Birch Park in Buckinghamshire. Your first appointment would probably follow in the August. I won't pressure you further. Once again, congratulations on the part you played in bringing that Cambridge lecturer fellow, his wife and their accomplices to book. I look forward to our October meeting. Meanwhile, good luck in your tripos examinations in the summer and I'm sure you will enjoy your summer in Italy.'

An official arrived to accompany me back to the reception desk and see me out of the building. On my journey back to Crawley, I realised I had to make a decision sooner or later in the next few months that would probably affect my whole working life. The present choice of careers appeared to be between the travel industry and the Army.

It was early June. I had taken all my examinations in Cambridge and was eagerly awaiting my departure date in mid-June to take up my summer job as a YTG travel representative in Italy. As usual on a Wednesday

evening after dinner in hall, I called in at the Junior
Common Room bar for a beer. James, a friend of mine
from the college chess club, soon came up to me. 'A chap
on my staircase called Martyn Fletcher was looking for
you earlier, John. I said you would probably be in here
after dinner. Oh! Talk of the devil, here he is.'

James bought Martyn a beer and we seated ourselves
in a corner. Martyn had a worried expression on his
face and he soon outlined his problem. There was a
British film crew in Cambridge, filming outside shots
and scenes for a romantic comedy. The stars were a
German actor, Hardy Kruger and the English actress,
Sylvia Syms. Martyn had landed the job of stand-in for
Hardy Kruger. This involved him being positioned
in certain outdoor locations so that the lighting and
sound technicians could get everything right for the
shooting takes of the real scenes with Hardy Kruger.
That very day he had received the distressing and
most unexpected news that his father had died. He had
already seen Dr. Hargreaves and had been granted
special dispensation to take the rest of the term off
so as to help his mother make the necessary funeral
arrangements. When he explained his predicament to
the film director, he was asked to find a replacement for
himself as Hardy Kruger's stand-in, as more filming was
due the following day. James had told him that I fitted
the bill in terms of the required fair complexion, build
and height. 'Unfortunately,' said James, 'I'm dark-haired
and shorter than both of you.' 'Well,' continued Martyn,
'Are you interested, John?' It took me a nano-second to
convince myself I was indeed interested. 'Sure, Martyn,
I'd love to do it.' 'There are about eight days of filming
left before they all leave Cambridge. You'll get paid £2 a

day plus refreshments. Be at the Market Hill end of Petty Cury tomorrow morning at eight o'clock. Report to the director, Wolf Rilla, and go on from there. Thanks a million for helping me out. I must go now and pack for tomorrow.'

I had already heard that there was a film crew in Cambridge but had thought nothing more about it. Once Martyn had left us, James did his best to give me some details as told to him by Martyn. All going well, the film was to be released at the end of the year with the title 'Bachelor of Hearts.' Hardy Kruger had already appeared in a British film in 1957, 'The One Who Got Away', the story of the only German prisoner-of-war to successfully escape from Allied custody abroad and return to Germany. Sylvia Syms was an attractive young actress who had already made 'Ice-Cold in Alex' with John Mills and Anthony Quayle.

In order to make a good impression, I arrived at the filming location a good twenty minutes early. Wolf Rilla was already there, attending to some casting details. I introduced myself and was told to listen carefully for any filming instructions. I soon met up with a girl called Janet who was Sylvia Syms' stand-in. Within the hour we had been positioned on a street corner at the end of Petty Cury, surrounded by lighting and sound equipment and the operating crew. There was a lot of shouting of orders and counter-orders before everything was to the director's satisfaction. Janet and I were removed from the scene and Hardy Kruger and Sylvia Syms took our places. Several other outdoor scenes were shot that day with long breaks between them. I thoroughly enjoyed my first day's filming experience. I duly received my £2 payment for having done little real 'work', reflecting on the fact that hard-working secretaries at the time only received £8 for a week's work.

In all, I had eight days' 'work', bringing me the welcome sum of £16. On several occasions I had brief chats with both Sylvia Syms, who was radiantly attractive in the flesh, and with Hardy Kruger, a very relaxed and friendly man. On one occasion, I was asked to perform a non-speaking role as an extra – a bystander looking into a large shop window. Janet joked that the scene would probably end up on the cutting-room floor. My final day's filming included a scene shot on the corner of Petty Cury and Hobson Street. Interestingly, Hobson Street was named after a livery stable owner who had his stables near a couple of colleges, students being his main customers. Hobson considered it was necessary to rotate his horses and any new customer was obliged to take the horse nearest the stable door or none at all. Hence the origin of the saying 'Hobson's choice', meaning one doesn't really have a choice at all, other than taking it or leaving it.

I saw the film in due course after its general release. 'Bachelor of Hearts' (1958) tells the story of a German exchange student (Hardy Kruger) who arrives in Cambridge for just one year. He joins in the very English non-academic high life, while at the same time romancing a pretty Girton College undergraduate, Sylvia Syms. There is some wonderful (now archive) footage of photogenic Cambridge itself, as it was in 1958. The film includes many amusing stereotypes of the English and of ideosyncratic Cambridge University life. It is true to its cinema period – no sex, no swearing and no violence but full of university japes and pranks. It has a certain charm about it and despite its lead actor being German, the film celebrates old-fashioned Englishness, having overtones of the old Ealing comedies. Incidentally, they didn't cut my starring role, looking into the shop window.

Many years later, Hardy Kruger (born in 1928), fluent in German, English and French, was ranked as one of the greatest German actors in the period from the 1950s through to the 1970s. In 1962 he appeared in the film 'Hatari!' with John Wayne, followed in 1965 by 'The Flight of the Phoenix' with James Stewart. His films in the 1970s included Richard Attenborough's 'A Bridge Too Far' (1977) and 'The Wild Geese' with Richard Burton (1978). Sylvia Sims (born 1934), has remained active in films, television and theatre well into the second decade of the twenty-first century.

Mid-June 1958 was a hectic time for me. As soon as I had finished my filming commitment with 'Bachelor of Hearts', it was necessary to travel to my parents' house in Crawley, Sussex with luggage containing my university books, personal items, clothes, etc. Most of it was left in Crawley before I then travelled to Manchester Airport to make contact with my first YTG Universal group bound for Torre Ligure. The travel company had now switched from train to aeroplane and coach. I met up with my group of twenty-four holidaymakers together with another YTG group of similar size bound for Alassio with another YTG travel representative. After landing at Nice Airport we travelled on to Italy in a chartered coach. We dropped off the Alassio group en route and half an hour later arrived at the 'Hotel Torre' in Torre Ligure. The first YTG group of the summer had already returned to Manchester and they had been looked after in Torre Ligure by a YTG staff member,

Pamela, who then stayed on at the hotel for a fortnight's holiday. Pamela met us at the hotel as we arrived and settled us in.

Torre Ligure and Alassio are both situated in the area of Liguria known as La Rivera di Ponente (western Riviera) which stretches from Genoa to the French border. Some of the towns closest to France such as Ventimiglia, Bordighera and San Remo had been favourite destinations for British tourists in the nineteenth and early twentieth centuries, especially during the winter months. The area to the east of Genoa is known as La Riviera di Levante (eastern Riviera) and stretches to Rapallo, Portofino and beyond towards Tuscany. That part of the western Riviera from Torre Ligure to Alassio and San Remo is also known as La Riviera dei Fiori (Riviera of Flowers), the most widely grown flower being the carnation. During the Second World War, which had finished only thirteen years before my YTG group arrived in 1958, Liguria had experienced heavy bombing and two years of occupation by German troops. Local memories were still very strong regarding that period but, in the main, German tourists were treated civilly.

The 'Hotel Torre' was named after a nearby mediaeval watch tower. It was owned and managed by a most devout catholic pair, Signor Angelo Antonelli and his wife, 'la Signora', neither of whom spoke a word of English. It was situated right on the promenade with its own private beach and could cater for about one hundred guests.

My group of twenty-four consisted of a dozen or so young women in their twenties, four couples and a handful of young men. They soon settled into a holiday routine of sunbathing, swimming, walking around the village and enjoying the evenings at the local bar/nightclub – the 'Rosa', run by Signor Luciano and his son. My YTG group were the only British tourists in Torre Ligure. The 'Hotel Torre' also had a German group of about forty holidaymakers and one or two other local hotels also had German groups. The' Rosa' was the main entertainment spot in the area and the tourists would flock there in the evenings – along with the local Italian men, both single and self-declared 'temporarily unattached' married. Men had to wear a jacket and tie and pay an entrance fee; women entered free.

Life for the local Italian men in Torre Ligure often mirrored 'la dolce vita' (the sweet life) in their pursuit of romantic interludes with the British and German holidaymaking females, especially the British. Progress in language learning was advancing on three fronts. First, my own spoken Italian was making excellent progress. Secondly, the whole YTG group were becoming well acquainted with 'vino', 'aranciata' (orange drink), 'gelato' (ice-cream), pasta and so on. For many, it was the first time they had eaten real spaghetti as opposed to the contents of Heinz tins. Thirdly, some of the young British girls were also acquiring new words and phrases in Italian. The main social ones were 'amore' (love), 'cuore' (heart), 'mare' (sea), 'ti amo' (I love you), 'luna' (moon) and 'bella' (beautiful). The latter Italian word was murmured by the eager Romeos to every British girl whether the description was really true or not. I was sometimes stopped in the street by hopeful young Italians armed with pen and paper, asking for translations of their romantic words into English.

As a result, many of my YTG client girls were romanced in two languages. My discreet research established that the Italian 'ragazzo' (boy) murmuring English words with a heavy, enchanting and seemingly irresistible Italian accent was the most successful approach to the heart of the 'ragazza' (girl) – especially when the 'luna' was above and the 'mare' nearby.

One of my young holidaymakers confided in me that her Torre Ligure boyfriend had told her he was a barrister and that he lived in a small 'palazzo' or palace. She was so pleased that he wasn't a basic waiter or perhaps working in a shop. His address must mean he came from a well-off family. I didn't have the heart to tell her that in Italian 'barista' meant barman, as in a cafe or bar – virtually a basic waiter. 'Palazzo' could translate as palace but it also meant an apartment building/block of flats. Her barrister living in a small palace was really a barman living in a block of flats.

For the British girls, the hit songs of the time, constantly being played very loudly on the juke-boxes in the local bars and cafes, would forever fix their holiday romance in their memory. 'Volare' (Flying up in the sky) was very popular as were 'All I have to do is dream' (Everly Brothers), 'Love-letters in the sand') (Pat Boone) and 'Come prima' (As before). Elvis Presley hits were other favourites. The music combined well with the Italians' protestations of eternal love. As the coach left 'Hotel Torre' on the Saturday morning taking their loved ones to the airport, the Italians would wave the tearful girls off on their return flight to Britain. As the coach arrived back at the hotel on the Saturday afternoon from the airport with the new group, the same Italians would jostle for position and crane their necks to view the arriving 'new talent'.

I soon got to know the two beach photographers, Roberto and Bruno. They were brothers and worked from their father's photographic shop opposite the hotel. The elder brother, Roberto, who was in his early twenties, had a good command of English and Bruno was doing his best to catch up. They would walk along the beach two or three times a day hoping to pick up orders. Holidaymakers could be photographed in the morning and collect their prints from the shop the same evening. When not on holiday at their parents' flat in Torre Ligure, the two brothers were studying at college in Turin. The family had a 1957 Fiat cinquecento (five hundred cc engine) and as the weeks passed, Roberto would occasionally collect me from the hotel in the evening after dinner and drive me to a variety of bars and night clubs in the nearby villages and towns. To relax linguistically, Roberto would only speak Italian and I only English. I had several invitations to dinner with the family at their flat in the centre of the village, situated in a very dark and narrow street with the walls of the buildings on opposite sides very close together. As their photographic business was booming, they were having a villa built on the hillside opposite the 'Hotel Torre' with wonderful sea views.

While the family always addressed me in standard Italian, I noticed that among themselves they usually spoke in a local Ligurian dialect. The regional capital was Genoa (Zena) and the dialect they spoke (Zeneize) had a heavy Genoese influence. There is no inherent intelligibility between Italian and Zeneize. Just as Swiss-German is unintelligible to the student of standard

German, so Zeneize makes no sense to the student of Italian. If anything, it has many similarities with French and is indeed closer to French than Italian. I found it fascinating to listen to the family speaking in dialect and it was agreed that Roberto and Bruno would give me a few basic lessons. I would do my best to have occasional practice with them and with the local shop-keepers – a few eyebrows were raised and I received some very funny looks.

One of the most enjoyable duties of my job as travel representative or courier were the trips. Two were planned each week at extra cost and as the Alassio YTG courier had expressed no interest in them, I led all four trips of the combined groups. Depending on whether we were travel-ling east or west, the Alassio group would board our chartered coach first or the Torre Ligure group were first on. The initial trip took us east to Genoa, Italy's main commercial port. We would visit the wonderful harbour and admire the fine statue of Christipher Columbus, before a visit to the monumental cemetery of Staglione with its hundreds of marble statues – evidence of the past wealth of the Genoese. I would always stop at the top of one avenue in the cemetery and announce that the compiler of the very first Italian crosswords was buried just thirty yards or so down the avenue – his grave was three down and four across. Some of my holidaymakers would smile and raise their eyes to heaven; others would look very interested and go down the avenue to find the grave. For good measure, I would also point out the grave in which Franco Froudini, the famous Italian escapologist, had been buried in 1936, 1937 and 1938.

After our packed lunches were finished, we would travel on to Rapallo and Portofino. We especially admired the fine villas in Portofino. Its mild winter climate and protection from the prevailing wind made the town a favourite of rich Italians from the north of Italy. Portofino still had elements of being an Italian fishing village. It was perhaps better known for its celebrity visitors, including the English actor, Rex Harrison. He was so smitten with Portofino that he bought a villa there.

The first week also saw a trip to Monesi, a ski resort on the French border but a sheer delight to visit in the summer. We would travel along the coast road to Imperia and then cut inland, taking the mountain roads to Monesi. Our first stop was at Pieve di Teco, a nearly intact fourteenth century village with fifteenth century frescoes in the Santa Maria church. Our holidaymakers would marvel at the village houses, which animals would share with their human owners especially in the winter months. The Monesi trip was so different. After we had left behind the coastal area with its kitchen gardens, olive groves and greenhouses of the flower industry, the coach climbed up mountain roads through areas of beech trees and chestnut woods, and fields of late blooming lavender. When we arrived at Monesi itself at an altitude of 4500 feet, there was a chair-lift to take us up to the hotel at the top where we could enjoy our packed lunches. The views from the hotel terrace were stunning – until low cloud descended, accompanied by a much lower temperature. I always advised my holidaymakers to take sweaters with them on the trip.

In the second week, we headed for Monaco/Monte Carlo, bordered on three sides by France and on the fourth by the Mediterranean Sea. We would initially make for the Royal Palace to watch the changing of the guard at twelve noon – well below the standard set by the Brigade of Guards at London Royal Palaces. It was only two years after the marriage of Prince Rainier to Grace Kelly, the American actress. We always hoped to catch a glimpse of the royal pair but we never did. Our packed lunches were consumed in a cafe in the square dominated by the Casino – no problem if we all bought an expensive drink on offer. The cafe's unisex squat lavatory (aka 'the hole in the ground') inevitably encouraged shared hilarity. After lunch, we would go into the Casino and wager small amounts of French francs on the tables offering black and red choice bets. There was then an hour or so when my group was free to wander around before we boarded our coach back to Alassio and Torre Ligure.

The final trip was a local one. After dinner, the Torre Ligure group would board a coach taking us on a short journey to Borgio Verezzi, a mountain village overlooking many miles of coastline. We would have a drink on the terrace of a trattoria offering splendid views, or walk around the village itself. The more adventurous of the holidaymakers would sample the local delicacy – snails. They were served either in a garlic, parsley and red wine sauce or in a tomato sauce. A complimentary glass or two of Valpolicella, a popular red wine, would also appear on the table. For those who had worked up a good appetite after dinner, there was good Ligurian food on offer, including a garlicky fish soup with shellfish and molluscs. Another attraction of the Borgio Verezzi visit were the fireflies. They could be guaranteed to be flying around for the duration of our trip, flashing their signals as a means of communication to attract a mate. They intrigued our holidaymakers and for some, along with the snails, they made the trip a more memorable one.

Village gossip as recounted by my two photographer friends, Roberto and Bruno, was that Signor Angelo Antonelli had arrived in Torre Ligure 'from the south' in the late 1940s. He had found clerical work in the village and in due course courted the daughter of a rich local landowner. Showing an entrepreneurial flare, the money that his marriage to her had brought, together with the financial backing of a Catholic Church organisation, enabled him to build the 'Hotel Torre'.

Signor Angelo and his wife, la Signora, were very staunch catholics and they wanted the village people to know that they were. In 1958, as usual, there was a parade and procession in the village to mark August 15th, the Assumption of the Virgin Mary into Heaven. As the procession passed the 'Hotel Torre', where a large crowd of onlookers had gathered, Signor Angelo rushed forward from the third rank of the marchers and relieved the stumbling cross-bearer of his heavy burden en route to the village church. Signor Angelo could just about carry the cross himself but he was sure his pain and courage were there for the whole village to witness and admire.

There was a 'Miss Torre Ligure' beauty contest held every August in the local bar-nightclub, the 'Rosa'. In 1958, YTG holidaymakers came second and third but the winner was a stunning Italian Gina Lollobrigida lookalike. The day following the contest, I happened to be outside the 'Hotel Torre' talking to Roberto when the new 'Miss Torre Ligure' sashayed past. Roberto and I stopped her to offer our congratulations and Roberto, confirmed photographer as ever, decided to take a photograph of me with the girl. At that moment la Signora emerged from the hotel and in quite basic Italian, all the while invoking the blessed Virgin Mary, she ordered us all to move on forthwith: the girl's presence on the pavement outside of her hotel was detrimental to its fine name and reputation.

La Signora, in her early forties with a young son of six, was not comfortable with my holidaymakers wearing skirts or dresses even just on the knee. I shudder to think of her raised blood pressure when, later in the 1960s, the mini-skirt and hot pants were in fashion. However, I could empathise with her to a certain extent. I am sure that many of the Torre Ligure womenfolk of her generation held much the same narrow views. They had missed out on so much in their lives due to the political upheavals in Italy during the 1930s, and then came the War. Two years of German occupation and the post-war austerity also had to be endured. They now saw the youth of the village enjoying the fruits of their older generation, post-war labours. The economy was taking off and there was plenty of leisure time for the young – something they themselves had been denied.

There was a marked division between the ways of the younger women in the village and of those in their forties and beyond, with many between forty and fifty appearing to be old well before their time. Dress preferences were especially different. For the older woman, their main choice of colour was mainstream black, although if they were feeling a little adventurous they might choose a shade of grey. If, on rare occasions, they felt unrestrained and modern, their dress or skirt length might be a daring three inches below the knee.

The top button of a dress or blouse might be left undone but discreetly undone, of course.

One morning, Signor Angelo called me into his office. 'Good news, Signor John,' he said. 'We've finished the conversion of the hotel's cancelled penthouse suite into a small concert hall area with a stage and seating for about seventy-five people. Installation of special stage lighting and wiring is now finished. I've been in touch with an agency in Turin and I've booked our first performers for three nights in mid-August. There will be an American singer to perform our traditional operatic arias and songs, and a young Italian lady who, accompanied by a small group of musicians, will sing the more popular songs of today. I'm preparing a publicity poster to put up in the hotel and around the village. I'd be grateful if you would do an English translation which we shall have printed. Herr Winkel, I am sure, will do a German one for his holidaymakers. We've got two weeks to get it all sorted out.' Giorgio, the hotel maintenance engineer, had told me about the cancellation of building a penthouse suite at the top of the hotel and that Signor Angelo had planned something else in its place. Signor Angelo's announcement was the first news I'd heard about a concert hall project, but he did tend to play things close to his chest.

A few days later, I accompanied him to view the new hotel facility. It looked an attractive venue and was more or less ready for the first performance. The seats had been arranged, there was a bar area and a large piano had pride of place on the stage. The stage area was quite generous and would easily take a small live group. Two lifts served the floor, each carrying six to eight persons. 'We'll see how the first three nights turn out and we'll go on from there,' Signor Angelo declared. 'I don't want to rush things. I'm relying on you and Herr Winkel to do your best to encourage your holidaymakers to attend at least the opening night and hopefully they'll return on one of the other nights. Performances will be on the Friday, Saturday and the Sunday.' 'I'll certainly do my best, Signor Angelo and I'm sure Herr Winkel will also crack the whip. We'll just have to wait and see what happens. Hopefully, tourists from other hotels and some of the townspeople will see the posters and turn up, too. What admission charge will there be for the evening's entertainment?' 'The whole project, including booking the two performers and the musicians, has cost us a lot of money and we must start getting some of it back. My wife and I reckon an admission charge of two thousand lire per head (just over £1) is reasonable.' The main nights at the local 'Rosa' nightclub were also Friday, Saturday and Sunday as well as for other other entertainment establishments in the area but I didn't want to say anything negative to Signor Angelo at this stage.

Photographs of the two performers duly arrived in the post from the agency in Turin. Albertina Bosco, the young Italian artiste, looked most attractive in her evening gown but the photograph of Paul Anderson Smith, the American singer, caused some surprise to Signor Angelo and the Signora. He was an American negro and for some reason they had imagined their singer to be a cross between Bing Crosby and Frank Sinatra.

I had agreed to meet Paul Anderson Smith from the Turin train at the local railway station on the Thursday morning before the Friday performance. I couldn't miss him as he stepped off the train – a massive six feet six with a body frame to match and a wonderful warm smile. I introduced myself and said I had a taxi waiting to take us to the hotel. As we sat in the taxi on the way from the station, I was struck by the charisma of our star performer. He was an excellent conversationalist and exuded a warm, sincere personality. 'He should go down very well with our audience,' I thought. Signor Angelo and the Signora met us in Reception and I carried out the introductions. They made an unusual looking threesome. Signor Angelo and his wife were both about five feet tall and Paul was towering over them with his height and body frame.

Albertina Bosco and the musicians arrived soon after one o'clock. It was agreed that signor Angelo and I would accompany our performers up to the concert hall at three o'clock. They would have plenty of time to rehearse before Friday's first performance. The hotel maintenance engineer was also present to operate lights and equipment as necessary. Signor Angelo and I stayed around for an hour or so. We were both impressed by the quality of the artistes. Fortunately, one of the musicians spoke good English, which took any translation pressure away from me.

Paul informed us that his act also included periods of chat when he told amusing stories and cracked a few jokes. Signor Angelo preferred the acts to be solely singing ones but Paul talked him into accepting the routine patter addition as well. For a couple of his songs, he would accompany himself on the piano. His first rehearsal, singing popular songs and an operatic aria or two, were well-known to the musicians. All looked well set for the following evening's opening performance. I did my very best to whip up interest among my group members. Most of them promised they would come along for the first night but they showed little excitement for a repeat attendance.

Dinner at the 'Hotel Torre' began at 7 pm. As the concert wouldn't begin until 8.45, there was plenty of time to enjoy one's meal and then make one's way up to the concert hall in good time for the start. In fact, I arrived at 8.15, just to see how things were progressing. The bar was operating and Roberto and Bruno had already turned up to take official photographs. By 8.45, there were about fifty people present, just as the live group played their first number. Albertina appeared and gave a terrific performance, singing a very popular song of the day, much to the audience's approval. She followed her opening number with a tearful ballad and finished her first appearance with a lively foot-tapping song. The musicians followed with three more numbers before there was a break for refreshments.

After the break, there was a roll of drums and Paul Anderson Smith appeared on the stage. He gave a marvellous rendition of both 'Santa Lucia' and 'O Solo Mio' followed by a Paul Robeson number 'Old Man River' – also well received. He then went into his patter routine which, unfortunately, was far from well received. His amusing stories and jokes would have undoubtedly appealed to an American audience but even the British members of that evening's audience found his broad American accent hard to follow and his regular use of Americanisms left them floundering. As for the Germans and Italians present, they were at a complete loss to understand anything. Paul redeemed himself with some more beautifully sung numbers, including two where he accompanied himself on the piano. Albertina returned, and after another break, Paul performed again, but this time without the patter. He had realised the communication problem, especially when none of his punch-lines raised the expected laughter.

The evening finished at 11pm and all in all it had been successful. Signor Angelo was beaming and congratulated his stars on their performance. Little did he realise what lay in store. Again on the Saturday evening, I arrived in the concert hall early and waited, and waited for people to arrive. By 8.30, in addition to Signor Angelo and myself, only five others had arrived; by the start of the show at 8.45, only a further two had shown up, making a total audience of nine. Sunday was even more disheartening – apart from Signor Angelo and myself, there were only four in the audience.

Signor Angelo, Herr Winkel and I discussed the problem the next morning. The reasons for the difference in numbers on the first evening and the other two evenings soon became clear. Of the fifty people present on the first evening, forty-five had come from Herr Winkel's group or the YTG group. Only one couple had returned on the Saturday and none on the Sunday. Despite the posters, there had been little if any interest from elsewhere.

On the Monday morning, I accompanied Paul Anderson Smith to the railway station. I expressed my sympathy for the poor Saturday and Sunday evening audience figures. He grinned, slapped me on the back and said, 'Well, look at it this way, John. You win some, you lose some. At least I got paid!' With that comment, he gripped my hand, smiled again and stepped onto the train. He really was an unforgettable character, a great performer and a very nice man into the bargain. As for

Signor Angelo, the disappointing outcome to his first foray into the entertainment business gave him much food for thought. The new concert hall remained closed for the rest of the season.

The YTG holidaymakers of 1958, were the first ever British holiday group to arrive in Torre Ligure but the German travel company for which Herr Winkel worked had been sending groups since 1955. By 1958, Herr Winkel had worked out which of the hotel rooms were the best and he had block-booked them all. As a result, some of my group members had rooms of an inferior quality or position to those allocated to the Germans. There was nothing I could do in the short term to remedy the situation. The hotel was full and all the rooms had been booked.

The 'Hotel Torre' occupied a fine position on the sea front with its own private beach. At a distance to one side, there was a block of flats, also with their own beach. On the other side of the hotel towards the village, and not at a great distance, there was a long stretch of open river-bed. I was told that in the winter it could be a rushing torrent emptying its water into the sea. It was mainly dry in the summer with just occasional pools of stagnant water – and therein lay a problem: mosquitos. It turned out that the rooms facing the river-bed were ones allocated to the YTC group. The summer nights in Torre Ligure were invariably hot and, although the rooms had ceiling fans, the British holidaymakers preferred to sleep with the windows open. Standard fitted air-condition systems in hotels of the 'Hotel Torre' star grading were still a decade away. Perhaps an hour before going to bed, the holidaymakers would have the light on and the window open. Despite my repeated warnings, some of the YTG group would come down to breakfast in the morning covered in mosquito bites. There was no way that mosquito nets could be fitted, especially as the the local mosquitos were not of the Anopheles malaria-carrying species. What I did manage to achieve was that every affected room was equipped with anti-mosquito powder pump devices and that the room-maids always closed the windows after servicing the rooms. The problem lessened but never did go away completely all summer; it was, indeed, a regrettable blot on the holiday landscape.

Signor Angelo assured me that there were municipal plans to cover over the river-bed with concrete arching and to construct a promenade in the area with benches, flower-beds and palm trees, but it took several years before the project was finally finished. However, in consultation with the YTG management and Signor Angelo, I ensured that YTG allocated rooms for the 1959 season onwards did not overlook the river-bed. Some other poor devils were to suffer– but not members of a YTG group.

Each YTG group at the 'Hotel Torre' had a 'last supper', finishing with cream cake and Asti Spumante sparkling wine. Signor Angelo would make a sentimental speech which I translated. He would milk the emotional evening for all it was worth – an excellent public relations exercise. Apart from the hotel concert hall episode, he was clearly an astute businessman, which is how he captured the YTG and the German contracts in the first place rather than their going to other hotels in the village. His final gesture at the last supper was to raise his glass of Asti Spumante and propose the toast: 'Salute' (Good health), sometimes adding 'cin-cin', an onomatopoeic Italian toast replicating the sound of glasses clinking.

Inevitably, my own last supper arrived in due course. It was at the end of the first week of October. I had been present at half a dozen or so such suppers during my fourteen week stint at the hotel but, for me, this one was different. Looking at the faces of my final summer group and listening to Signor Angelo making his farewell speech, I became quite emotional myself. After a full summer of courier work, I felt a distinct bond with Torre Ligure, a number of its inhabitants and with the 'Hotel Torre' itself. My daily routine would now be changing dramatically – and would I be looking for work in the travel industry as a career or would I be joining the Army? Within ten days, I would be sitting in front of 'K' in London discussing my future.

Roberto and Bruno came to see me off the next morning. Our coach called in at the Alassio hotel to take on their YTG group and courier. The flight from Nice to Manchester was on time. I duly arrived at my parents' house in Sussex very late the same evening. As I was drifting off to sleep in my bedroom, I found myself murmuring 'Arriverderci, Torre Ligure' – and agreeing on the nostalgic theme with the Everly Brothers as per the Torre Ligure bar juke-boxes: 'All I have to do is dream, dream, dream.'

CHAPTER 7

Within a week of my return from Italy, I was on my way to Curzon Street in London for another meeting with 'K'. The year had passed quickly and it was difficult to realise that it was over ten months since my last visit to his office. This time, however, I had a clear idea of how my employment future might take shape.

At the reception desk, as previously requested by 'K', I stated that I had an appointment in Room 101. I was given an identity tag to wear. An official soon appeared and accompanied me to 'K's' office. He greeted me with a broad smile and a firm handshake. After a few cursory enquiries about Italy, he came straight to the point. 'Well, Pluto young man, what's the decision to be? Are you to be a travel industry trainee or have you opted for a life in uniform?' 'Definitely the latter,' I replied. 'I'm one hundred percent sure it's by far the better option.' 'Excellent,' continued 'K', 'and it's the one I myself thought you would choose. I had already taken the liberty to arrange for my War Office contacts to forward me the necessary application forms. Take them away with you today, fill them in without too much delay and post them off. From what I've been told, it looks as if the Education Branch will be most happy to recruit you. I understand that linguists are the blue-eyed boys of the Education Branch, so your

Cambridge degree in Italian and French should prove invaluable. As I've said before, the application procedure takes several months but if all goes well, you should be joining the three-month induction course in Wycombe, Buckinghamshire in May. However, it's only mid-October now. What will you do in the meantime?' 'I've already given that point some thought,' I answered. 'Once I have posted off the application forms, I am going to check the 'Times Educational Supplement' for a supply teaching post from January in the Wycombe area. That would take me up to the Education Branch induction course start date in May.' 'Good thinking. I see from the notes accompanying the application form that a degree and all teaching experience will count towards your rank seniority. What with your Cambridge degree, your National Service and any extra teaching months, you should soon reach the rank of captain.'

'K' then shuffled a few files on his desk. 'One final point, and one I know I mentioned during your January visit earlier in the year. Once you have finished your induction course in August, you'll be ready to receive your posting to your first unit. I might well arrange for you to be of use to our Service if any relevant assignment surfaces. It probably won't but if you can be of use to us, do remember that as far as I am concerned you will be a unique hybrid – a full-time Army officer but with a certain connection to us. That is why the Education Branch is such a good cover for you. Had you opted for a career in the Intelligence Corps with its up-front connotations and with its being peopled by officers steeped in security matters, our special arrangement might well have been rumbled in due course. As it is, being in the Education Branch, you will be above suspicion and safe.'

'K' now switched the conversation to a totally new subject. 'I have a little surprise for you. Would you agree to be my guest for lunch?' 'Most certainly,' I replied. 'Well, I thought we'd go to my club, the Oxford and Cambridge in Pall Mall. Have you eaten there before?' 'No.' 'I'm sure you will enjoy lunch there. Let's be off! I've told my driver to be ready for 12.30.'

We went downstairs, walked past the reception desk, where I left my ID tag, and out through a rear exit. A car was waiting for us. The chauffeur opened the rear doors and we settled ourselves into the plush seats. Not long afterwards, we arrived at the Oxford and Cambridge Club. 'I'll be here for the rest of the day, Charles, and staying the night. Pick me up at 8.30 in the morning.'

As we approached the entrance door of the club, a uniformed doorman came towards us. 'Good-day, gentlemen. Nice weather for this time of year.' From the moment we entered the club, I could see it was a very special place to entertain friends and other guests. The decor and furniture were simply magnificent. A number of very large oil paintings hung on the walls. The atmosphere was unique. After a brief visit to the cloakroom, 'K' led me to a bar where we relaxed over a dry sherry. He was well known in the club, constantly greeting and acknowledging other members with smiles and nods, all the time remaining seated. He leaned over to me and said, 'They know me by sight here at the club from the doorman to the Secretary but there have no idea at all what I do.'

We entered a splendid dining-room at about one o'clock. Most of the tables were occupied, causing an animated buzz of conversation. 'K' had reserved a table for us. The menu choice was comprehensive and mouth-watering, including the main feature of my lunch – a beautifully presented sea bass. Our chief conversation topics were Cambridge, both town and gown, and Italy. 'K' had visited Italy a number of times, including some pre-war trips to Florence, Rome and Naples but he admitted to being ashamed at his lack of proficiency in the language.

I happened to ask if membership of the club was limited to just male graduates of the two universities. 'Yes, it is. Some avant-garde members consider we are living in a time warp here, but I am quite happy with the existing arrangements. Doubtless, the time will come when we shall also have lady members but I don't think that will happen in my lifetime. We are quite modern in our ways and thinking, really. We discuss a whole range of issues here.' 'Including the admission of lady members,' I queried. 'Oh, no!. We don't profess to be that modern. Not yet, anyway.'

At the end of my lunch visit to his club, 'K' escorted me to the entrance and the doorman hailed a taxi. 'K' settled my taxi fare to Victoria Station with the driver, added a handsome tip and bade me farewell. 'You'll be seeing me or hearing from me sooner or later,' he exclaimed and added with a chuckle, 'You won't be escaping from my clutches just yet.' His parting words immediately made me think of the popular acronym frequently shortened to 'TANSTAAFL' – 'There Ain't No Such Thing As A Free Lunch' or, for that matter, a free taxi journey.

The very evening I returned to my parents' house in Crawley from my meeting with 'K', I noted down three priorities in the memorandum section of my diary. The first was to read through the Army application form and notes very carefully before completion and posting off. The second was to buy a copy of the 'Times Educational Supplement' (TES) and check on supply teaching posts in the Wycombe area. The third was to buy a car so that I could be mobile, especially when moving away from Crawley in the not too distant future.

The first priority was completed within a day but I had to wait a few days before the next issue of the TES appeared. Hastily turning to the teaching vacancies in the Buckinghamshire area, I was disappointed to discover that there were no supply teaching posts at all on offer. I particularly wanted a school not far from Wycombe in order to get to know the area before starting my Army course in May. Further, I didn't want to impose much longer on my parents' hospitality. Their lifestyle was not mine and I wanted to be independent, anyway. I had to wait three weeks before a suitable post was advertised and by then it was mid-November. The one post that was available, starting in the January, required English and geography with some history, three subjects I was confident of being able to teach. The school was Wooburn Green County Secondary Modern School situated only a few miles from Wycombe, and no more than ten minutes by car.

Along with other secondary modern schools in the UK, the school catered for boys and girls who were not judged suitable for a grammar or technical-school place. Since the 'Butler Education Act' of 1944, schools had been divided into grammar, technical and secondary modern. There was no freedom of choice – where one ended up depended on the Eleven Plus examination result. A large majority of the children who went to school between 1944 and 1970 went to secondary modern schools – before comprehensive schools became the norm.

The teaching focus in the secondary modern school was placed on a wide range of basic practical skills including woodwork, technical drawing, handicraft and domestic science subjects such as cookery. Each school could decide on supporting subjects which usually included English, arithmetic, history and geography. The majority of the pupils would probably progress to semi-skilled and unskilled jobs in due course. School leaving age in 1959 was 15, having been raised from 14 in 1947. Very few of the pupils took the 'O' Level examination but opted for the lower qualification of the Certificate of Secondary Education (CSE). 'A' Levels were not on offer so no pupils could then progress to university. Permanent teaching posts in secondary modern schools were not seen as eminently desirable and there was a lot of staff turnover.

I sent for the application forms and they arrived within a few days. Having posted them off, I waited anxiously to learn whether I would be granted an interview or not. I needn't have worried – a letter arrived almost by return of post with an interview date fixed for late November.

My third priority was to buy a car. I had passed a particular second-hand car dealer's on a number of occasions when walking into the Crawley town centre. I had noticed a model which really attracted my attention. It was one which had interested me ever since my National Service days in Nottinghamshire – the A40 Somerset coupe, produced by the Austin Motor

Company between 1952 and 1954. A captain in my unit had purchased a brand new one which I had admired a lot. When new in 1954, the Crawley car had cost £700. It was now on sale in excellent condition for £425 with a low recorded mileage.

I was fortunate in that I could afford the purchase price of the car and pay cash. Thanks to my Major County Scholarship awarded by the London County Council as a result of my State Scholarship and 'A' Level results in 1952, fees relating to my three years at Cambridge following my National Service had all been covered. My scholarship grant had not only met all tuition fees, board and lodging charges and the provision of all books and stationery, but it had also provided me with a weekly pocket money allowance. In a sense, I had been paid to go to university. With the money I had saved as a National Service officer and with my YTG pay and day trip commission as a courier in Italy in 1957 and 1958, I had built up a very healthy bank balance of over £1000. Nearly fifty percent of that sum was now to be spent on the A40 Somerset coupe. It had two doors, separate front seats that folded forward to give access to the rear, and a column-mounted gear change lever. The car sported a 1200cc four-cylinder engine. My parents came with me to inspect the car before purchase. I took them on a test drive around the local area, at the end of which they seemed more bemused than anything else. Their own transport was limited to buses and trains and travel by car seemed completely alien to them.

Driving was less regulated in those days. The MOT test for motor vehicle roadworthiness wasn't introduced until 1960, and only then if the vehicle was ten years old or more. The test wasn't reduced to vehicles of three years or more until 1967. Further, seat belts didn't become compulsory until 1983. The A40 may have lacked seat belts but it did have a starting handle. If the weather was vey cold, I used to turn over the car engine several times on the starting handle, with the ignition turned off. Carrying out that procedure always ensured that the engine then fired first time. On one occasion at closing time in a pub car park after a heavy snowstorm, and with little room for manoeuvre, I reversed the car into a deep bank of snow. My companion made the bright suggestion that to clear the snow from the blocked exhaust pipe, I should insert the starting handle there and jiggle it about. That action on my part coincided with the arrival of the local policeman on his bicycle. He gave me a very funny look. 'Excuse me, sir. Could I have a word with you?'

My own new mode of transport certainly facilitated travel to the Wooburn Green school to attend my interview. No sooner had I arrived at the school reception desk than the headmaster himself appeared. Mr. Gordon was a friendly and relaxed man and I found it easy to relate to him. In his study, he explained that one of his staff would be going into hospital for a major operation in December and wouldn't be fit enough to return to teaching until April – hence the supply teaching vacancy. He referred to my application form, asked a few follow-up questions and then suggested that he showed me around the school.

The first thing that struck me on our tour was how smart the pupils looked in their uniforms. Pupil respect towards the staff was much in evidence. As we entered a classroom to observe a lesson in progress, the pupils immediately stood up from their desks and, looking at

Mr. Gordon, said, 'Good morning, sir.' Moving around the school, I could observe through classroom windows that the pupils in every classroom I passed were engaged in steady work with not a hint of disruption of any sort. 'I could work here,' I thought. The school had a large gymnasium, spacious playing fields for athletics, football, hockey and cricket, together with both hard and soft courts for tennis. 'We do our best to satisfy as many of our pupils' needs as possible,'explained Mr. Gordon. 'Because we are a secondary modern school and not a grammar school, some people label our pupils as failures. That thoughtless judgement is far from the truth. Our pupils have strengths other than purely academic ones. Over the years many of them have gone on to make a real success of their careers and lives.'

We finished our tour and returned to the study. 'Well, what do you think of us?' 'I am very impressed by what I've seen and I know I would enjoy the experience of teaching here.' 'And so you shall,' was the most unexpected reply. 'The post is yours. I've already seen three other candidates and my mind is now made up. There will be no need for you to wait and wonder about the result of your interview for the post – you already have it. You'll soon receive an official letter from me confirming everything, together with some notes from the teacher you are replacing. Term begins on Monday, 5th January.'

I thanked Mr. Gordon for his time and decision. Before leaving, I mentioned that perhaps he could help me with one matter exercising my mind – the question of local accommodation for me for the coming term. 'I might be able to help you,' he remarked. 'One of my staff, Tim Baker, has just got married. As a bachelor, he had rented accommodation not far from the school in Wooburn Grange. It's been converted into a number of flats and flatlets. There could be something at the Grange for you.' He gave me directions and added with a broad smile that he looked forward to my joining his staff in the January.

Wooburn Grange was about five minutes by car from the school. As I drove through the entrance, I caught sight of the Grange – a most imposing building on ground rising well above the road. To one side there were two or three new houses which I assumed had been built recently in the spacious grounds. The Grange itself was a two storey, white period building with grey slate roofing, and was almost certainly Victorian or Edwardian. It looked just like a very select and upmarket country hotel. Little did I know at the time that, one day in the future and for a very specific reason, it would become one of Britain's most famous 'hotels', and instantly recognisable to millions of people.

I parked my car and approached the front door, which was flanked by two evergreens in enormous tubs. I was about to ring the bell, when the door suddenly opened and a woman appeared. 'I saw you arrive. Can I help you?' 'I've been talking to Mr. Gordon, the local school headmaster and he mentioned that Tim Baker used to have a flatlet here. I'll be teaching at the school from January and I'm looking for accommodation until May.' 'Well, you've come to the right place. Come in.' She led me into the hall and then into a spacious drawing room. 'My name is Doris and I'm the housekeeper here. I look after the Grange for a couple who live locally in Bourne End. Tim's bed-sit hasn't been rented out again yet. I'll take you upstairs and show you around.'

'Bed-sit' was an apt description of the accommodation on offer. It consisted of a large bedsitting room with a kitchenette at one end dominated by a large refrigerator. 'You would share bathroom facilities with the lady next door who works full time and is away at weekends.' Doris confirmed a weekly rent to include electricity, radiator heating and gas for the cooker. She added that as for Tim Baker and given adequate warning, she would be pleased to provide basic cold suppers at an extra reasonable charge. Also 'at an extra reasonable charge', she would do my laundry weekly and return it ironed. Doris was obviously an astute businesswoman. She continued, 'As you are not paying rent until January and it's only November, I think it only right and proper that you pay a nominal amount of just two weeks' rent to retain the bed-sit accommodation empty for December.' I couldn't be bothered to argue the point. 'Oh! Plus you'll need to pay the first month's rent in advance, of course. A cheque will be fine. You'll get your keys when you arrive in January.' At least, I managed to get Doris to sign a receipt for everything. 'You will be very comfortable here, you know. Tim really enjoyed his stay with us.'

On arrival back in Crawley, I broke the good news to my parents about landing the teaching post and the booking of accommodation. They congratulated me on my success. I think they were relieved to learn that I would soon be flying the nest again, this time probably for good. I could now relax and enjoy December in the knowledge that 1959 should turn out to be a year in which I would be gainfully employed and starting out on my future career.

I had some family loose ends to tie up in December. I hadn't seen my brother, George, for some months or my sister, Amy, and her husband Michael. I had planned to visit Foyles bookshop in Charing Cross Road, London to look through their second-hand selection of bird books. On my way back to Crawley via Victoria Station, George and I could meet up for a chat over a beer and catch up on various topics. I telephoned him and we agreed a date and a meeting time.

George was four years older than me. I was easy-going whereas he was serious and studious by nature. He had preceded me at Cambridge, reading French and German, also after having completed his National Service. After graduating, he had endured a couple of trainee-graduate jobs before finding his real metier. He took up an appointment at Harrap's, the publishers, as a lexicographer and textbook author, employing his two foreign languages.

We both thoroughly enjoyed our evening, including reminiscing on our past family experiences together and discussing his job. In addition to his Harrap's foreign language work, George had started compiling notes on a book of boys' and girls' names. It was published a few years later by Harrap's and also by Pan in a paperback edition. He was most interested in my news regarding the Wooburn Green school and also my Army application.

George had done his National Service in the Intelligence Corps, 1947-49. After completing his basic training at Maresfield in Sussex, he was posted to Austria where he served many months in post-war Vienna. The battle-scarred city with its bombed-out streets had been divided into four sectors by the victorious Allies. It provided the setting for Carol Read's 'The Third Man' (1949), a thriller of the 'film noir' genre about friendship and betrayal, and filmed in black and white. It starred Orson Welles, Joseph Cotton and Trevor Howard. The zither music of Anton Karas provided a haunting musical score. George and I had been to see the film on general release in London. He was so entranced by it, bringing back as it did so many memories of his time spent in post-war Vienna, he returned to see it several more times. Many years later in 1999, the British Film Institute selected 'The Third Man' as the best British film of the twentieth century. Considering his intelligence and security work in Vienna during his National Service, I would have loved a discussion with George on my own recent experience in that field but, of course, my lips were sealed. We were still talking animatedly when they called 'last orders'. It was time to make our separate ways home, George to Twickenham and me to Crawley.

The next point on my December tick-list was to visit Amy and Michael in their flat in north London. They were both twenty-eight and had married earlier in the year. Michael worked in the family hardware business. Amy had long since opted out of academia and had become a successful dress designer for a well-known fashion house in London's West End.

The last family member to catch up with was my sister, Ruth. She was my parents' eldest child and was five years older than me. She came to Crawley to stay with my parents and me for Christmas and the New Year. Ruth was the most gifted member of the family in terms of academic ability. She had won an Open Scholarship to Cambridge at the end of the War to read ancient Greek and Latin (Classics) and she proceeded to achieve a rare starred First in part one of her tripos examinations. However, on leaving Cambridge, she spurned convention by spending her life living in a succession of small rented flats in London, studying and sleeping, sleeping and studying. Over the years, her studies had included pure and applied mathematics, biology, philosophy, logic and a variety of ancient and modern languages. She did the minimum of work in gainful employment. She was happy just to pay her rent and to retreat into her own special and very private academic world. She never married.

Her latest all-consuming interest soon became apparent during her Christmas sojourn at my parents' house – Egyptian hieroglyphics. She had enrolled in evening classes in the subject in London. She spent a lot of time during that festive break explaining the intricacies of the system to me and reproducing endless hieroglyphs on endless sheets of paper. Her latest hero was the French orientalist, Jean-Francois Champollion, whose classic work on the decipherment of Egyptian hieroglyphics in the early part of the nineteenth century so thoroughly intrigued and captivated her. Prior to Champollion, she had enjoyed a cerebral and linguistic love affair with Michael Ventris, the decipherer of the ancient Cretan script, Linear B. One could never relax in Ruth's company – her mind was forever in overdrive. Moreover, she expected others to keep up with her, if they could. I tried my best but, at least, I knew that as soon as Christmas and the New Year were over, it would be a case of pastures new for me.

I left Crawley for Wooburn Grange in my Austin A40 on 2nd January to give me a few days to settle in before the local school term began on the 5th. I had telephoned Doris, the housekeeper, to inform her of my arrival date and approximate time and also to book a cold supper for that evening. When I arrived at the Grange in the late afternoon, she greeted me warmly and accompanied me upstairs to the bed-sit. She had thoughtfully put on the heating and she informed me that my supper would be brought up at about six-thirty. By the time I had unpacked, checked out the bathroom and rearranged some of the furniture, Doris arrived with my supper. It was quite substantial, including ham and egg pie, beetroot, tomatoes and potato salad plus a couple of slices of buttered bread. I listened to an hour or two of programmes on the BBC Home Service on my wireless set before turning in for an early night.

As might be expected, I was a little apprehensive when I arrived at the school on the Monday morning. Some children were already milling around in the playground as I made my way to the staff-room. Mr. Gordon was hovering. He greeted me and introduced me to a couple of teachers who had already arrived. My first lesson was an English one to third-year pupils. They eyed me inquisitively but the lesson passed without a hitch and the fifty minutes just flew by. A history lesson followed before the morning break. In the staff-room, I chatted to several teachers over a cup of tea and without exception they were pleasant and quite friendly. I had the school lunch, the first hot meal I had eaten for several days – it was most welcome.

As the days and weeks passed, I settled comfortably into a routine of school and Wooburn Grange. In addition to my basic teaching commitment of English, history and geography, I stood in for teachers on sick leave. In that way, I also found myself teaching religious instruction and arithmetic; I even covered for the cookery teacher on one occasion.

In late February a letter arrived from Mr. Lewis Williams, the Managing Director of YTG Universal Limited. He had been approached by a group of Malayan primary schoolteachers on a two-year study course at the Malayan Teachers' Training College in Kirkby, near Liverpool. The group wanted to arrange a tour of northern Europe by coach during their Easter holidays from 1st – 17th April. The group size would be just over twenty made up of Malays, Chinese and Indians, all fluent in English. Would I be available to lead the group as a courier? My term at Wooburn Green County Second Modern School would end on 26th March and my induction course at the Army Education Centre in Wycombe wouldn't begin until May at the earliest. Mr. Williams had written in his letter that he appreciated the tour would include countries I had never visited. He added encouragingly 'but you are certainly capable of briefing yourself in advance on the main features of the towns and cities you will be visiting. Further, I know you will do your best to look after the group and keep them happy.' It was a challenge I couldn't refuse and I wrote back accepting the job offer.

Two further letters arrived at the Grange a few days later. One was from YTG giving me details of the group tour including a provisional itinerary. The second letter was from the War Office confirming my acceptance into the Education Branch. I would be appointed in the rank of lieutenant with sufficient seniority to indicate a promotion date to substantive captain in April 1961. Further details would follow in due course from the Education Branch.

The provisional itinerary for the Malayan teachers' trip was comprehensive. On day one, they would travel by train from Liverpool to London where I would meet them and we would board the boat train to Dover. Our coach driver for the trip would meet us at Ostend Harbour. Countries to be visited in the seventeen days were Belgium, Holland, Germany, Denmark, Sweden and Norway. A final figure of twenty-two trip participants had now been confirmed. The party consisted of eight women and fourteen men. We would be staying at hotels on a half-board basis – breakfast and dinner. I made a special point of travelling to Wycombe the following Saturday. I headed for the nearest bookshop where I bought two comprehensive travel guides to cover the six countries we would be visiting. All I had to do now was to study them and try to soak up as much information as possible on the main cities set out in the itinerary – no easy task. That input would all be supplemented in due course by further study in the evenings during the trip itself.

I had no discipline problems at all during my teaching term at the school. Although the pupils knew I was a supply teacher passing through, there were no incidents of misbehaviour. Mr. Gordon sat in on several of my lessons and was most complimentary as to how they had gone.

Towards the middle of March, I was most surprised by some news regarding Wooburn Grange. Doris, the housekeeper, looking somewhat shaken and unhappy, informed me it had been confirmed that the property had been sold. The new owners, who would be taking up residence in mid-April, planned to turn the Grange into a country club. It would all be a personal disaster for Doris as the new owners could not offer her further employment beyond the end of April. 'They'll give me just two extra weeks from their arrival so that the wife can learn about living in and running the Grange, just two miserable weeks. I'd love to just leave them to it, but I can't. I need the two weeks' extra income. As to my own future, I'll probably end up going to live with my sister and her husband in Manchester.' Doris confirmed that existing 'paying guests' such as myself would be given three months'grace to make alternative accommodation arrangements. As I would be moving to the Wycombe Birch Park Officers' Mess in May, I would not be affected.

One afternoon, about a week before the start of the YTG trip, I arrived back at the Grange from school and was greeted by Doris. She handed me a registered mail package which had been delivered that morning. On opening the package in my room, I found that it contained my own travel tickets for the return London – Dover and Dover – Ostend journeys, the confirmed itinerary, a list of the group participants and a large sterling float in notes. There was also a covering letter with many additional information points. One major item concerned the cultural make-up of the group – Malay, Chinese and Indian – explaining that dinner meals would exclude beef and pork. Our hotels had agreed on dinner menus which would concentrate on vegetarian dishes plus lamb, chicken and fish. We would be able to exchange sterling notes and travellers' cheques for the local currency at reception desks. The letter also declared that a Mr. Albert Wong was the appointed group representative. He would channel comments from the participants, both positive and negative, direct to me.

Mid-morning a week later, found me standing at the ticket barrier to the boat train at Victoria Station.

The rendezvous time was ten-thirty for the eleven o' clock train to Dover Harbour. A quarter of an hour passed and then I saw them. In fact, it would have been difficult to miss the group of Malays, Chinese and Indians making their way towards me. I stepped forward, smiled and introduced myself. Albert Wong approached me and thrust the train and ferry group ticket into my hand. 'Pleased to meet you,' he exclaimed. 'Our holiday begins now.'

The train and ferry were both on time and customs checks were a mere formality. On entering the arrival hall in Ostend, I immediately caught sight of a man carrying a large placard bearing the initials 'YTG'. In fractured English and looking rather daunted, he introduced himself as Paul, our coach driver. His face lit up when I started speaking to him in French. He later confided that with his poor command of English, he had dreaded the prospect of trying to get his travel messages across to the group. The coach was a thirty-five seater so there was plenty of room for our twenty-two participants to spread themselves out. It was equipped with a radio and microphone, together with a courier seat next to the driver. We stayed in Ostend the first night. Our hotel rooms were soon sorted out and we agreed to meet in the bar at half-past eight for a nine o'clock dinner. I had been learning and re-learning their names during the day and had made reasonable progress.

We left the hotel the following morning for Brussels with a scheduled stop at Ghent. We then travelled on for a two-night stay in Brussels. It would be tiresome to describe the travel details of the seventeen day trip. Suffice it to say that our major stopping-off cities with overnight accommodation were Brussels, Amsterdam,

Hamburg, Copenhagen, Gothenburg and Oslo. We visited other tourist hotspots en route including the Keukenhof Flower Gardens in Holland and the Hans Christian Anderson house in Odense, Denmark.

Chatting on the ferry from Ostend back to Dover on the last day of the trip, the group spoke of the highlights they had experienced. Their number one highlight had been our visit to a ski resort near Oslo. For almost all of the Malayans, snow was still an absolute wonder. They had enjoyed the opportunity to ski on some nursery slopes despite numerous slips and falls, all accompanied by hysterical laughter. Unexpectedly, their number two highlight was the evening visit to the Reeperbahn area of Hamburg, which happened to be only a ten-minute walk from our hotel near the harbour. They had all insisted on visiting it, encouraged by Mr. Wong, the group representative, who had done his own research on the subject. I had strong reservations regarding the visit but they turned out to be unfounded. We entered Herbertstrasse which was a screened-off side street. There were women of easy virtue seated behind plate glass windows in various stages of undress, waiting for any adventurous window-shopping customers. When one venturesome man did enter a front door, an enormous cheer went up from the assembled tourist onlookers although my party seemed to be struck dumb by it all. One young woman teacher commented later, 'Coming as I do from the morally strict country of Malaya, it was a mind-numbing experience – not exactly enjoyable but definitely unforgettable, and so a highlight.' The third agreed highlight was Copenhagen with its wonderful atmosphere, together with memorable visits to the Tivoli

Gardens and the bronze statue of Hans Christian Anderson's 'Little Mermaid' near the harbour.

We said our goodbyes at Victoria Station. They were travelling on to Liverpool and I was returning to Wooburn Green. When I arrived at the Grange, there was a pile of mail waiting for me in my room. The most important letter was from the Army Education Branch informing me of my joining date in May when I should report to Wycombe Birch Park. After a good night's sleep, I awoke the next morning with two priorities on my mind. First, to meet the new owners who had already been in residence a few days. Secondly, to send my trip report off to YTG.

Jack, in his mid-forties, was very much an extrovert, full of energy and very personable. He said that he and his wife had been considering running a country club for some years. Wooburn Grange had presented an ideal opportunity to put the idea into practice. He confirmed that it would open within a couple of months or so as the 'Wooburn Grange Country Club'.

Mr. Lewis Williams wrote to thank me for my 'comprehensive' trip report, adding that all the feedback received from the Malayan teachers confirmed a most interesting and enjoyable trip. 'Well done, John,' he wrote. 'I knew you would rise to the challenge.'

CHAPTER 8

In May 1959, I left Wooburn Grange, shortly to be renamed the 'Wooburn Grange Country Club'. I moved into my quarters in the Officers' Mess at the Army Education Branch Centre at Wycombe Birch Park. I was leaving a building which had been my home for over four months. Little did I realise at the time that it would become instantly recognisable to millions of television viewers in later years.

In planning the series of 'Fawlty Towers' – six in 1975 and a further six in 1979 – it was decided that Wooburn Grange Country Club would double for the hotel and that most of the exterior shots would be filmed there, including the opening shot of the building at the start of each episode. Unfortunately, Wooburn Grange Country Club is no more. It burned down in 1991 and a developer later built a number of houses on the site. I must be one of a very small band of people who can actually say, 'I lived for several months at 'Fawlty Towers' – in the very building shown at the start of each episode.'

I distinctly remember the first time I realised that the fictional hotel and Wooburn Grange Country Club were one and the same. Previously, I'd had a vague idea that they could be, but one day it rang really true as, yet again, I watched Basil Fawlty walk down the hotel steps. I was with some friends in a pub when I heard the familiar signature tune on the pub TV and we turned to see the start of an episode. As it progressed, there was a familiar exterior shot. I couldn't stop myself saying out loud, 'I lived there. I actually lived in 'Fawlty Towers'.' A man at the table next to ours leaned over and said, 'I don't know what you're drinking, mate, but whatever it is, I'm off to the bar to get myself a double.'

On our first morning at the Education Branch Centre, we had an introductory talk from Major Trevor, who commanded the Officer Training Wing. He introduced us to our course instructor, Captain Frank. I was the only one wearing civilian clothes that morning. The other eleven course participants had all just finished a basic officer cadet course elsewhere and were thus recently commissioned as second lieutenants. They were now reporting for their professional Branch training. Some were National Servicemen, others were hoping for a long-term Army career. My lack of uniform was rectified that very afternoon by a visit to the Centre Quartermaster. The Army tailor was also visiting, so I was able to be measured up for additional items such as service dress and mess kit. The Army granted a generous dress allowance which covered the purchase of most items.

Captain Frank gave us a synopsis of our course study subjects and it looked very much like a condensed post-graduate certificate of education. He was a pleasant and lively instructor with a ready sense of humour. His one failing was an occasional lapse in deep preparation of the specific subject in hand. An allotted hour's lesson could run out of steam in half the time, leading to another 'break for a cigarette or fresh air.'

Some cricket information appeared on the Officers' Mess notice-board during the first week of the course.

Was anyone interested in applying to play for the 'Wycombe Army Education Cricket Eleven'? If so, would they report to Major Ray in the Headquarter Wing. Matches would be played against local teams at the weekend. There was also a planned tour of some Oxford and Cambridge colleges in June, when the team would play as a representative Education Branch Eleven. Having been a very keen and moderately successful member of my grammar school first eleven team, I signed up the same day. Net practice would be that Friday afternoon with a match planned for the Sunday against a local team in Gerrards's Cross.

Major Ray was quite an extrovert character with a round, jovial face and a frequently exercised deep belly-laugh. I explained I had played as an all-rounder in my school cricket eleven, batting at number four and being a medium-fast bowler.. He gave me the address of a sports outfitter's in Wycombe which always had a good stock of cricketing wear. 'If, after our net practice on Friday, I think you'll pass muster for the Sunday game, then get youself kitted out in the Wycombe shop on Saturday.' Net practice went well and Major Ray informed me I would be in his eleven on the Sunday.

Captain Frank had told us that part of our induction course would be a two-week attachment to an Army unit. It was an innovation for our course although for some reason it wasn't repeated on subsequent induction courses. I was allocated a place at the Guards' Depot in Godalming, Surrey along with a National Service newly-commissioned second lieutenant. Bill Miller had graduated from London University in English but his studies seemed to have had little effect on his strong cockney accent or the basic idiomatic expressions he sometimes uttered. They weren't exactly in the 'Cor blimey, mate,' class but were not far from it. It had been during my own National Service days that I had managed to eradicate my own London accent, replaclng it with a more or less neutral one. I knew that in the rather snobbish Brigade of Guards of the time, a slight Scottish accent for an officer, even possibly a slight Irish one, were 'acceptable' but a strong cockney accent was conspicuous by its absence in a Guards Officers' Mess, except when employed by one of the mess waiters. I went to see the officer commanding our training wing but, having already met Major Trevor, I knew it would probably be like talking to the proverbial brick wall. I wasn't far from wrong. He maintained that Bill Miller had to go somewhere and the Guards' Depot in Godalming would rapidly increase his learning curve regarding Army mess life and customs. At least the major asked me to guide Bill and keep an eye on him. He would indeed be an Education Branch innocent abroad.

It was thus with some trepidation that I arrived at the Guards' Depot, Godalming with Bill Miller for our two week attachment and stay in the Officers' Mess. The First Guards' Depot was located at Caterham in Surrey; the Godalming Guards' Depot was referred to as the Second Guards' Depot. Having left our luggage in the rooms allocated to us in the Officers' Mess, we went across to the Education Wing. We were met by the incumbent instructor officer, Major Peter who, as a former member of the Royal Navy, welcomed us 'aboard'. He briefed us on the Depot and the Officers' Mess. He emphasised that with their unique atmosphere and routine procedures, we would certainly meet with some very unusual and seemingly odd customs. On the other hand, the Godalming Guards' Depot was a most efficient training unit with a first-rate commanding officer and adjutant. A number of the officers were from the landed gentry and even the aristocracy, exhibiting traits and personal mannerisms acquired during their privileged upbringing. As outsiders we could well find it difficult to adjust to the ways of the Mess and its officers. We should bear in mind that some of the Mess members would find us just as odd as we found them. He finished his briefing by saying, 'Professionally, the officers are first rate. It's just that they have some upper-class eccentricities, plus a few unusual habits and customs. So, my advice is to observe but refrain from comment.' The three of us didn't dine in the Mess that evening but went out for a pub meal in Godalming.

Major Peter's words of advice were still ringing in my ears as Bill and I came down to breakfast in the Mess dining-room the first morning of our stay. Initially, the kedgeree on the hotplate totally confused Bill who asked me in his loud cockney voice, 'What on earth is this weird-looking stuff, mate?' 'It's kedgeree, a mixture amongst other things of smoked haddock, rice, hard-boiled eggs and curry powder,' – as half a dozen heads turned to gaze at this odd intruder pair that perhaps a couple of their dogs might have brought in. Could they possibly be commissioned officers?

I couldn't help noticing that three or four Guards officers who were breakfasting were wearing their uniform service hats. I remembered hearing somewhere that if an officer was wearing his hat at breakfast, it meant, 'Don't talk to me: I feel somewhat 'fragile' this morning. I want to be left alone.' As chance would have it, Bill sat down next to a young lieutenant wearing an aforementioned service hat. There was no way I could alert him about the custom without drawing even more attention to ourselves. Inevitably, as April follows March, Bill with his cooked breakfast in front of him, chose to ask his neighbour, 'Would you please pass the salt,' which happened to be in front of the officer but well out of Bill's reach. Nothing happened. Bill repeated his request, not once but twice. Finally, with an exaggerated sniff, the Guards officer snapped his fingers. A mess waiter appeared by his side in seconds. 'Sir!' 'Brine, would you pass the salt to the officer on my right.' 'Yessir!' – the salt was duly moved some fifteen inches towards Bill by the waiter whose name I later learned was 'Brown'. Not a single glance was cast by the Guards officer in Bill's direction, not a glimmer that he even existed. My main thought then was, 'For heaven's sake, Bill, don't now ask the officer for the pepper or the waiter for some tomato ketchup.'

Some further embarrassment ensued during that first breakfast meal but fortunately it was way over Bill's head. I heard two second lieutenants whispering the letters 'HKLP' and looking towards Bill. That specific four-letter sequence reminded me starkly of my own first days at my officer cadet school in Aldershot in the early 1950s and of my own steep social learning curve. 'HKLP' translates to the initiated as 'Holds Knife Like Pen' and indeed that was how Bill was holding that particular piece of cutlery. A tactful word from me would be necessary later. Everybody, but everybody, of course, in the Guards' Depot Officers' Mess held their knife and fork in the 'correct' manner. Some lives can really circulate around such trivial social matters or they certainly did in certain circles in the

1950s. As soon as I could later, I briefed Bill on the service cap-wearing custom at breakfast. Further, as we were guests in their Mess, it would be 'diplomatic' to hold one's knife and fork as the Guards officers did – 'a typical Guards custom,' I explained. To his credit, Bill took the advice in good humour and promised he would conform.

We spent our first morning in the Education Wing observing Major Peter teaching recruits military calculations and accounts, followed by map-reading to a class of non-commissioned officers (NCOs). Then it was time for lunch. The three of us walked across to the Officers' Mess. I couldn't help noticing the large number of dogs that were around. It seemed that quite a few of the Guards officers making their way to the Mess for lunch, had two dogs each, mainly cocker spaniels and labradors. We went into the Mess, removed our service hats and left them on hooks in the corridor. The first feature one noticed inside the Mess was a large ornamental fountain gushing water. The second feature one noticed was that the cocker spaniels (well -named in the circumstances) and the labradors were cocking their legs against the fountain in an act of self-relief. Bill, with his eyes out on stalks, was about to pass a comment but I signalled to him to say nothing.

The first course happened to be an aptly named cock-a-leekie soup followed by a choice of dishes. The dogs were being fed under the table. Bill casually asked the officer next to him what his golden labradors were called. 'They are Rupert and George but they are not golden but yellow, don't you know,' was the curt response. Harrumph! Otherwise, our conversation was amongst ourselves. Major Peter mentioned that it very

much looked as if both of the Guards Depots would
be transferring to Pirbright near Woking in early 1960,
thus bringing to an end over fifty years of the Guards
Depot in Godalming. He and his family would have
to move from Godalming with the rest of the Depot
personnel. It would involve another schooling upset for
his three children.

As the days passed, I myself found one common habit
pertaining to several of the Guards officers quite
disconcerting. Admittedly, in their eyes, i was a low level
Education Branch 'schoolie', whereas being in the Foot
Guards, they were the cream of the cream. Occasionally
in the ante-room after a meal, I might get talking to an
officer about some subject or other. If he warmed to it,
such as perhaps when discussing cricket or Italy, he
would make you feel a valued companion with that
effortless charm and smooth social grace so typical of
the products of the more famous public schools. The
very next day, however, it seemed he didn't recognise you
and would look straight through you if you greeted him,
appearing loathe to talk to you again. One lunchtime, a
lieutenant actually commented to me in the ante-room
when I said something to him, 'Do I know you?'

Bill suffered more than me in that respect. When we
were having coffee with Major Peter one morning, Bill
admitted that certain characteristics of some of the
officers made him angry. He claimed they had an innate
sense of social superiority based on their privileged
background circumstances – 'an accident of birth' as he
called it. Sometimes when he was trying to engage in a
serious conversation, his comments would be met with
flippant or facetious replies. 'Oh! It makes me so mad,'
he said. 'They've also got such plummy voices, I can't

understand what they are saying half the time. Mind you, I suppose my cockney accent grates with them just as much as their accent grates with me. I've also acquired some new social vocabulary since I've been here. I notice they use 'napkin' instead of 'serviette', 'pudding' instead of 'sweet' and 'lavatory' or 'loo' instead of 'toilet'. I overheard one officer saying to some recruits, 'It's time for your dinner. I'll be back after my lunch.' Still, I appreciate that I must watch my step and take it all in good part. We won't be here for ever.' Fortunately, there were a number of Guards officers who were charm itself, genuinely engaging in conversation and regularly showing an interest in what their visitors had to say.

Major Peter did comment that, by and large now in the 1950s, many social barriers had been swept aside with regard to officers in the Foot Guards. 'Otherwise,' he said, 'they wouldn't be chatting to you two Education Branch officers in the first place. So consider yourselves lucky some progress has been achieved.'

In our second week of attachment, Bill and I were both programmed to teach at least three hours a day in the Education Wing. We were performing under the eagle eye of Major Peter. He always gave us an honest critique at the end of our teaching periods and invariably made valuable suggestions. I sat in on Bill's lessons and he sat in on mine. We both taught all the required subjects including English and map-reading. Major Peter would provide us with copious notes to read up in the evening before our next day's lessons. At the end of our two weeks, he declared his complete satisfaction with our performance and indeed with our progress in certain teaching techniques. He promised he would forward good reports to Wycombe.

Bill managed to make only one more faux pas or, at least, the only one I was aware of. It happened after lunch one day during our second week when we were sitting comfortably in the ante-room sipping our coffee. A General Election was due to be held the following day. Bill had been talking cricket to a Guards captain sat near him. 'Well,' said Bill, 'another General Election has come round. I've already voted by proxy but I suppose you will all be voting tomorrow.' 'I shan't be voting tomorrow', said Bill's cricket-chat companion, somewhat brusquely. 'Really?' replied Bill, 'I feel it's my duty to vote.' Well, let's put it this way,' replied the captain, 'I shan't be voting because I'm in the other 'Hice'.' Poor Bill had been talking to Captain The Lord Hetheringham who, as a hereditary peer of the realm and a member of the House of Lords, was ineligible to vote in a General Election.

There were two formal dining-in nights during our fortnight's attachment. The first was a regimental dinner night attended by all the Depot officers including Major Peter, Bill and myself. The Mess silver as set out on the tables must have been worth a king's ransom. Fortunately, Bill had already attended a couple of regimental dinner nights at the Wycombe Officers' Mess so, hopefully I thought, the procedures wouldn't be too alien to him. I had arranged with the President of the Mess Committee (PMC) to sit next to Bill so as to keep a friendly eye on him and to answer any procedural questions he might have. I also reminded him to drink very little before the meal, perhaps just one sherry, because when we sat down at dinner at 8pm, we would not be allowed to leave the table until after the port and the departure of the Depot Colonel and any guests – perhaps well over two hours later.

The meal itself went well and I noted how Bill was holding his cutlery 'Guards style'. Conversation to one side was dominated by three young Guards officers endlessly discussing the undoubted superwomen who had been their nannies. Each succeeding reminiscence seemed to aim at outdoing all others in the competence and love of nanny. Eventually, we reached the point where the port and madeira were being passed around the table, clockwise according to the standard military custom. One accepted the decanter with the right hand and passed it to the officer on one's left with the left hand. Bill performed the task accurately but soon absent-mindedly put the glass of port to his lips before I could kick him under the table. A few nearby 'tut-tuts' were sounded off but at that moment the PMC, having been informed by the Mess Sergeant that all glasses were filled, stood up. Silence reigned in the dining-room as he declared, 'Mr. Vice, the Queen.' The Vice-President then stood up at the opposite end of the dining-room and addressing the assembled officers said, 'Gentlemen, the Queen.' All present rose and holding their glasses, stood to attention as a small group of military musicians played a few bars of the National Anthem. All the officers then repeated the toast 'The Queen.' Officers of the rank of major and above were accorded the right to add, 'God bless her', before everyone drank Her Majesty's health. All in all, a complex procedure but one that has stood the test of time. Coffee and liqueurs were then served. Cigarettes and cigars were handed round and ash trays were placed on the tables.

Later, when we had all returned to the ante-room, Bill expressed his surprise to me at the three officers' comments in what he understood to be a discussion of their respective 'nans' or grandmothers. 'My nan would have been better than any of them but sadly, she passed away a couple of years ago at the age of eighty.' I didn't comment further.

Once the Colonel's guests had left the Mess at about eleven o'clock, it was time for the usual 'Mess games'. Jackets came off and sleeves were rolled up. The first game was the standard 'Moriarty challenge'. One volunteer was blindfolded, given a rolled-up newspaper and he then called out, 'Are you there, Moriarty?' Several nearby officers lay on the floor and shouted out, 'Here!' and then remained motionless. The volunteer with the newspaper had to judge distance and space before whacking it over what he thought was someone's head. It all went well until one volunteer was handed a rubber truncheon and soon managed to inflict a bruise or two. At one stage, a frozen chicken was obtained from the Mess kitchen and an ad hoc game of rugby followed until the chicken began to disintegrate into several pieces and both teams were scoring tries at the same time at opposite ends of the ante-room. A game of chair-borne polo was played with the dexterous use of soup spoons and an orange.

The Depot Mess ante-room had a number of very impressive oil paintings hanging on the walls from very solid picture rails. The final 'game' of the evening took place according to Mess custom at midnight. Two young officers challenged each other to cover a given length of the ante-room by clinging onto the picture rail, some nine feet above the floor. The agreed distance to be travelled by the two officers was to be timed. The quicker would be declared the evening's champion. 'Twenty pounds on Julian,' one major shouted, countered by 'Ten pounds on Archibald.' The betting continued with so much on Julian, followed by so much on Archibald until over two hundred pounds had been wagered. The Mess Treasurer was busy writing down all the bets before announcing, 'Time, gentlemen – the winner takes all.'

Julian, clearly an experienced and competent picture rail scrambler, covered the full distance in just under a minute. Archibald started well but then his feet caught in the stout cord holding a rather large portrait of a previous Guards general. He fell off the rail, crashed onto the floor and managed to bring the portrait down with him, inevitably smashing the glass. Half of Archibald's dinner also surfaced on the Mess carpet. The Colonel seemed to take it all in his stride but commented, 'See the Mess Secretary first thing in the morning, Archibald, so that you can settle the account for this evening's carelessness. Second thing in the morning, report to the Adjutant for two extra orderly officer duties for letting down the depot in front of visiting officers,' – eyeing Major Peter, Bill and me. 'Then we can forget about your below par performance this evening.' Meanwhile, three Mess orderlies (aptly named in the circumstances) had rushed in to clear away the evidence of Archibald's carelessness. Julian bought his defeated rival a glass of champagne and together they toasted 'the picture rail caper.' All very jolly stuff.

Our final evening at Godalming, happened to be a 'Ladies Night' with some very glamorous and titled ladies attending. They looked as if they had stepped straight off the front covers of the latest fashion magazines – which some of them might well have done.

I had a major's wife seated on my right. As we settled down at the table and waited for the soup to arrive, she fixed me with an inquisitive stare and said, 'You are not one of us, are you?' 'No. I'm in the Education Branch.' 'Oh! Which public school did you go to?' 'I didn't go to a public school. I went to a grammar school.' 'Oh! My husband went to Harrow.' 'But,' I continued, 'I did later go to Cambridge.' 'Oh! I love Cambridge. Humphrey and I have also been to Cambridge. It was when we spent a glorious weekend there last year, taking in the May Ball with our nephew, Nigel, who is at Trinity and the Ponsonby-Smythes. Do you know them?' 'Er, no.' 'Oh!.' Each 'Oh!' was uttered in a high pitched, squeaky voice and delivered with a distinct movement of the lower lip and a sharp twitch of the head.

Having passed enough time with this unusual and unworldly fellow on her left, the major's wife spent the rest of the meal talking animatedly with the Guards major on her right. I still picked up her occasional squeaky 'Oh!' in the general chatter of the dining-room but they were now being directed at him, while he had a much deeper 'Oh!' of his own.

Out of the corner of my eye, I had been checking on Bill's progress. He was sitting virtually opposite me next to a large lady with a strident voice. I couldn't help noticing that as we were finishing our soup, Bill was tipping his plate towards himself, whereas everyone, but everyone else, was tipping the plate away, enjoying the remains of the soup quietly and with conscious decorum. Further, I could hear from where I was sitting that Bill was definitely enjoying his soup. With Bill having spent two weeks rigidly conforming or trying to conform to unfamiliar social habits and customs, and when at times it had seemed to him like walking on eggshells, I thought, 'Good for you, Bill. Show them that you are different and that you don't always follow the crowd.'

I stayed on in the Mess ante-room until the last couples were leaving. I decided to take a stroll around the outside of the building to get a little exercise and some fresh air. As it began to rain, I sheltered under an arch behind a broad pillar by the Mess entrance. I could hear a couple talking at the entrance but they were out of sight. They were both speaking in the excessively strangulated and precise tones of received pronunciation or the clipped BBC English of the 1950s. The accent indicated a well-groomed social and educational background but gave no indication of the speaker's birthplace.

The woman was bemoaning the late arrival of their taxi home and her husband was insisting it would come along at any moment. I recognised his voice as that of a young captain by the name of Charles. There was a moment's silence and then, 'Charles, darling,' she suddenly began, 'I feel utterly squiffy and frightfully frolicsome this evening and so fruity, too. It must have been those final Tia Marias, darling. All I know, darling, is that when we get home, I want you to make passionate love to me. I just can't wait 'to have it orff', as the guardsmen would say, she giggled. 'Oh! Josephine,' he replied, 'I feel so awfully fragile this evening with ghastly stomach pains, don't you know. By the way, the guardsmen use another short Anglo-Saxon word, but never mind. Let's postpone our jolly for another couple of days. I'd be terribly grateful if you agreed, darling.' The only reply was a strangulated 'Oh! Darling!' And with that, their taxi arrived and they were gone – awfully quickly. It had indeed been a modern version of 'Not tonight, Josephine.'

Our final morning at the Guards' Depot duly arrived and Bill was determined to have the last word. He came down to breakfast wearing his service hat. I had to smile but, of course, I didn't speak to him. He saw me later and said, 'I just had to do it, John. I just had to do it.'

I really enjoyed the cricket matches throughout the summer and I managed to score a few runs and take some wickets. The highlight was the tour of the Oxford and Cambridge colleges when our team represented the 'Army Education Branch.' We played two matches in Cambridge, which were both drawn, against sides which included students and groundstaff. In Oxford, we played three matches, winning two and losing one. Our Eleven included three of us from the officers' induction course and three National Service sergeants who were also attending a Wycombe course. The Education Branch was seen as a very comfortable choice for graduates doing their two years' National Service. After just ten weeks of basic training and four weeks at Wycombe, they became sergeants. Although they were at the receiving end of a lot of banter and leg-pulling from the Regular Army sergeants, it was better than doing two years as a squaddie and the pay was good. After National Service ended in 1961, the Education Branch was staffed exclusively by officers. Selected regular sergeants and warrant officers were offered commissions while others left for alternative employment.

The cricketing highlight of the summer was not connected with the Army at all. I had gone over one evening to the newly-opened 'Wooburn Grange Country Club' to have a drink and a chat with Jack, the owner, with whom I had got on so well before leaving for Wycombe. He was very satisfied with the way business was developing and more than happy with the performance of the staff he had recruited. He mentioned that he had received two complimentary tickets for the third day of the England versus India Test Match at Lords on the Saturday. If I was interested in going with him, he would pick me up at the Wycombe Mess and drive on to Lords. I jumped at the chance and we made arrangements for the day.

It would be the second Test Match in the series, England having won the first match by an innings and 59 runs. On the car journey to London, Jack bemoaned the fact that England had been whitewashed four matches to none by Australia down under the previous winter. 'Let's hope for a better result against India this summer,' he said. 'At least, we are already one match up in the series.'

India had won the toss on the opening Thursday and had chosen to bat. They had made 168 all out, with Nari Contractor scoring a very useful 81. Tommy Greenhough had taken 5 wickets for 35 runs. England replied with 226, with Ken Barrington scoring a patient 80. We arrived in our seats as India were batting again. They were struggling and only managed 165. England soon knocked off the required 108 runs to win for the loss of only two wickets. Colin Cowdrey scored an unbeaten 63. It had been a most enjoyable day out – thanks to Jack. England went on to win all five matches in the series.

One day in mid-July just after I had finished lunch in the Officers' Mess, I was informed by a member of the Mess staff that I was wanted on the telephone. It turned out to be a call from 'K' himself. He disclosed that he'd had a hand in my forthcoming posting at the end of my induction course in August. He gave me a Dover telephone number to ring stating that 'Roger' would answer and arrange to meet me. Roger would give me full details including the background as to why a particular posting had been chosen for me. 'K' wished me good luck for the future and added that I was sure to be intrigued by the particular challenge that lay ahead.

I telephoned the Dover number that evening and sure enough Roger answered. I identified myself, adding that 'a caller from London' had asked me to ring and to arrange a meeting. I had an engagement on the coming Sunday but on Saturday I would be free. I had a car and could travel. Was Saturday a convenient day for our meeting? 'Yes, fine. I've got a suggestion. It's a bit of a journey for you but could you travel to the Dover area?' he asked. 'Sure, no problem.' 'Well, just a few miles east of Dover, there's a small village by the sea called St. Margaret's Bay. There's only one pub there, 'The Green Man', right on the sea front. Let's say we meet up at 12 noon on the Saturday before it gets too busy. I'll be in the lounge bar drinking an orange juice. See you there. You've got my number if there's a problem in the meantime.'

The journey on the Saturday was a little more complex than I had envisaged but once I was on the South Circular Road south-west of the river in London, it wasn't long before I found myself on the A2 heading for Dover. I arrived at St Margaret's Bay with half an hour in hand. Having taken my binoculars with me, I was able to do some birdwatching. I was pleased to find some kittiwakes ofshore and a couple of cormorants on the rocks. Entering the lounge bar of 'The Green Man' promptly at 12, I soon spotted Roger. It wasn't difficult for there were only two men at the bar, one drinking beer the other drinking orange juice. 'What are you drinking? "Just half of bitter, please.' I replied. He signalled for us to sit down in a corner. 'We'll just chat here', he began, in a low voice, 'and then we can talk business on a walk along the sea-front. How was your journey down?' 'A bit longer than I'd expected, but no hold-ups en route'. More casual chat followed until our drinks were finished and then we stepped outside. We made our way to the short promenade, came to an empty bench and sat down. 'Well', said Roger, 'you must be wondering what all this is about.' I nodded. 'I understand from London, you are a casual floater and that you have no past history with us. We have a specific problem here in east Kent and we need someone on the inside to give us a helping hand. As we are talking about a military unit and as you are an Army officer, the connection is clear. I must stress at this point that the military have no inkling of the problem themselves. It's all to be a Service job, and by 'Service' I mean our Service. We don't want the Army's Special Investigation Branch boots walking all over this one. They really messed up our last joint operation.

Roger began a detailed description of the assignment I was to take on. My posting would be as an Instructor Officer at Templer Barracks on Capel Heights just outside Folkestone on the Dover Road. The Barracks received an infantry battalion on a rotation basis every eighteen months or so. The present battalion had been there about three months. They had a regular Army Quartermaster (QM) who looked after the stores but he had a civilian assistant, by the name of Bill Morgan. He had worked as an Assistant Quartermaster (AQM) at the Barracks for over three years, seeing battalions come and go.

Bill Morgan himself had an interesting background. He had been taken prisoner in Korea in 1951 as an infantary battalion Company Quartermaster Sergeant (CQMS) running their stores. He had spent two years in a prisoner-of-war camp before being released and repatriated to the UK. He was divorced from his wife soon after and never remarried. He was subsequently selected for a QM commission but within a year had retired from the Army, having been given the nod that he would land the job of Assistant QM at Capel Heights as a civilian. In the last year he had come to the attention of British Intelligence and was classified as 'under suspicion'. Following the 'need to know' principle, Roger said that I didn't need to know how or why. He lived in the Mess, as I would on arrival and my assignment included getting close to him, observing him on and off duty and noting any visitors he had. He was being tracked on his car trips outside of the barracks but so far no useful information had been obtained. Further, he had become quite adept at outsmarting any tailing vehicles and would frequently just vanish. 'We believe he's up to no good but we just can't nail him,' continued Roger. 'Perhaps your input will help.' Driving back to Wycombe that afternoon, I wondered whether I had been too quick to accept the additional commitment of keeping tabs on Bill Morgan. On the other hand, I didn't have much choiceI. I realised I would be taking up a new appointment as an Instructor Officer in an infantry battalion and initially, at any rate, that would probably occupy me full-time. Further, it sounded as if Bill Morgan was no fool and I would have to watch my step very carefully if I wanted to avoid arousing any suspicion on his part towards me. After dinner in the Mess that evening, I played several games of darts and snooker in an effort to wind down from what had been a most unusual day.

When Captain Frank announced our postings a few days later, I tried hard to appear to be hearing the news for the first time and to look suitably intrigued by the words, 'John Reddisson, Templer Barracks, Capel Heights, Kent as an Instructor Officer.' Frank made further enquiries on my behalf and it turned out that I would be working as an assistant to a Captain Jack Smith.

CHAPTER 9

Templer Barracks on Capel Heights, located just outside Folkestone on the A20 Dover road, looked a grim and forbidding place. The rows of red brick buildings must have been buit in Victorian times. Perhaps because of the frequent winds, there was a distinct lack of mature trees. I arrived towards early evening on a Sunday in late August. This allowed me plenty of time to unpack and freshen up before making my way to the Officers' Mess bar for a pre-dinner drink. Most of the living-in Mess members were away for the weekend and the only people I met in the bar were the Orderly Officer, Bob Hodges, and the Assistant Quartermaster himself, Bill Morgan. It wasn't long before we all moved into the dining-room for dinner. I sat opposite Bill Morgan and next to Bob.

'What's your service record, then?' grunted Morgan. 'You don't look old enough to have had much, if any, service.' I replied that I had done two years' National Service including a posting as a lieutenant in Nottinghamshire. I had then decided to spend three years at Cambridge getting a degree before returning to the Army in the Education Branch. 'You know what we call you fellows? Schoolies!' he exclaimed with a mischievous smile and a wink towards Bob Hodges. 'Schoolies don't rank very high in the real Army's pecking order, especially here in an infantry battalion that's recently returned from counter-insurgency operations in Malaya.' I interrupted him to say that I understood the Army to be one large family in which we all carried out our specific roles according to our strengths and qualifications. 'We, serving officers (I stressed) all contribute accordingly.' 'Be that as it may,' he continued, 'but as far as the real Army is concerned, we just tolerate schoolies. Don't get any grand ideas about your Cambridge University status in this unit.' As far as I was concerned, his final comment laid bare his real grudge against the Education Branch – education itself and, for whatever reason, his own lack of it. Anyway, he had now finished his invective and he more or less ignored me for the rest of the meal, talking 'unit shop' with Bob Hodges. He declined the pudding and left the table with a cursory grunt in my direction plus a 'Good-night, Bob,' to the third member of our dining trio.

Once Bill Morgan had left the dining-room, Bob turned to me and said, 'You'll have to forgive our Assistant Quartermaster for his lack of manners but he does have a few personal problems. Two years in the bag in Korea certainly deprived him of the slightest trace of human kindness. He can be very aggressive and blunt when the mood takes him, especially after a few pre-dinner drinks, as you've just seen.'

Later that evening in my room, I reflected on Morgan's volatile nature, realising that my being on the receiving end at dinner that evening was probably the first of many future meals accompanied by a somewhat difficult dining companion. What on earth had I let myself in for? This specific assignment was going to be a lot more challenging than I had envisaged. Nevertheless, the overriding message had to be, 'Stay calm and carry on.'

The Education Centre was being run by Captain Jack Smith who had been at Templer Barracks for about a year. He had lost his number two officer three months previously and was very pleased to have me as a replacement. We went through the weekly timetable of lessons to be given and, rather apologetically, he said that I would be teaching the lion's share of the workload for the forseeable future. 'The filing system is in a bit of a mess,' he explained. 'I really must sort it out, update it and devise a more reliable system. Our office clerk, Mrs. Davies, is competent enough but she's allowed things to develop rather haphazardly. I hope now that you have been taken on strength, I can sort it all out.' Jack and I got on well together and he was a thoughtful and considerate boss. He was married with two small children and lived in one of the married quarters in the Garrison.

Weeks passed and my special assignment was no further forward. I had grown accustomed to Bill Morgan's sharp tongue at mealtimes and because I didn't bite, he had begun to ease off. In fact, he now addressed most of his sarcasm and banter towards a young infantry officer, Ian Sprackling, who had joined us fresh out of Sandhurst. Ian and I sometimes gave as good as we received, especially enjoying the fact that Morgan often couldn't quite catch the subtleties of our repartee. He couldn't be sure whether we were stringing him along or not. Such verbal revenge could be slow, drawn out and even sweet on occasions. During one meal, he was listening with half an ear to me and Ian talking about the poet, Keats. He decided to show some interest once we had finished and he asked us what a keat was.

Mess life would not have been traditional without its 'Bridge Evenings', held on the first Wednesday of every month. A section of the Mess ante-room was commandeered and two bridge tables were set up for eight players. Non-bridge players usually made themselves scarce for the evening. Table two was usually for a couple of unit majors and their wives. Table one was reserved for the Commanding Officer and his wife, together with Bill Morgan and a Kent Coastguard officer by the name of Jim Mitchell. Bill Morgan had apparently said that he had met Jim Mitchell in a harbour pub in Dover. They had become regular drinking pals, especially as both had a keen interest in the performance and fortunes of the Kent County cricket team. I had made it quite clear to the powers that be in the Garrison that, although I had played bridge in the past, I didn't consider myself a competent player. The truth was that I would rather spend the first Wednesday evening of each month doing something else or even nothing else rather than being regularly dragooned into playing bridge with the senior officers. It would have been too close for comfort in the event of poor play on my part.

Despite my plans to avoid the bridge clique, I was ambushed by none other than the Commanding Officer himself one Wednesday lunchtime. His wife was feeling unwell, so would I (please) make myself available for bridge that evening to make up a four for table one. Escape was impossible. I presented myself in the anteroom after dinner for my first bridge evening. I arrived about five minutes before the Coastguard officer, Jim

Mitchell, appeared. Heavily bearded and with a shock of grey hair, he was probably in his mid-forties – much the same age as Bill Morgan. As he walked into the ante-room, he strode up to Morgan and thrust a package into his hand saying, 'Here's the monthly 'Reader's Digest' for you to enjoy, Bill,' apparently a routine friendly gesture, having already read it himself as a subscriber. Bill Morgan put the package on the corner of the bar and I couldn't help noticing how tidy it looked, being neatly bound in a distinctive blue tape. Why couldn't Mitchell just deliver it in a paper bag, if a cover was indeed necessary? The Colonel now called us to order and we took our seats at the bridge tables. I performed adequately that evening and the Colonel seemed reasonably satisfied with his substitute playing partner.

Two months later, the same scenario was repeated. Mrs. Colonel was again indisposed, so I was drummed into bridge service for another evening. Once again, Jim Mitchell arrived with his copy of the 'Reader's Digest' for Bill Morgan, neatly sealed in a package with blue tape.

A breakthrough in my assignment came about in a most unusual and most unexpected way. I was a keen birdwatcher and as an additional spin-off hobby, I had built up a modest collection of antiquarian bird books. It included such gems as the first edition of William Yarrell's 'The History of British Birds' (1837) with the volumes bound in calf. The work went into several editions and was the standard reference for a generation of British ornithologists. Thomas Bewick was a master of woodcuts and I had the two-volume set of his work on British birds, well bound and with gilt lettering (1797-1804). I had located an antiquarian bookshop in Canterbury which had a number of desirable bird books, including several county books published in the nineteenth century. The owner was also able to source titles he hadn't got in stock. Once a month or so, I would drive over to Canterbury and spend a good hour checking out the stock. The owner William Smith, and his wife, were not English, despite their surname. Their accent sounded German and I heard the wife speaking German on the telephone on one occasion.

One Saturday morning, I arrived in Canterbury and walked along the High Street towards the bookshop. I was looking forward to collecting a copy of Alfred Newton's 'A Dictionary of Birds' (1896), which William Smith had obtained for me. When I was within some thirty yards of the shop, who should I see arriving at the premises but our one and only Bill Morgan with a package under his arm. He hadn't caught sight of me and he entered the shop. I loitered around at a safe distance until he emerged and disappeared down a side street. I noticed he was no longer carrying the package. That visit to an antiquarian bookshop was totally out of character for Bill Morgan. I had never even seen him reading his free copies of the 'Reader's Digest'. On the infrequent occasions English literature had been discussed in the Mess, he might as well have been a deaf-mute.

As I entered the shop, Mrs. Smith appeared, walking down the staircase from the first floor, where the Smiths had their living accommodation. 'Ah! Good morning. You've come for the Alfred Newton book. It arrived a few days ago. It's on my husband's desk in the office upstairs. Do go up and he'll let you have the book.' I went up the staircase and came to the open door of the office. William Smith greeted me warmly. 'Your book has arrived,' he said pointing to an opened parcel on his desk. What I also noticed at once was that my book parcel was lying next to another package, neatly bound in a distinctive blue tape. So that was what Bill Morgan had delivered. But how on earth could an antiquarian bookseller be remotely interested in receiving by special personal delivery a recent copy of the 'Reader's Digest? My mind was racing – if indeed the package did contain that item.

William Smith was too busy thumbing through the Newton book to notice my facial expression. He began to praise the book's contents and stressed what an excellent purchase I had made. 'Newton was a great ornithological figure towards the end of the nineteenth century,' he exclaimed. 'Professor of Zoology at Cambridge University and a veritable bird expert – hence his Dictionary.' He passed me the heavy tome to inspect, together with the invoice. I was delighted with my purchase and handed over my cheque. He carefully re-wrapped the book and ushered me out of his office. He led me down the stairs, opened the shop door for me and bade me a friendly 'Good-morning'. As I made my way back to the carpark, my mind was concentrating more on Bill Morgan's package than on my recent purchase. What could it have possibly contained?

That evening during dinner in the Mess, I found it difficult to talk trivialities with Bill Morgan. My thoughts were constantly returning to the package with its distinctive blue tape that he had delivered to the Smiths' shop in Canterbury. Was it an event of some real significance or, perhaps, a blind alley that would lead nowhere? Little did I know at the time that the answers to those questions would emerge sooner rather than later. After dinner, rather than use the Mess telephone with its echoing accoustics, I walked to the Garrison public box. I telephoned my handler, Roger, on his Dover number. Could we meet the following week, as I thought I had some useful information to pass on regarding Bill Morgan? We agreed to meet at 'The Green Man' in St. Margaret's Bay at one thirty on the Wednesday afternoon, when I would have no teaching commitment.

A couple of months earlier, I had joined the local RSPB group and had already been on some birdwatching trips with them. A few of the keener members had formed a telephone grapevine network to inform one another of local sightings of scarce and rare birds. I had established regular contact with Dave Roberts, a Dover birdwatcher. If anything interesting was about, Dave would be sure to know: he was an absolute mine of information. I knew I could get away from Templer Barracks by midday on the Wednesday, which would give me a good hour's birdwatching in the Dover-St. Margaret's Bay area before my scheduled meeting with Roger at one thirty. Dave came up trumps – there was a long-staying pair of black redstarts on the rough ground right in front of 'The Green Man'. Excellent news.

By twelve thirty on the Wednesday, I was already scanning the area in front of 'The Green Man' through my binoculars, but could find nothing of interest. There was another man about fifty yards away but closer to the beach and he was also scanning through binoculars. Suddenly, he turned towards me, waved and signalled that he had found something. As I approached him, he exclaimed, 'They are there, on the rocks, the reported pair of black redstarts – the first I've ever seen here.' A sudden flash of a red tail revealed exactly where the birds were. We got into conversation as we watched the birds together through our binoculars. 'Do you live locally?' I enquired. Puffing away at his cigarette, my companion birdwatcher informed me that he had lived in St. Margaret's Bay itself until a few years previously. He pointed to an attractive white house located on the very edge of the beach. 'Yes', he laughed, 'the first house in England as seen from the Calais-Dover ferry en route to Dover Harbour just down the coast. The house, as you can see, is very close to the sea and to the cliffs, perhaps too close. One day, part of the cliff may well end up in the back garden or even in the rear rooms, but it won't be in my time, I'm sure. When I lived there and used to look out to sea over the front flower-beds from the house windows, I could claim that I had ferries at the bottom of my garden,' he chuckled. However, I now spend a lot of time in Jamaica, especially during the winter. I'll be returning there very soon if all goes according to plan.'

There was a pause in our conversation as we silently admired the two birds in front of us. Then he continued, 'Do you often birdwatch here?' In birdwatching circles, you don't 'see' a bird, you 'have' it. So, it was quite natural for me to reply, 'Yes, from time to time. Last month I had two mediterranean gulls in the Bay and I also had a shag on the beach over there.' 'Really? That must have been something to be savoured, I'm sure. In my experience, shags are quite rare around here,' he declared with a twinkle in his eye. With that comment, he strode off towards 'The Green Man', leaving me to admire the black redstarts a little longer before I followed him.

Roger had also arrived early and we were soon sitting in a corner of the lounge bar enjoying a drink. Being a weekday in late autumn, there was a distinct lack of the throb and chatter of the summertime sunshine clientele. Roger and I would soon be sampling the November fresh air together on our walk and talk along the breakwater path below the cliffs. Meanwhile, I had noticed out of the corner of my eye that my erstwhile birdwatching companion was sat smoking at the bar with his back towards us. As he got up to go, he glanced in our direction. He must have recognised me, for he nodded and then made his way out. 'He's another birdwatcher,' I informed Roger. 'Yes, I know. He's also a novelist, by the name of Ian Fleming. He used to have a house here on the beach called 'White Cliffs' but he sold it a few years ago and moved away. He loves St. Margaret's Bay and still visits here from time to time, staying at the 'Granville Hotel' on the cliff top above us. He writes spy stories, you know; his hero is called James Bond. Have you read any?' To my discredit, although one way and another I had heard of the James Bond books, I had never read a single one.

As we walked along the gravel-strewn path below the cliffs, Roger asked me about the special news regarding Bill Morgan that I had referenced in my recent 'phone call. I related how by chance I had seen him enter a certain antiquarian bookshop in Canterbury carrying a package but emerging without it. I added that the package had been delivered to Morgan at the Templer Barracks Mess on a regular bridge evening by a certain Jim Mitchell, a Dover coastguard. It was one of a number of such packages regularly handed over to Morgan on bridge evenings by Mitchell. They were said to contain copies of the 'Reader's Digest' but such a publication was hardly antiquarian material. Further, for Morgan to visit an antiquarian bookshop was totally out of character for the man. I was sure it would now be worthwhile keeping an eye on the bookshop. It could all be nothing important but I had a definite hunch it was certainly worth following up. My phlegmatic handler noted down the details but seemingly took the information in his stride without revealing whether he thought it of real value or not. 'We'll put the bookshop under surveillance,' he said, 'and we'll check out this Jim Mitchell.' He finished off our meeting with one of his favourite sayings, 'Well, we'll see, won't we?'. The black redstarts were still around after he had left, and had now been joined by a solitary stonechat. I enjoyed watching them for another half an hour before making my way back to Templer Barracks.

Years later, I learned that Ian Fleming (1908-64) had made his home in 'White Cliffs' in 1951, revelling in its dramatic location at the foot of the cliffs directly on the sea-front. He had purchased the property from his good friend Noel Coward who had decided to move away in 1951 as more and more day-trippers – 'the noisy hoi-polloi', as he called them – were beginning to invade the privacy of his once tranquil St. Margaret's Bay.

Ian Fleming entertained many of his friends at 'White Cliffs' including the novelists Somerset Maugham and Evelyn Waugh. He had written some of his best books there, accompanied by a generous whisky, a cigarette (he smoked up to seventy a day) and the splendid views over the English Channel. Once he had sold the house, he frequently visited St. Margaret's Bay from his new homes in London and Surrey, often staying overnight at the 'Granville Hotel'.

Fleming's acquaintance with the world of espionage had begun in the very early days of the Second World War in 1939 when he was appointed personal assistant to the Director of Naval Intelligence. Initially he held the rank of lieutenant in the Royal Naval Volunteer Reserve (RNVR) before being rapidly promoted to Commander – the same rank as James Bond. The murky exploits of his war service provided ample material for his Bond novels.

Fleming also drew inspiration from Kent: even the 007 tag came from the number of the London to Dover coach service, which was later operated by National Express. The Royal St. George's Golf Club where he regularly played, became the Royal St. Mark's in 'Goldfinger'. The 'Granville Hotel', where I myself have enjoyed a good meal, was the same hotel which Bond and Gale Brand visited after the dramatic cliff fall in 'Moonraker'.

He took the name for his hero from that of the American ornithologist, James Bond, an expert on Caribbean birds and the author of the definitive bird guide, 'Birds of the West Indies'. Fleming, himself a keen birdwatcher, as I had witnessed, kept his own copy of Bond's guide on his desk in the study at his house 'Goldeneye' in Jamaica.

Sad to relate, Ian Fleming, his body worn out by excessive alcohol and tobacco, died after experiencing a heart attack in 1964, at the relatively young age of fifty-six. Once the Bond films appeared in the 1960s starring Sean Connery, and I went to see them, I often thought back to that birdwatching encounter with Ian Fleming on the beach at St. Margaret's Bay.

Following the meeting with my handler, Roger, British Intelligence put the antiquarian bookshop in

Canterbury and the Smiths themselves under close but discreet surveillance. Not only was Bill Morgan a regular visitor to the bookshop but also a certain Mark Pascoe paid frequent visits – and he was similarly watched. Pascoe was an engineer at an aeronautics factory in Sandwich which had several top secret War Office contracts. The Smiths were followed to London where they met up with a known KGB officer based at the Soviet Embassy. Matters came to a head and a top level decision was taken to strike.

Everything hinged on the precise time of 7.55pm on the first Wednesday of the following month. A number of synchronised arrests were made in Templer Barracks, in Canterbury and in Sandwich. While I was enjoying a good book in my room upstairs in the Officers' Mess, action was unfolding in the ante-room below. With the connivance of the Colonel, a Special Branch officer and three police officers burst into the room and arrested Bill Morgan and Jim Mitchell just as Mitchell was handing over his monthly 'Reader's Digest'. Meanwhile in Canterbury, the Smiths were arrested just as they were sitting down to dinner on the first floor of their bookshop. Similarly, Mark Pascoe was detained at the aeronautics factory in Sandwich, caught red-handed in the act of copying yet more top secret documents and drawings. The trap had been sprung and five people had been taken into custody.

According to Roger, it later emerged that Bill Morgan had been turned by the communist North Koreans during his two years as a prisoner-of-war in Korea. He had become a committed communist and had agreed to work towards global communism by acting as an agent for the Soviets. On his return to the UK, he had assumed the role of inactive sleeper for a couple of years. Once he had become a fixture at Templer Barracks in Capel Heights, he made contact with KGB officers at the Soviet Embassy in London. He began spying on training establishments and the deployment of troops throughout Kent. He was supremely well-placed to pass on details of activity at Templer Barracks but his local information gathering also extended to the garrison at Connaught Barracks at the top of Dover Hill only a few miles distant. It was arranged for him to run a Kent espionage ring and it had slowly taken shape with fellow members being the Smiths, Jim Mitchell and Mark Pascoe.

Jim Mitchell had been drawn into the ring after the KGB had begun blackmailing him over his homosexuality. His 'Reader's Digest' packages had contained highly sensitive material relating to naval exercises in the Channel, details of all Royal Navy ships passing through the Dover area, crew complements, weaponry and also naval codes. In addition, he had taken a close interest in the radar station on the Dover Heights.

As far as the Smiths were concerned, their real name turned out to be Schmidt, their being of communist East German origin. When their bookshop was raided by the police, several packages of top level information were discovered in their safe together with large amounts of cash to pay Morgan, Mitchell and Pascoe. Their own East German passports were also found in the safe, alongside faked British passports. The Schmidts had made occasional visits to London where they had met up with the KGB officer based at the Soviet Embassy. He was suspected by MI5 of having an extra-marital affair. The Schmidts would stay overnight at the same hotel as the Soviet officer along with up to two hundred other guests. It was concluded that the packaged material delivery would have taken place overnight - out of the Schmidts' bags and into the Soviet's suitcase. He would leave separately in the morning and make his way back to the Soviet Embassy. The clever ruse was that he was always accompanied by the same red-head lady. MI5 previously trailing him, had always assumed he was merely having an affair. It was all very neat on the part of the Soviets and, of course, a busy hotel with some two hundred guests is a very difficult stakeout to watch and monitor effectively.

At a subsequent meeting with Roger, he again expressed his gratitude for the Canterbury antiquarian bookshop lead. 'Your hunch certainly paid off,' he said. 'It all worked out vey nicely after that.' 'I haven't seen anything in the newspapers, yet.' I said. 'When will it all be reported?' 'You won't be seeing any reports in the newspapers,' Roger answered. The trials will take place behind closed doors in what is called a 'closed court'.' 'But isn't secret justice in such a court contrary to the British rule of law?' I continued. 'It's a form of justice that takes into account the necessity to guard national security,' Roger explained. 'We can't let the media report on matters that are deemed highly confidential. Material harmful to the national interest cannot be put into the public domain. The defendants will be represented by a security-cleared advocate rather than by a lawyer chosen by them. All relevant material will be examined by a judge. The system, I can assure you, is a necessary veil to protect state secrets. The number of cases affected is very small, anyway. Also remember that no country allows their spies to give evidence in open court. If they did, the public gallery would be full of KGB and other agents. It goes without saying that British Intelligence doesn't want to share with the general public or with potential aggressors the details of what they are doing and how they might be doing it.' It all reminded me of the similar cover-up in the Cambridge spy-case a couple of years earlier. I had thought the closed court secrecy might not apply in the present case but I was wrong.

Roger met me again a few months later. He gave me the news that the trials had taken place. The court had indeed been granted permission to try the accused in secret. The judge had warned the media that any reporting of the case would be damaging to national security and would be considered a contempt of court, punishable by imprisonment. The judge had been acting within his judicial rights to exclude the public and the press, and to issue a gagging order to prevent anything being reported of what had gone on in the courtroom. Roger said that Morgan, Mitchell and Pascoe had all been charged under the Official Secrets Act on two counts. First, for collecting confidential and classified information 'for a purpose prejudicial to the safety and interests of the State'. Secondly, 'for communicating such information to other persons'. All three had been found guilty and the inevitable prison sentences had followed. The Schmidts had also been jailed but Roger cynically reckoned that within a year or so, they would be exchanged for a couple of British agents languishing in an East German prison. Roger's final snippet of information was most Interesting. It had emerged that the Soviet KGB officer visiting the hotel wasn't having an extra-marital affair at all. The lady he was 'liaising' with at the hotel, turned out to be his blonde wife wearing a red wig – a very clever double bluff ruse by the Soviets.

'K' wrote to say how very pleased he was regarding my assistance in the successful outcome of the 'Capel Heights case' – his own judgement regarding my usefulness had been vindicated.

I wanted to go up to London to see a show but when I checked the late evening timetable of the Charing Cross to Folkestone trains there was a problem. I particularly wanted to see Agatha Christie's 'The Mousetrap' at the Ambassadors Theatre near Cambridge Circus. In order to catch the last train back to Folkestone, I would have to leave the theatre before the finish of the play. As it was a classic 'whodunnit', with the villain only being unmasked towards the end of the play, that option was unthinkable. A night's stay in a London hotel with their inflated rates was also out of the question. I had heard talk of an Officers' Club in central London where one could stay at a very reasonable overnight rate. I asked around in the Officers' Mess at Capel Heights and was directed to Major Brian, one of the battalion company commanders. He had spent a night at the London Officers' Club a couple of years previously. He informed me that the club was a bit run down but the overnight rate was heavily subsidised, being less than half the price charged by quite modest London hotels. He remarked that the club had an odd reservation system – you booked a bed, not a room. He promised to leave their telephone number in my Mess pigeon-hole. I rang the club and, sure enough, they booked me in for a bed overnight and not for a room. I didn't think anything more of the bed-booking reservation system and looked forward to my forthcoming London visit.

Agatha Christie's 'The Mousetrap' had already become famous as THE play to see in London. In April 1958 it had achieved the longest run ever of a show in the West End. By 1960, when I went to see the play, it had notched up its 3000th consecutive performance at the Ambassadors Theatre. Needless to say, watching the play was a most enjoyable experience. The scene towards the end in which the murderer was finally unmasked involved a classic Agatha Christie twist. At the end of the performance, one of the actors emerged from behind the stage curtain and came forward to the front of the stage to speak to the audience. He said he hoped we had enjoyed the play but then asked us not to reveal the identity of the murderer to anyone so as not to spoil it all for any future theatre-goers.

Having retrieved my coat and small overnight case from the theatre cloakroom, I made my way to the Leicester Square tube station to take my train to the Officers' Club. When I arrived there, I couldn't help but agree with Major Brian's description for the building – run down, and even seedy. In a brief conversation with the night receptionist, it was again pointed out to me that 'we reserve beds here, not rooms', and I had been allocated a bed in a room at the top of the building. It was a double room with two single beds and another late-arriving officer had made a provisional booking only, so the chances were that I wouldn't have to share – BUT, all the club's other beds had been allocated and filled. When I entered the room, I discovered it had a double bed not twin beds, so the receptionist must have made a mistake. Dream on!

I freshened up and went to bed about midnight. I was woken up at about two in the morning by someone entering the room and putting on a bedside lamp. Whoever he was, he was drunk as he fell over a chair and then a small table, talking to himself and burping all the while. Out of the corner of my eye, I saw him take off his coat, his jacket and tie. He was a portly individual, middle-aged and probably a major. He fell onto the far side of the double bed, turned off the light and almost immediately fell asleep – fortunately, with his back towards me. I was totally flabbergasted but remembered that the receptionist had said he understood it was a two-bedded room and that all the other beds in the club had been filled. I lay there wondering what to do and soon realised there was nothing I could do but grin (or grimace) and bear it. I tried to get back to sleep, edging as far away as possible from my new bed companion without actually falling out of bed. A new factor now entered this weird scenario. An ear-splitting snore erupted in the room, quickly followed by a series of high decibel foghorn-like snorts. I banged hard on the headboard, which had the effect of stopping the snores for about ten minutes – before they all started again. My banging the headboard procedure took place at least four more times before I finally managed to get some sleep.

When I woke up in the morning, my watch showed me it was seven o'clock. The other occupant of the bed hadn't moved all night, as far as I knew. In the half-light of the morning, I got out of bed, dressed, grabbed my overnight case and hurried out of the room. When I complained to the bleary-eyed night receptionist about my mind-boggling experience, all he would say was that he had told me it was a two-person bedroom and that all the club's beds had been taken. When

I accused him of making a bed-booking mistake, he denied it. I made tracks for the tube station and then on to Charing Cross Station for the Folkestone train.

When I returned to Capel Heights, I didn't mention the incident in the Mess, so as to avoid banter and ridicule. I wrote a strong letter of complaint to the manager of the Officers' Club but I never did receive a reply. I didn't return to London for another show for the rest of my time at Templer Barracks. I couldn't afford the standard hotel prices and I wouldn't have ventured back to the bed-only booking Officers' Club doss-house for all the tea in China. In future, I restricted my theatre-going to the Leas Pavilion in nearby Folkestone. It had a group of actors called the Arthur Brough Players and I reckoned they were as good as any West End theatrical group. The repertory company had been set up by actor Arthur Brough and his wife in 1929. The name Arthur Brough may sound familiar to some for, many years later, he went on to play Mr Grainger in the BBC television comedy series 'Are You Being Served?'.

The Folkestone company put on a different play every week – so there was always something new to see and enjoy. Travel costs to see a show were now kept to a minimum. More importantly, a comfortable single bed with no chance of an overnight intruder was always waiting for me on my return to the Officers' Mess at Capel Heights.

CHAPTER 10

It was late July and I was sitting in the office in the Education Centre at Capel Heights catching up on necessary paperwork when the telephone rang. It was a call from the colonel in charge of the Education Branch postings section in London. An emergency had arisen at the King Edward Army School near Ramsgate. A captain had been taken ill towards the end of the summer term and he wouldn't be returning to the school. The subjects he had taught were French, Latin and English. The colonel mentioned that I was suitably qualified to teach those subjects and he would prefer to move a bachelor at short notice rather than a married officer with a family. The school would be on holiday throughout August and the reporting date for the new post would be 1st September. In the circumstances, I would be given twenty-four hours to consider the post. I was asked to contact the postings section the following day with my decision. The colonel added, almost as an afterthought, that the new post would attract the acting rank, and pay, of captain.

It so happened that my colleague at the Education Centre, Captain Jack Smith, was himself a former pupil of the King Edward Army School (KEAS), a King Eddie, as he called himself. He had told me several stories about the school and the staff, always emphasising what a great educational establishment it was. The school had been founded in 1906 for the sons of serving soldiers. The school roll usually numbered about five hundred boys whose fathers had served a qualifying number of years as regular soldiers in the Army. Half of the teaching staff were Education Branch officers and half were civilians.

I broke the news to Captain Jack later in the morning when he returned to the office from a teaching commitment. He admitted that he would be sorry to lose me but added that it was an excellent posting and I should definitely accept the offer – especially in view of the promotion to captain. He mentioned that the school had a small Officers' Mess, or more exactly, a Teaching Staff Mess, which provided board and lodging. As far as he knew, there were only two teaching staff regulars at the Mess, two civilians, Charles and Ben. He had already heard about the emergency at the school. It involved Mike, an old friend of his, who had suffered a nervous breakdown following marriage problems. His wife had walked out on him, taking their three children with her. Mike had been admitted to Netley Military Hospital near Southampton and was now being treated in the psychiatric wing.

I telephoned the postings section the following morning and accepted the offer. I was informed that the headmaster, a serving Education Branch lieutenant-colonel, would be pleased to meet his new member of staff at an arranged date and time in early August. I duly arrived at the school for the appointment and made my way to the headmaster's house. I rang the bell at the door of a large detached house set in a spacious garden. The door was opened by a petite, bright-eyed lady who introduced herself as Nancy, the headmaster's wife. 'Ah! Robert is expecting you. I'll take you along to the study.' Colonel Robert met me at the door, ushered me in and we settled down in comfortable chairs. 'I won't sit at the desk,' he remarked. 'It's a chat not an interview. I wanted to meet you and show you around the school during the peace and quiet of the holiday period. By the way, you will stay for lunch, won't you?' 'I'd love to,' I replied. 'Excellent. I'll confirm with Nancy.'

Our chat ranged over a large number of subjects, both military and non-military. He and his wife were lovers of all things Italian. He had served in Italy during the War and he and Nancy had subsequently spent many holidays there. 'We don't know Liguria at all,' he pointed out. 'We always seem to end up in Tuscany or Rome.' It was arranged for us to tour the school first and then return to the house for lunch. We started our tour at the edge of the vast playing fields. 'We have well over one hundred and fifty acres here,' the headmaster declared, 'and our sports facilities are second to none. We have up to a dozen full-size grass pitches for rugby and cricket plus tennis courts. There's a gymnasium and indoor swimming pool. Plans are in hand to build a full-size athletics track in the next year or two. You will certainly be roped in to referee rugby and hockey matches and to umpire at cricket.' We then moved on to the Chapel and the large dining-hall. We visited a number of classrooms including my form classroom. 'You'll be the form master of one of our junior entry classes,' the Colonel explained as he led me to a detached block. 'You will enjoy teaching here in this light and airy classroom, I'm sure. Most of the junior entry boys are only ten years of age and they follow a pre-school curriculum. They wear military uniform, as do all our pupils. They have a smart civilian uniform as well, blazer, trousers, tie and so on. You'll be teaching them French and English, along with other classes. Latin is a subject for some senior classes and you'll be helping out the senior Latin master in that respect.

Our final port of call was the Teaching Staff Mess which was empty as Charles and Ben were away on holiday. 'You will be comfortable here although as there will only be the three of you, it won't exactly be buzzing with activity. Further, you'll be the new boy here in the Mess, joining a pair of confirmed bachelors with their firmly established habits and ways. Take it easy at first so as not to upset their routine and ways of doing things.' That sounded like a form of warning to me regarding life in the Teaching Staff Mess.

Over lunch, Colonel Robert mentioned that he and Nancy had two boys at boarding school in north Kent. He had recently received a letter from the school which included a typing error. The letter stated that the school fees would be increased from the start of the next calendar year by £500 'per anum'. He said he knew all about paying through the nose for school fees but the school's request was ridiculous. In addition to a first rate meal, accompanied by a glass or two of wine, Colonel Robert and his wife proved to be very good conversationalists. Nancy had the knack of seeming interested in everything I had to say and her softly spoken husband added touches of general knowledge and depth. I thought at the time that the day had been an excellent introduction to my future at the King Edward Army School.

I reported for duty at KEA School on Thursday 1ˢᵗ
September but as term didn't begin until the following
Monday, I had plenty of time to settle in. I had a comfortable room in the Teachers' Mess with radiator heating
plus en suite facilities, overlooking a well-kept lawn and
flower beds. Mrs. G, our housekeeper, appeared on the
Friday as did Charles, who turned out to be a history
teacher. We had our first meal together, dominated by
a detailed account of his recent visit to Copenhagen and
by cricket. He was pleased by the news that I had represented the Education Branch in the past and he looked
forward to our playing together in due course for the
staff cricket team. He seemed affable enough although
he could drift off into a rambling monologue in a very
soft voice and one had to concentrate hard to catch
what he was saying. Ben turned up over the weekend. He
was a large, somewhat unkempt individual but with a
friendly, pleasant personality. I heeded Colonel Robert's
advice not to be too forward, as it was soon clear that
I was joining a pair of bachelor teachers who had an
established, time-honoured working and living relationship. I was not only a newly-arrived intruder but also
very much the junior member of our trio.

All the staff and boys had filed into the Assembly
Hall by 8.45 on the Monday, the first day of term.
Colonel Robert addressed us for some ten minutes
before handing over to the commandant, a retired
brigadier who had served in the infantry during his
active Army career. The academic atmosphere as
established by the headmaster, now rapidly descended
into a purely military one. The commandant seemed
to be addressing the assembled schoolboys rather as a
battalion commander might address his soldiers. I heard

someone mumbling behind me, turned round and saw it was one of the civilian members of staff. He gave me a sly wink and I thought at the time, 'There goes a rebel.' Once the commandant had finished, the staff and boys alike made for their classrooms.

During the morning break, I found myself sitting next to the winking rebel. He introduced himslf as Chris, Head of English. 'I wish the commandant would realise this is an academic institution and not a battalion of soldiers about to attack the enemy,' he remarked. 'We can do without that rubbish. We've got a headmaster; why do we need a commandant as well?' As time passed at the school, I was to learn that such comments were typical of Chris – honest, forthright and with a touch of dissent.

Apart from the fact that all the serving officers wore uniform and the boys wore uniform, the military side of my job did not feature very large. Although the boys had endless parades, the military teaching staff had only occasional duty officer Sundays. That commitment involved attending Church Parade on the vast parade ground, followed by a Chapel service. There were eight Houses in the school and each House was named after a famous military figure. Four of the school Houses were headed by majors but relations were very informal and it was a case of first names all round.

As for most teachers looking back on their time spent teaching at a particular school, terms merged into terms, years into years. In all, I served three years at KEAS but the special events could be counted on the fingers of one hand. Further one of those special events was not connected with the school at all.. It was a six-week stint back in Torre Ligure as a courier/travel representative.

Being given the chance to return to my old job in Italy was a most unexpected development. Early on in my posting to the school, I had informed YTG Universal Ltd in Liverpool that as I was now teaching at a military school and had generous summer holidays, I could be available for up to six weeks if required. No offer of work came in the summer of 1961 and I had almost forgotten about it all until a letter arrived for me in June 1962. The courier contracted for the summer at Torre Ligure had withdrawn. They had arranged cover for June and most of July plus September. Could I possibly make myself available for the last week of July and the whole of August ? – the very period of the KEAS summer break. I immediately telephoned to confirm my availability. Charles Knott, the General Manager, was delighted and promised to send me all the necessary details.

My love affair with my Austin A40 Somerset coupe had begun to wear a bit thin. One of the main reasons for my falling out of love with the car was on account of repeated hood trouble. I could lower the hood into its appointed recess with no problems but stretching it back to its required position had become a chore and it didn't always fit correctly. Thinking about my forthcoming trip to Italy, I had a brainwave – why not drive out and back to extend the experience? That would clearly involve exchanging my Austin for a hard-top model. A more powerful engine for such a long return trip would also be a benefit. In the end, I opted for a Mark II Ford Zephyr, a six-cylinder four-door saloon, with a low recorded mileage. It had a 2.5 litre engine with a top speed of 88mph. I favoured a British model as did most people living in Britain at the time.

It wasn't until the Seventies that British drivers bought more foreign cars than home-made models.

The outward trip to Torre Ligure went without a hitch. I took the car-ferry to Calais and drove across France into Switzerland, where I spent the night. The following day, I drove down into Italy and reached Torre Ligure via Turin and Savona. I had a couple of days' grace with the on-site courier before she travelled back to Liverpool with her group at the weekend. The chartered flights to and from Liverpool were now centred on Albenga Airport close to Alassio and only a half-hour coach journey from Torre Ligure. Seventy-two YTG holidaymakers were arriving every two weeks, half bound for Alassio and half for Torre Ligure. Back in 1962, air travel was still viewed as a magical and glamorous luxury even on chartered flights with air hostesses fussing diligently over the holidaymakers. It made me think of my first group in 1957 which had numbered only eleven and which had endured the two-day train journey from Liverpool, and back.

Signor Angelo Antonelli and his wife, la Signora, at the 'Hotel Torre', greeted me warmly on my return and I very soon reverted from KEAS teacher to courier mode. I made contact with my photographer friend, Roberto, and his family, all enjoying life in their new villa overlooking the village. Roberto was no longer the footloose and fancy-free young man of previous years. He was now married. He had met Lynn, an attractive British school-teacher, when she was living in Alassio and working as a private English tutor. After the wedding, Lynn came to live with Roberto, his brother Bruno and the parents in the villa on the hillside.

However, it appeared that married life on the sunny Italian Riviera didn't quite turn out as Lynn had expected. As a single girl in Alassio, she had enjoyed plenty of free time sitting in the sun and relaxing on the beach. As a married woman now living with the parents, there were plenty of other things to do – with 'mamma'. These included shopping together bright and early every morning in the village to buy the day's fresh food; working together in the kitchen to prepare the family meals, including home-made pasta dishes; the 'joy' (mamma's word) of baking pizzas and bread, not forgetting the preserving of fruit and vegetables for the winter months; laundry, cleaning and polishing; sewing and darning; and most importantly, keeping all the curtains drawn and the shutters closed during the day so that the sun couldn't invade the rooms and blemish the furniture and rugs. Lynn told me it was like living in a cave and she couldn't even enjoy the sunshine through a window. As mamma explained, sitting in the sun doing nothing was all very well for those unmarried, frivolous and empty-headed British girls with nothing better to do – unlike lucky Lynn who had a loving husband.

Lynn made one or two unfortunate errors preparing food 'unsupervised' in the kitchen when mamma was absent. Unknowingly, she caused mamma to almost have a heart attack when she revealed she had added olive oil to the pasta while cooking it in boiling water rather than afterwards when it was fully drained. Further, she had once produced chicken with pasta – apparently another Italian culinary no-no. As Lynn discovered, although the British eat to live, the Italians live to eat and, by British standards, they can be very demanding and fussy eaters, and there is no doubt that 'mamma knows best.'

Meanwhile, with his wife absent on household duties with mamma, the 'loving husband' Roberto was busy photographing and chatting to other pretty British girls relaxing in the sun on the Torre Ligure beach. After all, someone had to carry out that time-consuming and demanding work in the furtherance of local tourism promotion and to earn some money. Roberto would explain to me, with a wink, that chatting to pretty girls on the beach was one of the downsides to his job but one he would do stoically anyway. He had tried to explain to Lynn that it was 'no big deal' but, from personal experience, she didn't seem convinced.

One particular episode, which took place during those sunny weeks spent in Torre Ligure in 1962, still sticks in my mind. Every village in Italy had its Conte or Contessa living in 'the big house', asset rich but income poor. Torre Ligure was no exception. La Contessa, in her seventies, lived in a large detached residence set in spacious grounds at the far side of the village well away from any peasant-type dwellings. Her husband, il Conte, had been shot by the Germans during the War and she had no children. A very attentive nephew, who lived in Turin, would appear in the village from time to time. According to local gossip,, the nephew was more interested in the undoubted future development potential of the villa and its surrounding land than in the elderly aunt herself. La Contessa had some sort of income but not enough to maintain the villa, and odd pieces would regularly fall off the building. Somehow, she or her nephew had discovered that there were British tourists staying at the 'Hotel Torre'. I received a message from Signor Angelo that la Contessa would like to meet the group's representative to discuss a business proposition. 'Be careful', warned la Signora, 'She is very unpredictable and quite a difficult woman.'

I arrived at the villa at an arranged time to meet la Contessa for a business chat. It was indeed a most imposing building but clearly in need of some external maintenance. An old, wrinkled woman appeared at the door and introduced herself as la Contessa's servant. She led me into a drawing-room where her employer was seated. 'Oh!' she exclaimed, 'I was expecting someone much older than you. You are the group leader, aren't you?' I nodded. Her Italian had none of the local accent, but was more Tuscan. She apologised for her total lack of English. The drawing-room was full of antique furniture and the walls were covered in oil paintings and tapestries. She noticed my admiring glances and said, 'Yes, it all looks lovely and impressive but the villa doesn't earn me any money at the moment. That's where you and your tourists come in. My nephew thinks that your holidaymakers would love to visit a genuine old Ligurian villa with a renowned aristocratic background. We could arrange an evening reception for them here after their dinner at the hotel. They could relax in comfort, enjoy a drink and see how an Italian Contessa still lives. My nephew will be here to look after the drinks' side of things – we don't want to be too generous with the alcohol otherwise the profits will disappear. He speaks good English so there will be two of you to translate any questions your people will ask me.' She mentioned an 'evening fee' to include a drink. It seemed reasonable for a one-off event for my group. 'By the way,' she added, 'we must limit the group size to fifteen and see how the first evening goes.' A date and time were agreed.

Perhaps it was the way in which I sold the idea to my group, but I soon had my fifteen 'villa guests'. We arrived at the villa at the appointed time. The old, wrinkled retainer opened the door and led us into the drawing-room. La Contessa came towards me with a worried look on her face. 'My nephew has let me down. He can't come this evening. I've bought some drinks in, mainly spirits, but please tell your group not to overindulge. I'm sure you understand.' I accompanied her on a couple of tours of the villa, with one half of the group on each occasion. I translated as required. Every room we entered brought gasps of admiration from the visitors. It was going to be a successful evening.

It did indeed prove to be a most enjoyable evening for my holidaymakers and the following day they were busy telling the others about the visit. However, the enjoyment and pleasure turned out to be one-sided. Signor Angelo received a telephone call from la Contessa in which she bitterly complained about the 'English' and their behaviour the previous evening. Apparently, while the tour of the villa was taking place with one half of the group, the other half were doing their best to empty every drinks' bottle in sight. Her whole stock seemed to have disappeared. Further, someone had spilled a glass or more of red wine on one of her precious and priceless rugs. Far from making a profit on the evening, she was facing a considerable loss. There would be no more 'English evenings'.

Three or four days before my planned return to England, my replacement arrived in Torre Ligure. He was a young student reading French and Italian at Oxford. I briefed him on his courier duties and explained as best I could what to do and what not to do to achieve a happy group of tourists. He would be accompanying the present group to Albenga Airport at the weekend and welcoming his new one. Meanwhile, I travelled back to Kent in the Zephyr. It proved to be another long journey without a hitch.

On my return to KEA School, it took me quite a while to get back into the swing of things. My mind was still dwelling on courier life in sunny Italy and on all its pleasures and advantages. Here I now was back in cloudy, chilly Kent facing another term of attempting to persuade British schoolboys that there was real merit in mastering the intricacies of French and Latin, let alone English grammar. Further, for the next six months, I would personally be facing the challenge of mastering the intricacies of a far more complex set of subjects. I would be taking my practical captain to major examination at the beginning of October and then in the following spring, the half-dozen papers – each of two or three hours' duration – of the written examination. There would be a lot of burning the midnight oil to master the syllabus requirements of military law, military history, aspects of tactics and so on.

The first hurdle was overcome when I passed the practical examination. It took place on some god-forsaken hill in deepest Sussex with much of the county spread out below. Initially, I had to calculate distances to various features in the far off countryside. The main test followed, which involved giving battle orders as a battalion commander in a rigid, time-honoured sequence, for my troops to attack an isolated village located a few miles distant. In due course, I also passed the written examination and was informed that my promotion to substantive major would occur in April 1967.

Every school has its own special characters and KEA School was full of them. Perhaps the most interesting of all the teaching staff characters was the original mumbling dissenter from day one – Chris, the Head of English. He lived with his French wife in a school house in the KEAS grounds. He was a most competent French speaker and had served on espionage duties in France during World War Two. Towards the end of the War, Chris had been attached to an American forward unit as their British Liaison Officer. In late April 1945, his unit met up with the Soviet forces of a Guards Division at the River Elbe near Torgau, south of Berlin.

The front line was flexible for a few days. Three German SS officers had come out of hiding and had surrendered to the American unit. Chris and a couple of guards were to accompany the Germans in a truck to a rear US formation for debriefing. En route, they met a Soviet patrol manning a road block and they were asked to get out of the vehicle. Without warning, the Soviet captain commanding the patrol walked up to the three German SS officers, pulled out his revolver and shot each of them in the head, killing them on the spot. He then smiled broadly, shook Chris's hand and indicated that the truck could drive on. Well outnumbered, there was nothing Chris and his colleagues could do but obey the request. They loaded the dead Germans into the vehicle and returned to their unit. The Americans logged the incident and made an official protest to the Soviets but there was no follow-up. The German SS had been particularly brutal in their treatment of Soviet civilians and, if captured in their readily recognised SS uniform by Soviet soldiers, they were summarily executed. Surrendering to the

Americans was a way of escaping such a fate or so the three SS officers had thought.

Chris had written a number of books and was much sought after as a ghost writer. He was an excellent raconteur with a fund of stories about his wartime experiences, some probably true, others questionably so. It was well known that the boys loved his lessons, rating him an excellent teacher and a fair one, loathe to use the slipper or the cane. In that respect, he was unlike a number of his contemporaries at the school who not infrequently punished boys physically. He spoke highly of Colonel Robert but held the commandant in low esteem, considering him 'an abrasive and puffed-up martinet, inhabiting his own considerably limited micro-world'. Chris and his wife invited me to dinner on a number of occasions. He would say that it gave me an opportunity to enjoy a meal in peace, away from the bickerings of 'those two old women in the Teachers' Mess '– Charles and Ben. He was an accomplished pianist and on my visits to his house he would often sit down at the piano. His favourite party piece was to play and sing a particular number, Hoagy Carmichael style.

Another unforgettable character was Paddy, the volatile Irish Head of Art. He had a love of flamboyant clothing with brightly coloured shirts and knitted ties – a rebellious statement against the school's military uniform. He was prone to delivering endless banter in the staff-room, often bouncing his witticisms off Chris, a seasoned accomplice. A valued client of the staff pub, he could often be found there propping up the bar with a few other regulars. Stocky and short, he was not easily offended but he did object to a cartoon of him which appeared in the school magazine 'The Eddie'. It was the caption that annoyed him – ars brevis – a corruption of his classroom motto 'ars longa, vita brevis' (art endures, life is short). Paddy was a good cricketer and regularly appeared for the KEAS staff cricket team. He was a solid opening bat and a safe pair of hands as a slip fielder. He lived in Manston, a village only a ten-minute drive from the school and he occasionally played cricket for the village team.

One July morning in the staff-room, Paddy mentioned to me that he was turning out as opening batsman for the Manston team the following Sunday. They were short of players so could I join them to play as his opening batsman partner. He added that village cricket was something special and I would enjoy the experience. The game in question was against a village team from the Canterbury area.

Our captain won the toss and decided to bat. Paddy and I padded up and we went out to bat. In the second over of the match, Paddy neatly clipped the ball for four runs past third man. Unfortunately, Charlie, the poaching lurcher belonging to Jim Figgins the Manston star spin bowler, had slipped his lead. He seized the ball as it rolled over the boundary line and was last seen racing across a nearby field with the cricket ball in his jaws. It was as well that our team could produce a reserve ball and the match continued. A few overs later. I was bowled a short ball. I advanced down the pitch and gave it an almighty swipe over mid-wicket. The ball flew high and far, crossing the boundary line for a six as it headed for the local Rectory and its garden. 'Oh! No!' exclaimed Paddy. 'That'll be trouble'.'Sure enough, the sound of breaking glass echoed in the distance. 'That'll be the vicar's new conservatory', continued Paddy, 'and he'll be hopping mad. We've had trouble with him before. You'll have woken him up from his Sunday afternoon nap between morning service and evensong.' What with Charlie the lurcher having run off with our first match ball, and the reserve ball being somewhere in the Rectory, play was temporarily suspended. Our twelfth man was despatched to retrieve the match ball but the furious vicar refused to hand it over. Our cricketer returned, totally deflated. 'I told the vicar we needed the ball to continue our match but what with his smashed conservatory roof and a broken aspidistra pot where the ball had landed, he told me to push off. Well, anyway, an unchristian, anglo-saxon version of that request - he was really livid with steam coming out of his ears.' Tommy Cakebread, our opening fast bowler, volunteered to cycle home to get a replacement cricket ball which he said was in a kitchen drawer. The match scorer and his wife now appeared from the pavilion with refreshments – two large jugs of beer and some glasses, together with pickled onions and crisps, while we waited for Tommy Cakebread to return. It all ended up with Manston winning the match by six wickets. It had been my introduction to village cricket. Watching county cricket at the Kent county ground in Canterbury later in the summer, I thought that they never seemed to have the dramas that village cricket experienced.

Bill (W.C. Harris), known as 'Flush Harry' to the boys, was a former Royal Artillery major and an expert meteorologist. He had the knack of instilling a love of geography in his class students. His father aged 90 lived with Bill and his wife. The old man was still active, both physically and mentally. He occasionally appeared in the staff pub for a pint of beer, which he would drain with gusto.

Peter Richardson, a captain at the school, lived with his wife in an attractive detached house called 'Windrush' on The Droveway in Manston. We had struck up a friendship and I often went birdwatching with him to local hot-spots. He had a good eye for plumage detail and was quite knowledgeable about many aspects of bird life. Our main haunts were around Sandwich Bay – very good for yellow-browed warblers in the autumn and for snow buntings in the winter – and Dungeness which was good for birds throughout the year. Peter and his wife had moved out of school accommodation and bought 'Windrush' in 1961, paying £2500. They had spent another £500 installing central heating. The five bedroom property was in good decorative order and was set in an attractive garden extending to a third of an acre. It overlooked the valley fields towards Ramsgate and was a mere fifteen minutes drive to the beach. Peter reckoned that his property investment of roughly three times his annual salary was a good one. He would rent the house out as and when he was posted. The average comfortable family saloon car cost about £1000 in 1961 – such were the relative prices of property and cars in those days.

As the months and years passed at KEA School, I began to find the Charles-Ben relationship in the Staff Mess quite exasperating at times. They had lived their bachelor lives at the Mess for so long that they had begun to resemble some long-married couples in their interactions, reciprocal fussiness and occasional lapses of patience. Meals would sometimes present oppportunities for cheap point-scoring, with occasional glances in my direction for approval. Little things would intensly annoy the other – the repositioning on the table of the condiments or the sugar bowl; the rustling of a newspaper at breakfast; the slurping of soup; the form of dress: Charles wore a tie at every meal but Ben would occasionally (and deliberately) appear tie-less, much to Charles's annoyance; and so on and so on. Sometimes they weren't on normal talking terms, with me having to act as an intermediary. In short, there wasn't always the best mealtime atmosphere to aid good digestion.

When I had initially visited KEA School and had been shown the extensive playing fields by the headmaster, he had mentioned that I would be roped in to help out with sport. Charles was a very keen cricketing and rugby coach of the school teams and he did indeed rope me in to act as his coaching assistant and also to be the nominated supervisory member of the KEA School staff for various matches. On one memorable Saturday afternoon, the Kent public school, Dover College, sent two representative teams to play KEA School at rugby. We were victors in both games. Charles was extremely pleased at the school's successes. At the meal in the dining-hall afterwards, he and I sat with the Dover College coaching staff. One particular young games master from the college rather annoyed Charles by his claim that KEA School were lucky to win both matches. Charles fixed him with his beady eye and insisted it had all been down to team skill, stamina and perhaps good coaching. 'You'll have to forgive young Jeremy,' said their senior member of staff, 'but he takes defeat very personally. He is a very dedicated sports coach and that can only be a good thing.'

KEA School and the surrounding area, situated in open countryside near Ramsgate, seemed to have its own micro-climate, especially in winter when the 'beast from the east' would blow in. An area of high pressure would become established over the area sucking in freezing air from Siberia and causing the thermometer to plunge dramatically. Strong winds of up to 50 or 60mph would frequently follow and the wind speed would have the effect of making low temperatures feel even colder. Frequently in winter, East Kent would register lower temperatures than cities much closer to the Arctic Circle, such as Oslo, in Norway, and Stockholm in Sweden. I found that snow, often resulting in deep drifts, was a regular winter feature of life at KEA School in the early 1960s. No-one, however, not even local residents who had lived in the area for decades, were prepared for the 1962-63 winter.

The Big Freeze of 1963, as it became known, was one of the coldest winters ever recorded in Britain. When the snow began falling on Boxing Day 1962 and continued throughout next day, it was considered to be an opportunity – especially for the children – to enjoy a belated White Christmas. Little did anyone guess what lay ahead. Temperatures plummeted to almost minus 20c and rivers and lakes began to freeze over. Arctic conditions were to last for over two months. Exceptional snowfall led to huge snowdrifts, crippling road and rail transport. Blizzards were common in East Kent, driven on by gale force easterly winds. Many villagers were cut off and fallen powerlines added to the misery. Snow drifts of eight feet were not uncommon around Ramsgate, and January 1963 proved to be the coldest month of the 20th century.

The sea froze for one mile out from the shore at Herne Bay in North Kent.

Somehow our KEA schoolboys managed to struggle through the chaos so as to arrive for the new term at the beginning of January. Groups of boys armed with shovels, spades and brooms were soon seen all over the school site moving the snow from roads and paths. Radio and television kept us up-to-date with what was happening in other parts of the country. Various snippets brought us news of a car being driven across the frozen Thames at Oxford; people being rescued by helicopter after being snowbound in some isolated area for over a week; whole areas relying on water from road tankers because the mains had frozen and two hundred London buses being put out of action when their fuel froze.

Sports fixtures were a main casualty of the weather as snow blanketed the ground week after week. Events were cancelled wholesale or postponed. The third round of the FA Cup was scheduled for 5th January but the round wasn't completed until 11th March – 66 days later.

The thaw did not set in until early March; 6th March was the first frost-free day of the year. Despite the extreme weather extending over many weeks, families had done their best to carry on with normal life. The generation that had come through the War just got on with their lives as best they could. As for the boys at KEA School, most of them viewed the disruption as a minor inconvenience and the snow itself as a welcome addition to their daily life.

I received an unexpected message from 'K' in early April. He wanted to talk to me about a couple of points affecting my future in the Army. He thought it best on this occasion to meet outside London. Having heard from Roger, my Dover handler, that 'The Green Man' was a suitable out-of-the-way rendezvous, he nominated the St Margaret's Bay pub as out meeting place.

As I arrived in the car park, a large chauffeur-driven limousine pulled up next to me. Out stepped 'K' himself. He greeted me with a broad smile and a handshake. 'That's good timing,' he exclaimed. 'We obviously both share a love of punctuality.' It was such a fine and warm spring day that we decided to have our pub lunch out on the terrace, overlooking the sea. 'It's a great locale here,' commented 'K'. 'We've got the sun, the sea, something to drink and our food will be arriving soon – what more could we want?' Our lunchtime conversation in the public setting of the terrace was limited to general conversation and reference to KEA School and to one or two current affairs of the time. I raised the subject of the Cuban Missile Crisis of the preceeding October, a time when the world was the closest ever to nuclear war. During the crisis, both the USA and the USSR had been at their highest state of military readiness. Fortunately, President John Kennedy and Soviet Premier Nikita Khrushchev had managed to come to a solution acceptable to both sides. The installations in Cuba were dismantled and the nuclear missiles were returned to the Soviet Union. 'Our discussion concerning the Soviet Union is closely connected to something we'll betalking about later on our walk,' said 'K' enigmatically.

Having left the terrace after our meal, we enjoyed the privacy of the beach promenade. 'K' soon broached the two subjects he had on his mind. First, had I thought about where I might go on my next posting? 'You'll have been at KEA School three years in September. It will be time to move on and hopefully gain some more linguistic expertise that would sit nicely on your CV. I've been in touch with my contact in the postings branch and you could well fill a vacancy coming up in August.' 'Where might that be?' I enquired eagerly. 'Singapore,' was 'K's' immediate reply. 'Every Education Branch officer posted to Singapore is put on a basic Malay course soon after arrival, with opportunities to enrol on a higher level course later. Further, as Indonesia is now flexing its muscles and talking belligerently regarding its neighbours, there could well be a chance to study and use Indonesian as well. What do you think?' 'It sounds an excellent idea,' I replied. 'I would love to see the Far East and your suggestion sounds perfect.' 'Right,' continued 'K', 'leave it to me. It can all be arranged.' We continued our walk in silence for a few minutes, came to an empty bench and sat down. 'My second suggestion is long term but well worth some consideration now. Further to our recent discussion regarding the USSR, I would predict that the Cold War will continue for many years. Inevitably, Russian speakers will be in high demand. Some of the Army postings for qualified Russian linguists are very special and extremely interesting. I would suggest that after your Singapore posting, rather than return to some routine military education job, you join the eighteen month Russian course your Branch runs at its Centre in Wycombe Birch Park in Buckinghamshire. The students spend a year at the Centre in Wycombe followed by living in Paris with a White Russian family for a further six months. If you are interested in the idea in due course, like most things, it can be arranged.' The thought of my posting to Singapore was filling my mind and I could just about muster a few words to say how interesting the Russian proposition sounded. 'Well, Pluto young man, you've got plenty to think about in the short term and something to think about in the long term if the idea of a Russian language course appeals to you. I haven't been able to find you another suitable intelligence assignment since you've been at the military school in Ramsgate. Still, after the two successful outcomes in Cambridge and Capel Heights, I think you deserve my personal input regarding your next posting and even the one after that. I've enjoyed my visit today to St. Margaret's Bay but it's high time I was heading back to London.' I accompanied him back to his limousine in the car park and we said our goodbyes. As the vehicle passed 'The Green Man' on its way up the steep cliff road, I couldn't help but think, 'That was some meeting, it really was. Singapore with Malay and then a long Russian course. I must be dreaming.'

A month later, Colonel Robert called me into his office. 'I've got some good news for you, John,' he said. 'Your posting has come through and in August you will be posted to ------.' He broke off. 'Where do you think?' he continued. 'I've no idea,' I replied with tongue in cheek. 'Well, it's to Singapore, you lucky chap – a really plum posting that we'd all like. Anyway, congratulations on your good luck. I'm sure you will enjoy Singapore immensely.'

My final weeks at KEA School were dominated by talk of the Profumo scandal, both in the staff-room and in the Teachers' Mess at mealtimes with Charles and Ben. At the height of the Cold War, John Profumo, a married MP and the Secretary of State for War, had carried out a clandestine affair with an alleged call-girl, Christine Keeler, in the privacy of Cliveden, the Astors' country house in Buckinghamshire. The problem for Profumo was that Keeler was also in a relationship with Yevgeni Ivanov, a senior naval attache and spy based at the Soviet Embassy in London. The obvious threat to national security was emphasised in the media.

When challenged in the House of Commons in March 1963 regarding the liaison, Profumo lied to the House, denying any relationship between him and Keeler had ever existed. When the truth eventually emerged, Profumo resigned and he disappeared from the public domain.

Meanwhile, the reputation of Harold MacMillan's Conservative Government had been badly damaged. MacMillan himself resigned a few months later, soon ushering in Harold Wilson's Labour Government in 1964.

In the midst of all the euphoria regarding my posting to Singapore, one difficult and sensitive task lay ahead. Throughout my time in Kent, I had been visiting my elderly parents in Crawley, Sussex every couple of months. On my next visit, I would be facing the problem of having to tell them that I would soon be going overseas and probably not returning for three years. For parents accustomed to seeing their son every couple of months, a three-year absence would be a very long time indeed.

I visited my parents in Crawley a month later to say goodbye prior to my posting to Singapore, probably for three years. My mother was 56 and in robust health but my father had reached 73 and was in poor health. A big surprise awaited me on my arrival in Crawley. I was greeted by my mother and Ruth and informed that my father had been taken ill with bronchitis and was now a patient at a hospital near Brighton. Arrangements were made for me to visit him a week later.

In an exchange of letters, my father had asked me to meet him at a certain point in the grounds rather than in the hospital itself. He was no longer a bed-patient and enjoyed an occasional short walk in the July sunshine. He met me as arranged at a bench in the rose garden. A uniformed male nurse, whom I assumed had arrived early for his shift and was also enjoying the sunshine in the rose garden, sat not far away from us. I noticed he was looking in our direction a few times but thought nothing more of it. My father and I chatted away on a broad range of subjects.

He was not one to dole out much praise but at one stage in our conversation he said, 'You know, John, you've done very well to achieve the educational and social progress that you have. In my day, the universities of Oxford and Cambridge, and a commission in the Army, were the preserve of the sons of the gentry and the well-heeled professional classes – doctors, lawyers and so on. Here you are, the son of a working class engineer, as a Cambridge graduate and an Army captain. You have done well. Fortunately, it's no longer who you know but what you know that matters. The higher educational and Army commissioning systems of today no longer mirror the wretched class system endured by the likes of us in former years.'

We continued to reminisce and laugh together for a good hour. Apart from his bronchitis, he came across as perfectly normal with his mind as sharp as ever. He commented that he was pleased with the treatment he was receiving. I looked at him a few times as he was talking and looking into the distance. My mind was focusing on that inevitable question that all sons and daughters ask themselves as they share time with an elderly parent who is not in the best of health. The question in my case was compounded by my knowing that we would not meet again for some years. 'Will you still be alive when I return?' I thought. As we embraced on parting, I believed I detected a tear on his cheek but he was a proud man and would never have acknowledged any emotional weakness. I felt intensely sad at leaving him. The uniformed nurse now approached us and said,' Come on, Sam, it's high time to go back.' My father muttered, 'All right, Bill, I'm coming.' Turning to me, he commented, 'They look after you well here, John. They make sure you come to no harm.'

He got up from the bench, wished me well and set off with the nurse up the path back to the hospital building. I stayed by the bench watching them. My father and I managed one last wave to each other before he disappeared inside the building. Little did I know what the establishment really was and the manner in which he had ended up there. As we shall see, I only discovered the terrible truth from Amy after my return from Singapore. I also learned what role Ruth had played in it all. Had I known the full circumstances at the time, I would have been heartbroken.

CHAPTER 11

'Will those passengers travelling on Flight 301 to Singapore, please report to gate number three.' The announcement at RAF Lyneham brought a rush of activity in our waiting area. Servicemen, young and not so young, mothers with babes in arms and children, passed through the necessary controls. We all made our way up the boarding steps onto an RAF Transport Command plane. As we taxied along the runway prior to take-off, I looked out of my window and thought how I wouldn't be returning to the UK for the next three years.

After a five-hour flight, we arrived at the RAF staging post of El Adem, situated in a stony desert about twenty miles south of Tobruk in Libya. Our arrival was greeted by dazzling, bright sunshine. King Idris I had reigned since Libya gained independence in 1951. He was to remain king until the Army coup of 1969 when a small group of officers led by a certain Muammah Gaddafi overthrew the government. As a young officer, Gaddafi attended an English language course in the 1960s run by the Education Branch at its Centre in Buckinghamshire. In conversation with a young RAF serviceman during the stopover, he said he must have done something wrong to end up in the desolate wastes of El Adem, but he couldn't remember what. We later had a short stopover in Bahrein.

RAF Gan, situated on Addu Atoll in the Maldives in the Indian Ocean, was a complete contrast to El Adem. It was considered to be a plum posting. The weather on Gan was characterised by continuous sunny days for about ten months of the year, followed by two months of the monsoon season with its virtually non-stop rain. Circling around the atoll before we landed, and then approaching the runway, I have an enduring memory of an island of matchless beauty. I asked one of the RAF officers stationed there whether Gan was indeed such a good posting. 'I'm not married,' he explained, 'and for me it's an absolute paradise. The monthly temperatures remain static in the eighties and the palm-fringed beaches are as white and pristine as you could possibly imagine. The scuba-diving, snorkelling and night fishing are fantastic and the coral reefs are teeming with fish. Only last week, we saw a couple of whale sharks beyond the lagoon along with some giant manta rays. It certainly beats being back in Lincolnshire, which was my previous posting, at RAF Waddington.' He sounded like a really happy man and a living advertisement for the Maldives.

Gan was our last stopover before we reached Paya Lebar Airport in Singapore. As I left the plane, a blast of hot air hit me and my nostrils caught the sweet, sweet smell of the tropics. A number of us on the flight were going on to Nee Soon Garrison in the centre of the island. An Army coach carried us through open countryside and built-up areas presenting us with an ever-changing kaleidoscope of Singapore life.

On first appearance, Nee Soon Garrison Officers' Mess seemed comfortable enough. Although the malaria-bearing anopheles mosquito was absent from the island, the Mess Sergeant pointed out that it was advisable to use the provided mosquito nets around my bed as other biting species were around. 'There's always the chance of getting dengue fever from an infected bite,' he added. 'It's very unpleasant and I wouldn't wish it on my worst enemy. There's no vaccine against it.' About a year later, I was to find out just how unpleasant dengue fever could be. My room was large, equipped with an effective ceiling fan and it overlooked a well-maintained lawn with a few scattered bushes. The only drawback was the heat, and sweating was the order of the day. 'It stays in the eighties all year round,' said the Mess Sergeant, 'and the nights can be uncomfortably hot. Still, we mustn't complain. Everything considered, Captain Reddisson, there are few postings that match up to Singapore.'

After dinner in the Mess that evening, I had a visit from Mark, the Education Branch captain who ran the Centre where I would be working. We chatted over a beer in the Mess bar. He was about ten years older than me, most affable, married with four boys under fifteen and lived in a married quarter in the Garrison. He explained that to escape the oppressive heat of the afternoon, our working hours were from 7.15am until 1.30pm. 'I play a lot of golf,' said Mark. 'Those working hours are a boon as they mean I can play eighteen holes any afternoon I wish at the Island Golf Club.' He went on to explain that I would be teaching English to Malay soldiers, as well as map-reading, current affairs and military calculations to British servicemen. 'There are plenty of teaching materials in the Centre for you to look through,' Mark said, 'and in any case, you won't be teaching for a few days.' He added with a wry smile, 'I shall probably be losing you for a while within a month or two, John, as all Education Branch officers arriving in Singapore are sooner or later put on a five-week Malay course. I did the course myself and found it very worthwhile.' Before we finished our chat in the bar, Mark made a suggestion which I gratefully accepted. 'If you agree, I'll collect you tomorrow morning in my car and give you a tour of Singapore, including a spot of lunch.'

After an early breakfast the next morning, I went for a short walk around the Officers' Mess area. I was delighted to see several birds which I recognised from the guidebook I had purchased in the UK. They included a yellow-vented bulbul, black-naped oriole and a tailor-bird. Large tropical butterflies were flitting around. All in all, it was an enjoyable welcome from Singapore's natural world.

It took Mark and me about half an hour to reach Singapore city. Our first visit was to CK Tang where Mark's wife had tasked him to buy certain items. It was a vast department store on Orchard Road, Singapore's most vibrant shopping and entertainment area. Fortunately, the store was air-conditioned, which meant Mark and I could wander around the various departments in complete comfort, well away from the perspiration of Orchard Road itself. Mark pointed out a section selling camphor-wood chests. 'Those chests seem to be the number one priority for people returning to the UK. They have some beautiful carvings and retain that special camphor smell to remind people of the days spent in Singapore.'

We next visited 'Raffles Hotel', the famous colonial-style hotel named after Stamford Raffles, the founder of modern Singapore. It had been built at the end of the nineteenth century and was an iconic building of the colonial days between the wars. It boasted a ballroom, grand verandah and a billiards room. Mark and I chatted over a coffee before we toured the hotel looking at the public rooms.

From 'Raffles', we went for 'a spot of lunch' to the Tanglin Club, Singapore's oldest and most prominent social club. It had been founded in the 1860s 'to meet the social needs of British expatriates living in Singapore.' Somehow, the ambience of the club still evoked the past, rather like 'Raffles Hotel', more British Empire than the 1960s. When our drinks arrived, Mark formally greeted me to Singapore with the Singapore Chinese toast 'yum seng' (bottoms up). The lunch menu was comprehensive and I selected one of the club's specialities – Lobster Thermidor, an absolutely delicious choice. I noticed that when Mark wished to attract the attention of one of the waiters, he would call out 'Boy!' The waiters were Malay and Chinese, mostly over fifty, and I thought Mark's 'Boy!' was a bit demeaning. 'It's the custom here in the club, John,' explained Mark, 'and has been for the last hundred years. Anyway, if you think about it, we address waiters in France the same way. After all, 'garcon' means 'boy' in French, doesn't it? "You're right, Mark,' I answered, 'but I've never thought about it in that way before.' 'While we are on the subject,' continued Mark, 'there's another thing about addressing people in Singapore. As a British officer, you will be respectfully addressed as 'tuan' by Singaporeans such as shopkeepers, taxi drivers and general workers, but if they are Malay, you will address them as 'enche.' A Malay NCO greeting you in the morning will say, 'Selamat pagi, tuan.'(Good morning, sir.) You would reply, 'Selamat pagi, enche.' One other thing to remember, John, regarding names, is how to address the Chinese. For example, the Singapore Prime Minister is Lee Kuan Yew. He would be Mr. Lee, not Mr. Yew. The sooner you know these things the better, I suppose.' Mark mentioned that the club's Sunday curry lunches were something special and most enjoyable after a morning swim in the large club pool. He suggested it would be a good idea for me to join the club. We tracked down the club secretary. Mark sponsored me and I joined then and there.

After lunch, we paid a visit to the harbour area and the nearby Padang, one of Singapore's major recreational areas. 'If you are interested in playing cricket,' said Mark, 'this is where our Education Branch cricket team plays.' Mark, himself, was a good opening bowler and we subsequently enjoyed a number of games together on the Padang ground.

Mark mentioned that it was essential to have a car in Singapore. We called in at a dealer's and after a a number of false choices and much hemming and hawing, I eventually chose a second-hand Standard Vanguard Vignale saloon. It was the two-litre, four door model with a front bench-seat and a steering column mounted gear-change lever. It was polished up and prepared for me to collect the following day.

Instead of making for the Officers' Mess on our return to Nee Soon, Mark drove me to his married quarter to introduce me to his charming wife, Sally. Over a cup of tea, they said what a great posting Singapore was, especially in terms of social activity. 'A generous overseas allowance means that we can eat out regularly, enjoy the Tanglin Club's facilities and entertain at home. We have a 'wash amah' who can also help out with the children, a 'kebun' (gardener) and a 'cook amah'. Three servants, not bad for a captain. But that's the sort of life one can enjoy in Singapore.'

Mark and I were two of the many thousands of UK servicemen arriving in Singapore and the surrounding area in the early 1960s. The history books tell us that the reason for the rapid build-up of UK service personnel had its origins in the 'Confrontation' conflict between the Malaysian Federation and Indonesia. The Malayan prime minister had proposed a federation to be composed of Malaya, Singapore and the north Borneo colonies of Brunei, Sabah and Sarawak. These colonies bordered Indonesia and their President Sukarno had hoped that all the projected Malaysian Federation countries would join Indonesia in forming a Greater Indonesia. The idea of an independent Malaysia delivered a death blow to that dream. Sukarno declared that the new Federation was merely a way of maintaining British colonial influence in the area. In 1962, he engineered a revolt iin Brunei, led by a radical Muslim group, but it was soon put down by British forces. Indonesia now widened its aggressive tactics by sending irregular military 'volunteers' into Sarawak and Sabah where they engaged in sabotage and subversion. Indonesian regular troops also began crossing the border in Borneo. On 16 September 1963, Malaysia was formally created and it asked for military assistance from Britain to be increased so as to counter Indonesia's political and military aggression. Singapore agreed that the island could act as the military headquarters of the campaign. The British and Malaysian armed forces were later joined by Australian and New Zealand servicemen.

Over the months, the number of British and Commonwealth servicemen deployed in the area grew to some fifty thousand. In Borneo the troops were in position along a nine hundred-mile front in some of the world's worst jungle terrain. Cross-border operations into Indonesia were initiated using special forces on long-range patrols, enabling the SAS to perfect their jungle tactics. After the undeclared war had dragged on for three years, a peace agreement was finally established in 1966 and Indonesia formally accepted the existence of Malaysia.

Mark's prediction that he would soon lose me from the Education Centre to a Malay course proved to be accurate. In October, I started the five-week language course in the Far East Training Centre (FETC) language wing, situated only a few hundred yards from the Education Centre across a vast parade ground. The military authorities had decreed that every unit arriving in the area should send representatives to Nee Soon to attend the Malay language course. There were forty-eight students on my course, divided into four classes of twelve. The language wing had two Education Branch teaching staff, two civilian teachers seconded from the UK and six Malay military instructors. There was a set timetable to be followed, consisting of twenty-four printed lesson handouts, one of which was followed daily. The final Friday of the five weeks was reserved for the Army Colloquial Test for students who had shown promise. If candidates passed, there was a generous financial award. During our first week, we had a placement test. Based on the results, the four classes were streamed. I had studied hard and found myself in the top stream under Captain Phil, the wing's Chief Instructor, and Sergeant-Major Hassan. One morning in late November, Phil walked into the classroom and wrote a new Malay word for us on the whiteboard – 'membunoh' (to kill, to assassinate) adding underneath 'President John F. Kennedy'.

I continued to work hard throughout the course. On the final day, I took the Army Colloquial Test, obtaining, so I was later informed, a very good mark in the nineties. Later in the day, I was asked to report to the officer commanding the language wing, Major Tim. He explained that the Chief Instuctor, Phil, was due to be posted in a couple of months or so and no successor had yet been appointed. He added that he had telephoned Education Branch HQ that very afternoon to make an urgent suggestion. HQ had just returned his call, agreeing to the suggestion. Would I be interested in joining the wing as an instructor with immediate effect with a view to taking over from Phil as Chief Instructor two months later? It was, as they say, an offer I couldn't refuse. Poor Mark at the Education Centre, had not only lost me for the five-week Malay course, he had lost me for good. I hoped he would soon find a replacement for me as there was clearly a need for the young Malay recruits from up-country to learn English as soon as possible. Coming back to Nee Soon from Singapore city late one night soon after starting my language course, I was challenged at the FETC barrier by a young Malay on guard duty. He had probably worked hard on trying to learn his guard duty phrases but muddled them up under pressure. As he challenged me, he blurted out, 'Halt! Who there goes? Stop or I'll shoot me!'

I cut my Malay teeth on my initial class group the following Monday. Most evenings were spent studying Malay from non-language wing material so as to widen my knowledge base. By the time I took over from Phil,

I had acquired a much deeper knowledge of the language. One of the problems in learning Malay is that it is considered 'an easy language'. The basics are indeed deceptively uncomplicated. It was only after further study that I began to realise the subtleties of the language and then draw the conclusion that it wasn't so easy after all. Malay has given the English language a few words including amok (amuk), bamboo (bambu), cockatoo (kakaktua), orangutan (orang-utan: jungle person), ketchup (kichap) and tea (teh).

As the months passed, the build-up of UK servicemen increased considerably and we also received students from Royal Navy and Fleet Air Arm units, as well as Australian and New Zealand personnel. Our classes increased to five, totalling sixty students, with further instructors helping out. Living in the Mess with a number of the officer students, I got to know some of them very well, including great characters from the Fleet Air Arm and 22 Special Air Service (22 SAS).

An unforgettable character who developed into the life and soul of one of my classroom groups was 22 SAS Trooper Talaiasi Labalaba, a Fijian. We called him 'Laba'. He did well on the course, making particularly good progress in the spoken language. Some years later as an SAS sergeant, he was to show outstanding courage and commitment to his colleagues and regiment in an under-reported and brutal war in Oman in 1972 during the Dhofar Rebellion. Holed up in a desert fort at Mirbat with some local troops and eight other soldiers from B Squadron, 22 SAS Regiment, fighting an enemy force estimated to be around three hundred, he carried on engaging the enemy when seriously wounded. He died of his wounds at the scene. He was held in such high regard by his Regiment that a statue of him has been erected at their Hereford Headquarters.

I carried on studying Malay intensively in my free time and passed the more difficult Linguist examination, followed six months later by the advanced Civil Service Interpretership examination. The latter included the need to master the Jawi or Arabic-based alphabet. A CSC Interpretership examination is considered by educational authorities to be the equivalent in study level of a UK university degree. The language wing had also taken on the task of teaching Indonesian to Linguist level. Indonesian was then considered to be a separate language from Malay but in the last fifty years, steps have been taken to merge them into one language. I duly passed my Indonesian Linguist and Interpretership examinations after much burning of the midnight oil.

Mention of Singapore in the early 1960s would not be complete without a reference to the notorious and very busy Bugis Street. It was characterised by the 'pasar malam' (night market) with its numerous outdoor bars and roadside hawker stalls, situated close to the rat-infested monsoon storm-drains. I visited the area on a few occasions in the company of two or three young officers from Nee Soon Garrison (safety in numbers). It was a bustling tourist target at night, especially on account of the showy main attraction – the extravagantly dressed transvestites who strutted their stuff around midnight. They were known to the regulars as Kai Tais or Beany Boys. One could indulge in a decent plate of nasi goreng (fried rice) or mah mee (soup noodles) while watching the nightly parade of the exuberant main attraction and seeing the new onlookers' reactions as they glimpsed a beautiful girl's adam's apple or unusually large hands or feet. A sub-attraction was the inevitable losing game of noughts and crosses against the quick-witted and persistent Singaporean youngsters, still very active into the early hours.

Despite my extended language studies, I made sure to allow myself time for leisure activities. I joined the Island Golf Club and in due course obtained my (twenty-six) official handicap. I enjoyed playing in cricket matches at the Padang. The Tanglin Club was a great venue for social occasions, including their wonderful Sunday curry lunches. I also regularly spent evenings at the club, when dancing was very much in evidence. One memorable evening, a particular brigadier, newly arrived from the UK and, let's say, in an excessively convivial state, mistook the Singapore national anthem 'Majulah Singapura' (Onward Singapore) for the last dance. He pulled his wife onto the dance floor and, in the circumstances, gave a fair rendition of a foxtrot. I believe the Club Secretary spoke to him afterwards. Not unexpectedly, the brigadier and his wife did not return to the club to give a repeat performance of, by now, their legendary dancing skill.

One of my favourite films is 'Breakfast at Tiffany's' (1961), starring George Peppard and Audrey Hepburn as Holly Golightly. I first saw the film in Singapore. Its theme music is centred on the wonderfully evocative 'Moon River', composed by Henry Mancini with lyrics by Johnny Mercer. It was a favourite number of the resident Chinese chanteuse at the Tanglin Club and she sang it beautifully. Whenever I hear the song today, it transports me back to the Tanglin Club and conjures up memories of Singapore life in the 1960s.

I joined the Services Scuba-Diving Club and went on a most enjoyable weekend diving trip to Tioman Island off Malaya's east coast, where the water was crystal clear to a considerable depth. Butterfly and birdwatching trips were regular events. With two expatriate UK birders, John Darnell and Mike Webster, I recorded Singapore's vey first sighting of a vagrant spoon-billed stint, later called spoon-billed sandpiper, at the Jurong Prawn Ponds in the west of the island.

During my three years in Singapore, one of the more memorable visits away from the island was to the Cameron Highlands in Malaya. I drove there to spend a two-week 'change of air' leave period as provided by the service authorities. Road signs in Malaya were infrequent but sooner or later one came to a sign bearing the single word 'Utara', especially at road junctions. Many a British driver had pulled over and consulted his map to locate the town of Utara. It was not shown on the best of maps, causing one to give up in disgust. The general concensus would then be that it must mean 'caution' or 'take extra care'. In fact, 'Utara' is the Malay word for 'North', for that was the direction to take when travelling 'up country' in Malaya.

I had been warned to drive extra carefully when passing through any Malay 'kampong' (village) en route and to keep a vey sharp lookout for any Malay children playing by the roadside. There had been a number of incidents in which British drivers had experienced Malay children running into the path of their car and causing a serious accident resulting in a badly injured child or even worse. I was advised If that happened to me, I wasn't to stop but drive on to the next police post and return to the scene of the accident with some Malay police officers. Some drivers had stopped only to be brutally attacked by the Malay villagers, intent on some sort of revenge. It is not a coincidence that one of the few words Malay words in the English language is 'amok'. To have Malay villagers run amok after an accident would be something best avoided.

The Cameron Highlands, designated a military services' leave-station, were some 5000 feet above sea-level, where the air was fresh and cool, unlike the heat of the steaming jungle below or of Singapore. As I drove up the winding mountain road with its hairpin bends, I had occasional views of the (so-called) 'Malayan aboriginals' along the roadside, some with their six-foot bamboo hunting blowpipes on their shoulders. My two weeks spent in a holiday bungalow included evenings when the area was enveloped in a swirling cold mist but with me sat comfortably in front of a log fire. Blankets would be needed later on the bed as night temperatures dipped below 10 C.

It was a most relaxing yet surreal holiday in the 'tropics'. Bird and butterfly species were totally unlike those I was accustomed to seeing at virtual sea-level in Singapore and southern Malaya. On walking around the local residential areas one frequently came across roses in bloom in the well-tended gardens. One retired tea-planter told me that his roses bloomed three times a year, such were the climate and growing conditions. The Malayan Emergency (1948-60) was well in the past and it was perfectly safe to wander around the area on one's own. Among the typical birds of the Cameron Highlands, special mention may be made of white-tailed robin, large niltava, mountain bulbul, slaty-backed forktail and silver-eared mesia. Close observation of such birds added greatly to the interest and pleasure of my visit.

The following year, I visited Fraser's Hill, some 4,500 feet above sea-level and another 'change of air' station. Although the birdwatching was more productive, Fraser's Hill somehow lacked the supreme charm and charisma of the Cameron Highlands.

I suffered a temporary setback in my work and in my leisure pursuits when I contracted dengue fever. I went down with a high temperature, pain behind the eyes, accompanied by bone, muscle and joint pain. I was allocated a bed in the Garrison sick-bay and had regular visits from the Medical Officer. He prescribed pain relief tablets and plenty of fluids. It cleared up in about two weeks but was most unpleasant while it lasted.

One evening in January 1965, I was having dinner with other officers in the Nee Soon Mess when the Garrison commanding officer arrived unexpectedly and made an announcement. He had just heard on the wireless that Winston Churchill had passed away at his home in London. All the officers stood up and we toasted 'Sir Winston Churchill'.

When I had met 'K' at St. Margaret's Bay near Dover, he had raised the question of an eighteen month Russian language course after my Singapore posting. He had said that if I was interested in applying to attend the course, it 'could be arranged'. In the spring of 1965, I received a lengthy telegram. To my surprise, it was from 'K' referencing the Russian course. He stated that if I was still interested in the long Russian course, I should apply without too much delay for the course beginning in Wycombe in September 1966. Nominal rolls were usually drawn up many months ahead of the course start date. I should apply through the usual Education Branch channels and he would monitor selection at the London end. There was a PS to 'K's telegram: 'Keep up the good work at the FETC Language Wing,' Major Tim, the officer commanding the Language Wing, gave me an excellent recommendation to be selected for the course, as did the Education Branch staff officer at the main HQ in Singapore, Lieutenant- colonel Len. He and I had met a number of times in the Tanglin Club at their Sunday curry lunches, and he had already mentioned that the long Russian course would be a good career move for me.

As an interesting diversion from studying and teaching Malay and Indonesian, I began to learn Iban, a language close to Malay and spoken by the Iban people of Sarawak. A number of my Malay language students had passed through the Far East Training Centre in Singapore on their way back to the UK after having served in Sarawak, often along the border with Indonesia. Using their Malay as a basis for communication with the locals, they had also picked up a fair amount of Iban at first hand. In due course, I produced a small handbook of Iban for any of my future students who could be ending up on the Sarawak-Indonesian border. What I hadn't reckoned on was that I, too, would end up on that border in the near future. One morning in May 1965, Major Tim called me into his office. Headquarters had received a number of requests from units in Borneo for their Malay speakers to be examined for the Army Colloquial Test, a generous financial award being paid on a successful result. Would the language wing provide an examiner to hold the test in a number of locations in Borneo? Major Tim said that he was too busy in developing Indonesian language course material to go himself. He assumed I would jump at the chance to satisfy the request from Headquarters. He was certainly correct in his assumption. A list of test centres was drawn up and units in Borneo were invited to submit names of candidates. A full itinerary was worked out covering a two-week tour, with the furthest-flung outpost to be my first test centre – Nanga Gaat on the Sarawak-Indonesian border itself.

I left RAF Changi at some ungodly hour in the early morning – or 'at sparrowfart' as it is so eloquently called in the Army – aboard a Bristol Freighter bound for Kuching, Sarawak. It was a most uncomfortable flight, with me being sat in a corner of the metal-floored freight compartment. A Malaysian Airways DC3 took me on to Sibu. A Whirlwind helicopter of 845 Naval Air Squadron of the Royal Navy Fleet Air Arm was my next mode of transport. The Squadron had become known as the 'Junglies' for their work in Borneo. By coincidence, the Wessex helicopter was piloted by one of my former students at the language wing. We landed at Kapit for an hour's break before proceeding over many miles of dense jungle. We finally reached Nanga Gaat in the Indonesian border area. I had now been travelling for over sixteen hours since leaving RAF Changi and was pleased to have the chance to freshen up in the makeshift 'Naval Mess.' I spent the next three days examining British and Gurkha candidates for the Malay test. Each test lasted about half an hour and I managed to examine six candidates in the morning and a further six in the afternoon – tiring work in the humid and hot tropical conditions.

One evening, the local service personnel rigged up a screen in a large clearing. In addition to assorted servicemen, about fifty Iban of all ages turned up and we watched the Burt Lancaster film 'Elmer Gantry.' It was a memorable, magical setting for the 'cinema show,' with nothing but hundreds of miles of jungle all around us. Our perimeter security was in very safe hands. In addition to Gurkha sentries on patrol around the camp area, elements of 22 SAS Regiment were not far away. Based on previous contact experience, Indonesian forces would stay well away from such formidable soldiers.

Another evening and night, were spent in an Iban longhouse, 'Rumah Tinggan,' about five miles up- river from Nanga Gaat. I was informed the Iban were celebrating a good harvest and combining it with a wedding feast. As a special guest from far-off Singapore, I was asked by the Iban headman to prepare a bowl of food with him in celebration of the good harvest. I carried the bowl up some rickety wooden steps to deposit it in the loft area. My next task was something completely different. The headman thrust into my hand a fluttering cockerel. I was invited to follow him around the longhouse, pausing at groups of people. I was to hold the cockerel over their heads momentarily so as to bring luck in the months ahead, leading to the next harvest. As a foretaste of their luck to come, some Iban had an initial blessing of chicken bird-lime. For my efforts, I was presented with a copper bracelet and introduced to the recently married couple.

The wedding feast consisted of several courses accompanied by large amounts of tuak – a potent rice wine. When we had finished eating and drinking, a group of young Iban girls, clad only in their traditional skirts, sang to us for about ten minutes. Wedding speeches followed and I was pleased to understand parts of them, further to my Iban studies. Mosquito nets were provided for us as we settled down to sleep in the longhouse. The Iban had been headhunters in the past and headhunting had been temporarily revived during the Second World War. The Iban had played an important role in guerrilla warfare against the occupying Japanese forces. I couldn't help grimacing as I'd mounted the steps to the longhouse after the meal, and passed a wooden pillar from which dangled several skulls. Two of the skulls were adorned with spectacles and I reckoned I knew their provenance.

Before I left Nanga Gaat, I paid a personal pilgrimage to a heart-rending and tragic spot, where I said a silent prayer. It was the site on the river where two Wessex helicopters of 845 Squadron had collided and then crashed into the fast-flowing river a few weeks earlier, resulting in the deaths of eight service personnel. The list included a pilot who had been in one of my Malay classes and whom I had befriended at Nee Soon. I had been to several parties with him on the island. It was a tragic end for such a fine, fun-loving young man.

I had arrived at Nanga Gaat by helicopter from Sibu, but left by river. Arriving at Kapit, I transferred to a speedboat and we reached Sibu mid-afternoon. The best part of the boat journey along the river had been in seeing a number of tropical birds along the way – including hornbills, herons and several species of kingfisher. I had also glimpsed a number of butterflies including the majestic Rajah Brooke's birdwing, a huge butterfly named after Sir James Brooke, the first white rajah of nineteenth century Sarawak. Over the next week, I visited other test centres in Sibu, Kuching and Brunei before flying back to RAF Changi, from where I returned to Nee Soon.

One November morning later in the year, the Garrison Adjutant handed me a telegram. I immediately thought it was another communication from 'K' regarding the Russian course. I opened it on the spot. It was in fact from my mother – 'Dad passed away yesterday. Funeral next week. Will write soon. Love. Mum'. The Adjutant must have seen the expression on my face. 'Bad news?' he enquired.'Yes, my father has passed away.' 'Why not spend a few minutes in the Garrison Church?' the Adjutant continued.' 'It'll help. We only have one father.' I sat in the church for a time, reflecting on my father's life and on how well we had got on together. He had never physically punished me and had always been calm and philosophical, but he had endured one saga of a troubled, personal life. Born to a quarryman and his wife in the 1880s and growing up in a small cottage in the wilds of Hessle in Yorkshire couldn't have been much fun. The First World War arrived and he lost an eye in the carnage of Gallipoli in 1915. He lost his first wife to tubercolosis and the Spanish 'Flu epidemic of 1919-20. His young son of eight went off to live with relatives in Australia and he never saw him again. Only a few years after he had married my mother, the Wall Street Crash and the Depression arrived and he was thrown out of work. A qualified engineer, he had been forced to find work pushing a barrow around the Southwark fruit and vegetable market to keep himself, his wife and four young children afloat. World War Two then followed with his house being destroyed by the Luftwaffe and his family being dispersed to distant parts of England and Wales. He had experienced a very challenging time with his eldest daughter, Ruth. He had ended his days in a hospital miles away from home, passing away at the age of 76. There was enough misery there, I thought, for half a dozen men but I had never heard him complain or bemoan his lot in life. He really had remained calm and had carried on. 'Rest in peace, Dad,' I exclaimed aloud. 'Rest in peace.'

A few months later, I received a posting order. I was to leave Singapore in August 1966 and was then to report to Wycombe Park in Buckinghamshire in early September to attend the eighteen month Russian course. I immediately thought: 'Thank you 'K'.'

CHAPTER 12

I arrived at the Wycombe Birch Park Officers' Mess on the Sunday afternoon before the start of the Russian course. Since my last visit some years before, the Mess had been relocated to a multi-storey block that towered over the surrounding Buckinghamshire countryside. My first thought was that only the MoD could get away with building such a vertical monstrosity in the previously attractive rural setting.

I made for the Mess bar before dinner, hoping to come across some officers who would also be attending the Russian course. I was not to be disappointed. Two young lieutenants were sat at the bar deep in conversation. One of them looked vaguely familiar, possibly from the media. Nigel, an officer in the Foot Guards, introduced himself first, followed by Edward in the Cavalry. It turned out later that both of them were scions of well-known English families, with Edward's being particularly prominent – and both were Old Etonians into the bargain. Some MoD course planner had ensured that having officers from the Cavalry and the Foot Guards would bring a touch of class to the Russian course nominal roll. Further, both officers proved to be first rate students and popular with their fellow 'kursanty' or course members. By a twist of fate, as a grammar school product, and by virtue of my age and rank seniority, I was to be declared the 'course senior'. Life's social and material advantages had not come into the equation.

By the time we had assembled in our classroom in the Russian language wing the following morning, the number of students on the course had increased to ten. Additions were two Royal Navy officers, two infantry subalterns, a Ghanaian lieutenant and two Intelligence Corps NCOs. We had an opening address from the major commanding the wing who then handed us over to the Chief Instructor for a brief description of the linguistic content of the course. Not long afterwards, the ten of us began our very first lesson under Ray, a civilian tutor. It was assumed that we students had no prior knowledge of the Russian language or of its cyrillic alphabet and we started our studies from the very basics. Ray informed us that he would be our tutor for the whole year leading up to the start of the six-month Paris study period the following September. Our classroom was set out 1960s style with rows of desks.

After a few weeks solely under Ray's guidance, we began having occasional lessons from the wing's non-British teaching staff. They consisted of a Pole, an East German and a Yugoslav. They had all learned Russian as a second language in their respective countries. The Cold War had precluded the wing's chances of recruiting a Soviet tutor, whose first language would have been Russian, to help us in our studies.

We always had lunch with our tutors in the Officers' Mess during the week, so as to continue our practice in the spoken language. One noticed at lunch how the non-British tutors would sit down at the table and then proceed, little by little, to surround themselves with the meal accompaniments such as vegetable dishes, salad, bread, butter, water, condiments and any sauces. Presumably, it was an automatic reaction to zero supplies during the War, which they were still unable to shake off.

About a month after the start of the Russian course, I received a telephone call from Amy. She and her husband, Michael, would love to have me over for lunch in their north London house. Further, she wanted to bring me up-to-date on a family matter of which I knew little if anything. Amy and Michael had now been married for about ten years and they had two bright and chirpy young daughters, Debbie and Joanne. After our lunch, they went to play next door. We adults were relaxing with our coffees in the sitting-room when Amy broached the subject of 'the family matter'. 'John, did you notice anything unusual about that hospital where Dad was being treated for his bronchitis and where he subsequently died?' 'Well, only that Dad commented on how good the treatment was and how well they looked after you,' I replied. 'I don't quite know how to put this,' Amy continued, 'but they had to watch their inmates closely. It was a hospital that treated patients who were mentally disturbed. A number of them had been sectioned and Dad was more or less put into that category.' 'But he was totally sane when I saw him there before I went to Singapore,' I protested. 'I would have soon noticed if he'd had any mental problems.' 'Exactly,' countered Amy, 'and when I visited him up to his death, he always came across as perfectly normal and sane. He must have known where he was but he was too weak and depressed to do much about it, and clearly he didn't want to make a fuss.' 'How on earth did he end up there? Surely Mum and Ruth could have done something about it?' 'You've hit the nail right on the head, John,' replied Amy, 'They certainly did do something about it. They were the ones who put him away.'

Amy explained that long before my visit to Crawley before I went to Singapore, matters had been building up to a head. My mother and Ruth had been refusing to have any communication with my father. Fuelled by an atmosphere of Ruth's ingrained and vindictive dislike of my father, they wouldn't speak to him and ignored him when he tried to speak to them. Ruth was very much the driving force and, once again, she had taken exception to something he had said or done – and so, he had to be punished, irrespective of the fact that she was a visitor in his house. My mother's love for Ruth was unconditional. Where Ruth led, my mother followed and Ruth could be very manipulative. Over the years, her abnormal behaviour had created pressures, arguments and divisions within the family. Her uncompromising attitude and behaviour had undoubtedly led to my parents splitting up in Llanelly at the end of the War when I was twelve. 'The crunch came,' continued Amy, 'when Dad was ill in bed with one of his bronchial attacks. He had run out of his pills and medicines and needed a repeat prescription. Dad was too ill and weak to go to the doctor's or the chemist's himself but, apparently, neither Mum nor Ruth would help. By all accounts, Dad lost his temper and smashed some crockery against the bedroom wall and started shouting at them. Ruth went straight out of the house to the nearest phone-box and she telephoned the police on 999. When they arrived, Dad had calmed down but it was too late. Mum and Ruth claimed he was violent and unstable. One thing led to another and my mother and Ruth signed the necessary papers. Dad was taken away to that hospital, which they considered 'a place of safety'.

'I went to visit him,' continued Amy, 'and while I was there in the hospital talking to the staff, the awful truth dawned on me. I just couldn't believe what they were telling me. I tackled Mum and Ruth at the first opportunity later but they both claimed it was for everyone's good. There was nothing I could do.'

Michael interrupted to say how upset Amy had been about it all with frequent tears and sleepless nights. 'It was so unnecessary and so unjust,' he added. Meanwhile, Amy had become distressed and it took a few minutes for her to compose herself. 'And that's not all,' she exclaimed. 'Dad's funeral service was a mockery.' She went on to explain how Ruth had briefed the officiating vicar on my father's life. 'I sat there in the church,' said Amy, 'and I just couldn't believe what the vicar was saying in his address: Dad had not been a good father, he was prone to violent outbursts and had ended his days in 'a place of safety' in view of his troubled mind. Nothing was mentioned about his fighting at Gallipoli or his difficult life during the Second World War. No mention was made of the fact that although his mother was illiterate, signing his birth certificate with a cross ('the mark of the mother') and although he himself had been denied secondary education, he fathered three children who all went on to become Cambridge University Masters of Arts, and a fourth who became a successful dress designer in the highly competitive world of fashion in London's West End. I started crying. Ruth leaned across and told me to be quiet and to pull myself together. Michael went to the graveside afterwards but I just couldn't go. I sat in the car crying and wondering how a man of the cloth could say such damning things at someone's funeral.'

Michael now continued. 'Your father had subscribed to a funeral plan, so all expenses were met. There was also some money in a savings account, a couple of hundred pounds or so. Ruth decided how the money should be spent. A week after the funeral, she and your mother went on an away-day excursion to Canterbury. They visited the Cathedral, went shopping and had a first-class lunch in a hotel restaurant. A final visit to a jeweller's meant that all the money had disappeared in a day.' 'Have you tackled Mum and Ruth on the subject?' I asked Amy. 'Mum just clams up and Ruth will only say that it's all water under the bridge now, so I get nowhere. The truth of the matter is that if anyone in the family had mental problems, it's Ruth herself. In addition to her difficult nature, she never socialises and she takes everything you say so literally. If I asked her how I might look in a particular dress or coat she might reply in such a blunt way it could be taken for rudeness. She takes a delight in forensic attention to detail. That's fine if you are studying ancient Greek and Latin but it can be most unsettling in social situations.' And there we left the subject of Ruth and her unusual personality.

In April 1967, seven months after the start of our course, I received the welcome news that I had been promoted to major. It was with great pleasure that I removed the three pips or stars on my various items and replaced them with a crown. I also welcomed the generous pay increase. Amongst other things, it allowed me to upgrade my car to a comfortable and reliable Rover 2000 with fully synchromesh transmission. It was the first car I had owned to have seat belts fitted, although their compulsory use didn't apply until 1983 – and then only for the driver and front passenger. Rear seat belt legislation didn't become effective until 1991.

That April saw another communication from 'K'. Would I meet him to discuss the question of my posting at the end of the Russian course. There were several possible options and he would present them to me. He was scheduled to attend a conference in Oxford in the near future and suggested we met at a hotel in the centre of the town for lunch on the Sunday before the conference. Oxford was easily accessible for me, being only a few miles further along the A40 from Wycombe. We lunched in a fine restaurant on Banbury Road between Keble and Somerville Colleges. 'K' showed great pleasure and interest in my telling him how much I had enjoyed the Singapore posting. 'I am so pleased,' he enthused, 'especially as I had recommended it in the first place.'

After lunch we walked along Keble Road and entered the Park. After we had found a comfortable bench, 'K' broached the question of my posting after the end of the Russian course in early 1968. 'There are postings for trained military interpreters in Germany,' he began. 'You could serve in BRIXMIS, the British Exchange Mission, located in Potsdam near Berlin in East Germany. Essentially, you would be one of a number of British personnel going on spying tours around the country attempting to establish details of Soviet and East German barracks, troop strengths and movements, their equipment and so on. Not quite James Bond but there could be elements of danger. There is always the chance of being spotted by the Soviets or by the East German police. If you are detained by them things could turn nasty and abusive. On the other hand you could serve as BLO to SOXMIS, the British Liaison Officer to the Soviet Exchange Mission to the Commander-in-Chief, British Army Of the Rhine (BAOR), West Germany. In that appointment, you would have a small support staff under you and you would liaise with the Head of Mission, a Soviet Major-General, and his staff as directed by Headquarters (HQ) BAOR. Your tasks would include presenting letters from HQ BAOR to SOXMIS and transmitting back their replies. You would accompany SOXMIS officers on trips outside their Mission when they are invited to attend British military events in the area. SOXMIS hold two large receptions every year and you would be involved in drawing up the guest list of high-ranking service personnel. You would certainly use your Russian much more in SOXMIS than in BRIXMIS. Finallly, there's always the chance of a post at the Government Communications Headquarters, GCHQ, in Cheltenham, the centre for the Government's Signals Intelligence, or SIGINT, activities. You would be employed in interpreting signals intelligence messages being transmitted in Russian. What do you think, John?' 'Listening closely to what you have been saying, my first choice would be for BLO to SOXMIS with its interesting job description and the apparent independence from superiors on site. Secondly, it would be for BRIXMIS and finally GCHQ. I must say that GCHQ doesn't appeal at all.' 'Well, you may have to do a spell at GCHQ whilst waiting for a vacancy at BRIXMIS or SOXMIS.

I'll check out the posting dates of present incumbents and let you know.'

'K' now changed the subject of our conversation to a most unexpected one. 'Pluto, or John, if you prefer,' he began, 'it's now ten years since I first came into your life when I visited you in St. Luke's College, Cambridge. Initially, I planned to use you in a project I had conceived, a mere flight of fancy. You didn't exist at all on paper and you never have. You were meant to satisfy my curiosity as to whether I could handle an amateur in the field without arousing any suspicions on the part of my peer colleagues in the Service. It was almost a game, if you like, and despite one or two close shaves, I got away with it. I then came to realise the arrogance of my project in as much as I was really playing God with your career and even your life. At the beginning, I had targeted you to deal with the traitorous lecturer in Cambridge. I then influenced you in choosing the Army as a career and arranged your posting to Capel Heights, leading to the uncovering of the espionage activity there. You responded so well to the challenges I set you, I began to develop an almost paternal sense of responsibility for you and came to realise I had to repay you somehow. My conscience was eased by my influencing your plum posting to Singapore and then latterly to the Wycombe Russian course. Now, of course, here I am again tinkering with your next posting. Perhaps I am not explaining myself terribly well, John. What I am leading up to is the fact that by the time you finish your next posting, I shall have retired, probably to the sunny clime of Andalusia in southern Spain. I shall be playing no further part in your Army career or indeed in your life. The project has now been played out to its end. I apologise for my initial arrogance but trust I have made amends in helping you to engage in work that you have enjoyed, and hopefully will continue to enjoy for another three years. We shan't be meeting again and I wish you every success in the future. I trust you understand my position.' There was little I could find to respond to 'K's outpourings. I did, however, mention that several times since the Capel Heights affair, I had wondered why 'K', from his lofty heights in the Intelligence Service in London, should bother to take an interest in this minnow called Pluto and influence my postings. No more was said on the subject and we walked back into the centre of Oxford. As we said our goodbyes, we shook hands and to my surprise, 'K' leaned forward and embraced me. "Take care, John,' he said, I've enjoyed our ten -year journey together. Now it's not 'aurevoir' but 'adieu'.' However, fate and its co-conspirator, coincidence, were to combine and our paths were to cross again, many hundreds of miles from Oxford and many years into the future.

A few months later, the major commanding the Russian language wing at Wycombe called me into his office. 'John,' he said, 'I've just received news of your posting at the end of the course. It's a real plum - to Germany. You're to be the next BLO to SOXMIS with an effective date of 5th March 1968.

Meanwhile, I had been making excellent progress in my Russian studies and had achieved consistently high marks in the weekly progress tests.

The next stage in our course duly arrived – a six-month stay in Paris, living with a White Russian host family. The parents of the family heads of the small pool of White Russians had fled Russia after the Revolution and had settled in the French capital. They had continued to speak Russian to their children over the years and it was now those children, several decades later, who provided that small pool of host families for the Wycombe students. As the course senior, I had first choice of host family with whom I could stay. On the recommendation of a former 'kursant,' or course student, who had stayed with them, I chose a family living in a flat in a northern Parisian suburb. It turned out to be a monumental mistake and a monumental disaster.

My host 'family' consisted of a widow in her fifties, her twenty-three year-old university student son and the mother's sister. On arrival, I was allocated a bed-sitting room but on checking where the radiator might be, I discovered that the room had no heating. I knew that Paris with its continental type climate would get very cold indeed in the winter. I told the mother that the MoD was paying for a room with heating. 'But,' she protested, going to a wall in the room, 'feel here. The wall is hot – there's a radiator on the other side.' I insisted that the room was not suitable. To placate their seemingly awkward guest, I was transferred to the other room with the radiator, which had been the sister's room. Not a good beginning to my six-month stay with a White Russian host family, especially as the whole matter had been discussed in French. Both the original room and my new room overlooked a sprawling railway network of some ten tracks running into Paris so any noise level would have been the same in either room. The first meal I had in the flat was taken in a cramped entrance hall on a table pushed against a wall with the bathroom/loo opposite. I realised my new bed-sitting room had been the original dining-room. Within two weeks of my arrival in Paris, fate really intervened. Apparently, every ten years there was a requirement for the complete maintenance overhaul of the local railway bridge and of those ten tracks into and out of Paris. That railway bridge was about a hundred yards from my single-glazed room window – and 1967 was the tenth year. The maintenance work was to be carried out at night to prevent disruption to busy daytime timetables. The work began in mid-September, from 10.00pm to 6.00am, and lasted until mid-January. The first night as I lay in my bed trying to get to sleep, I could initially hear the clang, clang of the men working on the tracks below my bedroom window. Some powerful arc-lights were switched on, flooding my bedroom through the thin curtains with their powerful yellow beams. I sprang out of bed and drew back the curtains. At that moment, a railworker appeared, carrying what looked like a trumpet. In fact, it was a trumpet, and the man blew it loud and long as a train approached, in order to warn his colleagues working on the tracks. In turn, another railworker further up the line, also equipped with a trumpet, blew his instrument in response. There is a piece of music called 'Trumpet Voluntary' but I was undergoing a third-degree 'Trumpet Involuntary.' It went on every night from 10.00pm to 6.00am except Sundays, week after week, month after month. I received little sympathy from my host family, Their view was that the railway system needed a ten-yearly maintenance overhaul – and that was that. I made urgent enquiries so as to move to another White Russian host family, but all the families had been allocated. Unfortunately for me, or perhaps fortunately, a 90 year-old widower, the one reserve possibility, had died in the August. There was no escape other than an expensive one. I booked into a local hotel, well away from the railway lines on two nights a week so as to get some much needed uninterrupted sleep. I always requested the same quiet room overlooking a cemetery – no chance of noise disturbance there. Inevitably, my studies suffered badly. I did get some sleep on the other nights in the flat between 6.00am and 10.00am but then I missed breakfast. Lunch was often an indifferent meal; for example, lamb chop and rice three days in a row. I started going regularly for lunch to a nearby Chinese restaurant, returning to the flat about 3pm. I managed to get some study work done between 3 and 6.30pm, when supper was ready, but that was all. I found it increasingly difficult to focus on my studies.

Once a week on a Thursday evening, we ten expatriate 'kursanty' met up in the bar of the British Embassy in the smart Rue du Faubourg St. Honore. As the course senior, I collected in the homework as set by Wycombe and gave out the new homework. Edward was ever present with his completed Russian exercises and he never missed a Thursday get-together, unlike one or two less conscientious 'kursanty'. He remained a very approachable, affable young officer and I certainly enjoyed his company. Nigel, the Guards lieutenant, and I went out together a few times, including to one or two Embassy receptions. He was another excellent companion as well as being a most competent linguist, including speaking fluent Italian. Like Edward, he was a first rate officer and gentleman.

As far as I was concerned, the time spent in Paris, which had been declared the icing on the Russian course cake, was a great disappointment. Overall, I found my French improving by leaps and bounds – an excellent refresher course. On the other hand, my Russian stagnated.. My host family and railway problems apart, I felt the Paris part of the course, no less than one third of the eighteen months, was a complete waste of time as far as meaningful Russian studies were concerned. I considered it not fit for purpose. Had I stayed in Wycombe instead, I would have benefited so much more following a closely structured, monitored and supervised course programme of advanced Russian studies. In Paris, the two White Russian tutors we went to weekly for 'military Russian' spoke excellent emigre Russian, I am sure, but they had no idea how to teach.

In a lifetime of learning and teaching languages, it has been my experience, invariably upheld and reinforced over the years, that, except at university level, non-British speakers of the language being studied have to be used with supervision and great caution. It looks so neat and attractive when the management of an educational establishment, be it a school, college or institute, can trumpet that their staff list includes native speakers. All very good and fine if they are essentially used in a conversational capacity. Let them loose as class teachers with translation passages and I have found time and again there will be problems. Their foreign mindset and their teaching skills, or lack of them, will so often provide a limited and low standard of presentation and explanation to the detriment of their students' progress.

So it had proved at Wycombe. Ray, our British tutor, was excellent and we had learned so much from him, especially as the grammar bullet points were put across in a way we students could understand and from which we could benefit. I had usually come away from a lesson delivered by a non-British tutor, feeling short-changed and even irritated. It also soon became apparent that none of them were teacher-trained but had picked up a few valuable pointers after practising on their students over the years. In teaching Russian, Ray knew only too well the relative difficulty of certain linguistic stumbling-blocks because he himself had been forced to overcome them in the past. The non-British teaching staff at Wycombe were unable to get inside their students' English language mindset. As a result, they were prone to teach a relatively easily understood grammar point with the same emphasis as one that was difficult to grasp. Ray varied the emphasis accordingly as he had experienced the problem himself and fully understood the relative difficulty.

I found it a blessing to return to Wycombe from Paris. I could now enjoy a couple of weeks consolidating my Russian knowledge in structured lessons under Ray before the Civil Service Interpretership examination in mid-February. At least, I had a good night's sleep at the end of each day. I duly passed the examination but reckoned I would have achieved much the same mark if I had taken it six months earlier, before going to Paris.

I would be leaving the UK shortly for three years in West Germany and might not be returning on a visit for a year or two. During my course at Wycombe, I had occasionally visited my mother in Sussex. In view of the way she and Ruth had treated my father, it was more out of a sense of filial duty rather than anything else. After the death of my father, she had moved from the house into a two-bedroom flat. Ruth had left Crawley to live in a flatlet in London, finding work from time to time. On one of my visits to Crawley, I had met up with Ruth but we didn't have a lot to say to each other. The subject of my father was never mentioned by either my mother or by Ruth.

The course had finished and the CSC examination had been taken. All that remained now was to bid farewell to the other nine 'kursanty' and to Wycombe. It was time to make tracks for West Germany and to take up my appointment as the British Liaison Officer to the Soviet Exchange Mission (BLO to SOXMIS). As I drove south on my way to Ostend and the car ferry, I wondered what liaising with the Soviets would be like. At least, I was now a qualified speaker of their language. I was soon to find out about the Soviets and their ways by being at 'the sharp end' itself.

'The John Reddisson Saga – My Later Years': scheduled for publication in early 2014.

Following on from 'My Early Life', we observe John Reddisson from the age of thirty-five to eighty, (1968-2013). Initially, he spends three memorable years as the British Liaison Officer to a Soviet Military Mission (SOXMIS) in West Germany at the height of the Cold War. On his return to London, he meets and marries the fragrant Maria but not before completing an intelligence assignment in Hong Kong, involving much scheming and intrigue. Disillusioned by later Army life, he retires and joins an English language school on the Kent coast, becoming the Principal in due course. Retirement to a villa on an Andalusian mountainside to live 'the Spanish dream' brings several initial shocks and later unexpected problems. John and Maria decide to return to England after three years in the Spanish sun, settling in Lincolnshire.

Lightning Source UK Ltd.
Milton Keynes UK
UKOW05f1610111113

220836UK00001B/9/P